D0396558

COURT TROUBLE

A PLATFORM TENNIS MYSTERY

COURT TROUBLE

MIKE BEFELER

FIVE STAR

A part of Gale, Cengage Learning

GALE
CENGAGE Learning·

Farmington Hills, Mich • San Francisco • New York • Waterville, Maine
Meriden, Conn • Mason, Ohio • Chicago

GALE
CENGAGE Learning

LIBRARY OF CONGRESS CATALOGING-IN-PUBLICATION DATA

Names: Befeler, Mike, author.
Title: Court trouble : a Platform tennis mystery / Mike Befeler.
Description: First Edition. | Waterville, Maine : Five Star, a part of Cengage Learning, Inc. 2016.
Identifiers: LCCN 2016001562 (print) | LCCN 2016006279 (ebook) | ISBN 9781432832223 (hardback) | ISBN 1432832220 (hardcover) | ISBN 9781432832056 (ebook) | ISBN 1432832050 (ebook)
Subjects: | BISAC: FICTION / Mystery & Detective / General. | GSAFD: Mystery fiction.
Classification: LCC PS3602.E37 C68 2016 (print) | LCC PS3602.E37 (ebook) | DDC 813/.6—dc23
LC record available at http://lccn.loc.gov/2016001562

Find us on Facebook– https://www.facebook.com/FiveStarCengage
Visit our website– http://www.gale.cengage.com/fivestar/
Contact Five Star™ Publishing at FiveStar@cengage.com

Printed in Mexico
2 3 4 5 6 7 20 19 18 17 16

In memory of Phil Geil and to my platform tennis buddies including Greg Johnson, Chris Bowman, Mike Merritt, Bob Ziegenhagen, Tom McCormick, Tim Conarro, John Miller, Jim Warner, Mike Small, Don Sherwood, Curt Corrigan, Pete Kelley, Brock Borman, Gary Horvath, Robbie Robertson and Tom Scott.

ACKNOWLEDGMENTS

Many thanks to my critique group, in particular Chris Goff; my wife, Wendy; the Five Star team including Deni Dietz, Tracey Matthews and Tiffany Schofield; and all the platform tennis players, partners and opponents, over the last twenty years.

CAST OF CHARACTERS

Mark Yeager: retired entrepreneur and platform tennis player

Woody Thorp: engineer and one of Mark's regular platform tennis foursome

Ben Quentin: lawyer and one of Mark's regular platform tennis foursome

Shelby Prescott: university professor and one of Mark's regular platform tennis foursome

Manny Grimes: platform tennis player and Mark's friend

Ken Idler: businessman and platform tennis player

Lee Daggett: investor, gambler and platform tennis player

Jacob Fish: owner of Creo Tech and platform tennis player

Howard Roscoe: gun dealer and platform tennis player

Carl Peters: detective

Sophie Yeager: Mark's wife

Al Lawson: *Denver Post* business editor

Davie Randolf: ex-employee of Jacob Fish at Creo Tech

Norm Yeager: Mark's son

Dawn Yeager: Norm's wife

Audrey Yeager: Mark's daughter

Julia Ruthers: attendant at rec center

Barbara Grimes: Manny's wife

Cheryl Idler: Ken Idler's wife

Melinda Daggett: Lee Daggett's ex-wife

Dr. Gallager: Mark Yeager's physician

9

Norborne Marston: friend of Mark Yeager's and CEO of Marston Electronics
Chip Deever: vice president of sales at Marston Electronics
Paul Crandall: replacement platform tennis player for Mark Yeager
Old Mel: street person
Clyde: ex-military and drug addict
Reagan Caldwell: Manny's accountant
Seth Pinter: Jaguar dealer sales manager

CHAPTER 1

An unexpected shiver ran through Mark Yeager's body as he slammed the door of his seven-year-old, gray BMW and zipped up his sweat suit to block the cool autumn air. Staring up, he noticed the broken light at this end of the parking lot. Probably shot out by one of the kids from the neighboring low-rent apartments. Beyond the lamppost, he could discern several stars in the moonless night sky.

Gripping the worn handle of his equipment bag, he marched up the dark walkway that wound between the windowless, brick North Boulder Recreation Center building and a park. Ahead of him, lights shown on the two outdoor platform tennis courts, reflecting off the wire-mesh fence. Off to the north and east, acres of open space lay fallow, but during the summer these fields shimmered with the kaleidoscope of irises growing in neat rows.

Mark liked to arrive early to loosen up his well-taped elbow by hitting a few practice serves. He put his hand to his groin, a habit since his prostate surgery. Then he stretched his six-foot-tall, fifty-six-year-old frame, thankful that he remained alive and able to play again.

He climbed the stairs to the raised deck of the nearest court and focused on four players already on the adjoining court. Three of them stood at the net, waving their paddles at each other. Mark heard, "You asshole," and "Like hell I will," and "Give me a break, you fuckwit."

Mark squinted and recognized the fourth bundled-up person on the other court—his friend Manny Grimes. Manny stood calmly at the baseline in a light-blue sweat suit. He waved to Mark. Why did Manny team with these jerks? Most of the players here wanted to enjoy a good workout, but those three guys acted like they wanted to kill someone.

Mark cradled the eighteen-inch-long Viking "Wow" paddle in his hand, admiring the strength of the composite wood and fiberglass surrounded by a solid steel rim. He had once witnessed an opponent put a half-inch-deep dent in the net post when angrily slamming a paddle into it.

He placed his left toe an inch behind the baseline and sniffed the air, catching the faint aroma of grilled hamburgers drifting in the slight breeze. Eyeing the other side of the court, he launched a ball skyward. He connected and the ball shot forward into the service box and ricocheted off the back screen. The muscles tingled in his right arm.

As he prepared to hit the next practice serve, two of his group, Ben Quentin and Woody Thorp, clambered up the stairs. While Mark had retained all his brown hair, Woody had a shining bald head above his gold-rim glasses. Ben met Mark's gaze with his serious, lawyer's blue eyes magnified by small, oval glasses.

Only after the three of them had started warming up did Shelby Prescott, who reminded Mark of a skinny Santa Claus, make his appearance. Shelby, a sixty-year-old sociology professor at the University of Colorado, always arrived last with an explanation such as "The dog ran out and I had to find him" or "The phone rang as I was getting ready to leave."

"What's the excuse this time, Shelby?" Mark asked.

Shelby stroked his beard, then ran his hand through his equally white hair. "You're never going to believe this, but I found this huge buck in the backyard, eating my hedge. I had to chase him away and clean up the deer poop on my grass."

Mark rolled his eyes. "You're right, Shelby. I'm never going to believe it." Gingerly, he stretched out one leg on the top of the net to loosen his hamstring.

Shelby looked toward Mark and winced. "Look at that grubby duct tape on the bottom of your shoe. As a retired entrepreneur, you should be able to afford new footwear."

Mark reached out with his gloved hand and smoothed a corner of tape that had come loose from the sole of his left tennis shoe. He lowered his leg and rested his hand on the net. "These Nikes are comfortable, and I don't want to break in new ones."

Shelby now rolled his eyes.

The rough court with its sandpaper-like covering ate through tennis shoes like a grinder on balsa wood. If Mark attached duct tape to the bottoms of his shoes every time he played, they lasted much longer.

Shelby sauntered over to Mark's side of the court. He waved his arm in a circular motion to limber up and settled in to hit a few practice ground strokes and volleys.

"Up or down?" Mark called, holding his hand over the Viking label on the end of the paddle handle to determine which team served first.

"Down and dirty," Ben called.

"Too bad," Mark said with a smile, showing the right-side-up V. "We'll serve. I'll start."

He squeezed the new ball in his left hand. This game entered his bloodstream like a dose of illicit drugs. The finesse of placing the ball so it would bounce off the corner of the wire mesh screen reminded him of solving an ever-evolving math puzzle.

He tossed the ball up, his eyes riveted on the yellow-green sphere against the black sky. His paddle made contact and sent the ball spinning over the net. He dashed forward and hit a volley that bounced deep in the court and rebounded off the back screen.

A high lob came back, and Shelby backpedaled to retrieve it, hitting an overhead deep into the corner.

Then a weak return, very short.

Mark lunged forward and chopped a drop shot that landed barely over the net, out of his opponents' reach.

Mark wiped his forehead, while his heart raced, sending adrenaline surging through his whole system. Although 2002 had not been his best year, now every cell in his body seemed to shout, "Yes, I'm back! I'm here! I'm alive!"

At the sound of a paddle clattering to the surface, his head jerked up. Two of the men on the adjoining court stood face-to-face, shouting, "Goddamn loser," and "Retard," at each other.

Mark made eye contact with Manny Grimes. Manny shrugged his shoulders as if to say, "See what I have to put up with."

Trying to ignore the noise, Mark focused on serving the next point.

After winning the first game, Mark gasped for air. As they changed sides, Mark put his arm around Shelby's shoulders. "I know you like to charge the net when we're returning serve, but hold back. We can beat these guys if we play steady and don't over-commit. Patience."

"Right, Coach," Shelby replied with a salute.

Mark prepared to receive a serve when he heard someone yell "Shit!" behind him. He turned around to see who had shouted.

A man in a gray sweat suit ascended the stairs of the adjoining court. "I'm supposed to play tonight," he bellowed. "Lee, what the hell are you doing here?" He thrust open the door and stomped onto the court.

"You're not scheduled for tonight," a voice shouted back. "I told you I'd call you if we needed a sub. Besides, we started at seven."

"You said you'd call me if you didn't need me. And you said seven-thirty, not seven."

Mark turned away from the other group to look at the members of his foursome. Shelby looked skyward and said, "Oh, brother."

Suddenly, all the court lights went out. Mark blinked in the sudden darkness, seeing spots.

The sound of a loud crack broke the night air, followed by a thump.

Mark's eyes adjusted to the darkness, but with little ancillary light, it still remained impossible to clearly see anything. Then moments later, the lights came on again.

Mark shielded his eyes from the sudden glare and looked at the next court.

Someone lay slumped by the net with a paddle resting next to him. The other four stood motionless nearby.

Mark charged to the screen to position himself for a better view.

Blood oozed from a gash on the top of the man's head. He wore a light-blue sweat suit.

"It's Manny!" Mark shouted. He ran to his equipment bag, grabbed his cell phone and punched in 9-1-1.

CHAPTER 2

Manny's body splayed lifeless on the court. The EMTs had arrived too late to do any good.

Mark's hands shook. He had trouble focusing. His head throbbed.

He needed to pull himself together. He took a deep breath and scanned the other court. This was no accident, and four potential murderers sulked on the adjoining court. Any of them could have bashed Manny with a paddle. For all the bluster and noise earlier, the four remained suspiciously quiet now.

Mark twisted his paddle in his hands and watched in silence as a police officer spoke with each of the players on the adjoining court and then separated them to wait along the recreation center outer wall.

Wanting to watch the proceedings more closely, Mark tried to go out the court door, but a policeman stopped him. "Please wait in the court for a few more minutes. Detective Peters will want to talk to you."

Mark shrugged, shut the door and continued to watch the activity alongside the rec center building.

A photographer shot pictures of each of the suspects, and then a man in an overcoat wiped swabs over their sweat suits before dropping the samples in separate paper bags. Finally an officer escorted them individually out to waiting cars. Mark recognized the last suspect to leave. Jacob Fish.

Jacob began to yell and wave both hands in the air.

Mark rubbed his cold chin. Here Manny was dead, and Jacob was putting on an Academy Award–acting performance.

Turning his attention away from the parking lot, Mark noticed an officer wrapping yellow tape across the handrails leading to the other platform tennis court. Then a man in a dark coat entered their court. He stood approximately six-foot-two with the build of a University of Colorado linebacker. Mark estimated his age to be early forties. He addressed Mark and his companions. "I'm Detective Carl Peters. I need to take a statement from each of you and search your equipment bags. We can either do it here or down at headquarters. Your choice."

Shelby looked at his watch. "I have to head home. Why don't you interview me first?"

"Shelby, you just got here," Mark protested.

"I know, but I have term papers to grade tonight."

Mark decided to drive to the public safety building on 33rd Street rather than stand in the cold. After showing his driver's license to Peters, who wrote the information on a pad, Mark excused himself and strode toward the parking lot. So much for a friendly platform tennis game.

Mark drank a cup of lukewarm coffee while sitting in the lobby of the public safety building watching people go in and out through the glass door. Thoughts ping-ponged around in his head, rebounding from the awful events of this evening to his recent bout with cancer. He felt his stomach tighten at the memory.

He divided his life into two periods: before cancer and after cancer. He had been healthy, rarely missing work and never bed-ridden. Sure, there had been occasional colds, but he always bounced back within days. He hadn't been a hospital patient since his birth. He took his good health for granted, accepting it as the way things should be. Then came the news that he had prostate cancer. That changed everything. Nothing like a dose of mortality slapping him alongside the head.

What a hell of a wake-up call. Even people who did all the right things could die. It could happen to anyone.

Look at Manny.

If it hadn't been for Manny, Mark might be dead or dying by now. He thought back to that fateful day six months ago.

He and Manny had sat on a bench outside the recreation center, chatting after a lunchtime platform tennis game. The conversation meandered around until, finally, they broached the subject of health. Mark always felt comfortable with Manny and found himself saying more than usual about some physical problems he had experienced.

Manny looked him in the eyes. "You have symptoms of prostate cancer. You need to go in immediately for a checkup."

Mark laughed. "I don't like doctors. Haven't been to see one in probably five years."

Manny grabbed his arm. "Come with me. I'm taking you over to the Boulder Medical Center right now."

"You're kidding me."

"No! This could be a matter of life or death."

Manny drove him the four blocks to the medical center and waited while an on-call physician tended to Mark. Sure enough, he had a malignant, enlarged prostate. And if Manny had not insisted . . .

A hand touched Mark's shoulder. Startled, he jumped.

"Mr. Yeager, would you please come this way?"

Mark sighed. He'd continue with his life, just as he did after his cancer surgery.

He followed the officer along a hallway covered with pictures of past police chiefs, into a small, bare room with hard, wooden chairs on each side of a table that looked like surplus from a local middle school.

"Detective Peters will be with you shortly."

Mark waited and waited and finally closed his eyes. He imagined a meadow with butterflies, but the butterflies turned into flying paddles. Then a firm hand shook him.

"Mr. Yeager, I'm ready to speak with you."

Mark blinked. "Sorry. I was daydreaming." He looked into the intense eyes of Detective Peters.

"Mr. Yeager, this has been a trying evening for you. I'll let you leave as soon as possible. I'd appreciate it if you would please describe the scene as you witnessed it."

"I'm not a suspect, am I?" Mark asked.

"No. It's clear you remained fenced into the other court when the murder happened."

Mark recounted arriving and observing the men on the other court, playing for a short while, being surprised when the lights went out and then receiving the shock of seeing a bludgeoned Manny Grimes when the lights came back on.

"Describe specifically what you noticed the men doing on the adjoining court right before the lights went out."

"They had all gathered at the net. The fifth man, whom I don't know, had just arrived. We stopped our game when he stomped onto the court and started an argument with one of the players, Lee Daggett."

"Did you know the victim?"

"I've known Manny for over two years. He often filled in when one of our regular foursome couldn't play."

"And the other men on the court with Manny?"

Mark thought back over the last several years of platform tennis games. "Manny is the only one I've played platform tennis with. I've seen the others at the courts once in a while, but that's it."

"Let's review the situation before the lights went out. Continue."

"The players on the other court acted pretty heated. They swore at each other. But, strangely, Manny seemed above it all. The other three argued like spoiled kids."

"Describe any threats you heard."

"Nothing specific, but they constantly badgered each other as they played."

"What else did you notice?"

"The man who came late. His timing was impeccable. Moments after he arrived, the lights went out."

Peters wrote on his notepad.

"Can you describe the positions of the men on the other court when the lights came back on?"

"I really didn't notice them. My attention was only focused on Manny. I saw a paddle lying next to him. Then I picked up my cell phone."

"Anything else you observed?"

Mark thought for a moment. "Nothing else."

"I won't keep you any longer, Mr. Yeager. If you think of something that might be useful, please give me a call."

Peters gave Mark his card.

Mark looked at the blank wall in front of him and thought of the crime shows he'd watched on television. "I have some questions for you. Wouldn't there be blood spatter from the victim on the killer? Since the suspects were probably wearing gloves, I don't imagine you found fingerprints on the murder weapon, but did you discover anything suspicious in their equipment bags?"

Peters looked thoughtfully at Mark. "Astute questions, but I can't discuss the investigation at this time."

"Why not?"

"We don't divulge any case details."

As Mark left the room, he noticed one of the suspects, Ken Idler, standing in the hallway, dressed in tennis shorts and a turtleneck shirt. His build approximated Manny's, but his face held dark, darting eyes, a brown mustache and a goatee.

"Look, you've asked your questions and you know where to find me if you need me again," Idler said. "I was bending down to tie my tennis shoe when the lights went out. One of the others killed Manny. Now I need to return home to my wife."

"We need to run one more test, Mr. Idler," the policeman said.

"You've already taken my sweat suit. I assume you'll give me something warm to wear home."

"We have a jacket we'll loan you when you're driven back to the recreation center."

"How good of you," Idler said, turning and kicking the base plate of the wall.

CHAPTER 3

When Mark entered his house at eleven-thirty, he found Sophie in the living room. She lowered a legal thriller held in her soft, white hands and gave him a smile. Their eyes met in the way that comes from thirty years of marriage.

Mark admired her short, blond hair and well-conditioned body, the result of yoga and walking. Who would guess that she would turn fifty-two in three months? He hoped that one of these days the aftereffect from his cancer surgery would wear off and he would once again be able to enjoy the pleasures of intimacy with Sophie.

"Quite a late game tonight," she said.

"We hardly played at all. There was a murder on the courts."

"What?" Her eyes widened, and she dropped her book.

"You remember Manny Grimes?"

"Yes."

"Someone bludgeoned him to death with a paddle on the next court."

She put her hand to her cheek. "How awful. You must be in a state of shock."

"I was shaken by it, but I'm okay now."

"Manny's poor wife. Do the police know who killed him?"

"Not yet. They have four suspects."

"Tell me the whole story."

Mark recounted the events, exactly as he had related them to Detective Peters.

"I hope the police do a better job than with the Jon Benet Ramsey murder," Sophie said.

"The police interviewed the four suspects. Any of them could have done it. They all stood near the body when the lights came on."

"Do you know any of them?"

Mark suddenly remembered an event he should have mentioned to Detective Peters. "I know three of their names and had a run-in with one of them, Jacob Fish, a year ago."

He thought back to last fall when Jacob insisted that he had rights to the north court when, in fact, Mark had reserved it. The reservation had been confirmed by the perky blonde at the desk. Jacob had only relinquished the court after they had all trooped inside to examine the reservation schedule.

"This dumb broad obviously made a mistake!" Jacob had shouted, mustache twitching and bald head flushing.

"No," Mark had replied, clenching his teeth. "She's right and you're wrong."

The taller and younger Jacob had made a fist as if he would punch Mark in the nose right on the spot.

Mark snapped back from his reminiscence when Sophie asked, "And the other suspects?"

"Ken Idler. He's a local businessman. I've seen him on the courts several times. He's another 'winner.' Threw a tantrum at police headquarters tonight."

"Not the passive type."

"No. None of them are shy or retiring. They spent most of the evening arguing. And Lee Daggett. He's another sweetheart. Poster child for verbal abuse."

"But I don't understand—you said four suspects."

"That's the strange part. Seconds before the lights went out, another man arrived. I've never seen him before. He and Lee Daggett argued over who was supposed to be playing."

"Why would one of them have it in for Manny?"

Mark scratched his head. "I can't figure that out. These other guys all shouted at each other, but Manny seemed to stay out of the fray. He and I made eye contact during one of the arguments on their court. I still can't understand why he associated with those jerks. Manny is such a nice guy."

Sophie leveled her gaze at Mark. "I know you liked Manny, but I've never shared your enthusiasm for him."

Mark blinked. "Why not?"

"It goes back to a party several years ago. One of the guys you used to play platform tennis with had a group of your buddies and their wives over. Now, I like your regular group and have always enjoyed Ben and Woody and get a kick out of the scatterbrained professor, Shelby, but something about Manny didn't strike me right."

"I've never had any problems with him, and he did me a big favor once."

"Yes, I know your feelings, but Manny didn't seem genuine." She sighed. "To be blunt, he struck me as a phony."

Mark laughed. "Well, he's always been genuine with me. Maybe he had a hidden life."

"That just might be, Mark."

"In any case, he certainly didn't deserve being murdered with a paddle."

"I agree, and there may be some additional fallout from the murder," Sophie said.

Mark knew his wife had keen insights into events, often giving him a perspective he might have otherwise missed. "How so?"

"You've been telling me there's a snafu with the expansion of the recreation center, resulting in a hearing on Monday to relocate the courts."

"Yes."

"Well. You're fighting this issue—the people living near the courts consider them a disruption to their quiet neighborhood. They dislike the lights and noise from the courts. In their place, I'd play up this murder. This loud, obnoxious sport brings the wrong element into our neighborhood. Down with murderous platform tennis players and their despicable sport. Protect our children from this threat. Bulldoze the courts."

Mark had to laugh in spite of himself. "You'd make a great lawyer. I'm glad you're on my side."

"Am I? Maybe without the courts you wouldn't be associating with murderers until almost midnight."

"Then you'd be stuck with me around here more."

She smiled. "I know you. You'd jump full speed into some other project. You'll never be one to sit at home. It may frustrate me at times, but it's also what I love about you."

"Thanks for the vote of confidence."

Sophie stood and strolled over to Mark, wrapping her arms around his neck.

He put his hand under her chin and gave her a kiss. There was a time when this would have aroused him, but ever since his prostate-cancer surgery . . .

He released her and stepped away. "I better go take a shower."

Two days later, with Manny's murder on his mind, Mark sat in silence at Vic's coffee house with Ben Quentin and Woody Thorp after their midday game. He surveyed the white wall covered with pictures of a smiling Buddha surrounded by naked women. Heating pipes ran along the ceiling and intersected a curved arch of galvanized steel that separated the customers from the kitchen. A bearded, young man in a white T-shirt stood behind the coffee bar, wiping the counter with a dishcloth. The room emitted staccato bursts of background conversation, coffee grinding, a baby crying, cups striking saucers and laughter.

Ben Quentin, the youngest of their group at forty-eight, shook his full head of brown hair. He rubbed his chin covered with its ever-present five o'clock shadow and stared blankly through his small, oval glasses. "I keep replaying what I saw. It reminds me of when my wife died three years ago." He gazed sadly at the far wall.

Woody Thorp adjusted his gold-rim glasses and wiped his high forehead. "I know what you mean. It's been hard for me, too. It brings up the awful memories of my son dying in that car wreck."

Ben turned to face his two friends. "We're all survivors, recovering from bad situations," he said firmly. "Trying to return to normal, staying active. Then some asshole kills our friend." He slapped the table for emphasis.

"I've never heard anything good about anyone in that group," Woody said. "I'm sure they're all capable of murder."

"But no arrest yet," Ben added, taking a sip of his cappuccino. "The article in the *Daily Camera* only referred to a police investigation underway."

"And, of all people, the victim is the guy who substituted for Mark while he recovered from his cancer surgery," Woody said. "We've all enjoyed a good game with Manny. Always genial and helpful. Gave me a ride home one time when I had a flat tire."

"Offered to provide a new ball each time we played, not like some people," Ben said, elbowing Mark. "The consummate gentleman. Played a good solid game. Never tried to drill people. Always made effective passing shots."

"Now someone bludgeons him with a paddle," Woody said, wincing. "And we all saw it happen. I mean, we were there when it happened. I can't clear that scene from my mind."

"Oh, like we can?" Ben asked.

Ignoring his sarcasm, Woody continued. "I've never witnessed anything like that before. I keep seeing it like a reoccurring movie scene. That group in the enclosed court—"

"And I remember the closed door," Ben interrupted. "When the fifth guy, Howard Roscoe, came stomping up the stairs, he slammed it shut after he entered the court."

"So that's the latecomer," Mark said. "I've seen him before, but didn't know his name."

Shelby Prescott slid onto a chair.

Ben looked at Shelby. "Speaking of latecomers, we've been here for fifteen minutes. How come you're even late making a five-minute drive from the courts?"

"I had to retrieve this book out of my trunk for Woody," Shelby said, plopping a hefty reference book onto the table.

"You're setting a bad tome with such a large book," Woody said with a straight face.

Mark and Shelby groaned.

"Don't encourage him," Ben said, glaring at them. "Woody loves to have people groan at his bad puns. You have to ignore him."

Woody smiled in acknowledgement. "Now, as I was saying before Shelby's once-again late arrival, five of them stood on the enclosed court. And the lights go out for, what do you think, fifteen seconds?"

"I would state twenty seconds," Shelby confirmed in his most professorial tone.

"Okay, say twenty seconds," Woody continued. "We look over and see Manny dead and a bloody paddle lying on the court. Four, and only four, suspects. No time for anyone else to come into the court, kill Manny and leave."

"Well summarized," Ben said. "A good engineer's analysis. The conclusion: no outside intruder."

"Maybe the squirrel did it," Shelby said.

"Huh?" Woody opened his eyes wide.

"You remember," Shelby said, waving his hand at Woody.

"Must have been last year. While the four of us played, a squirrel climbed the fence, scurried down the inside, ran across the court, scampered back up and sat there chattering at us."

"We can rule out the squirrel," Ben said, swatting Shelby with a newspaper that had been lying on the table. "We have to find the motive. One of those guys had a good reason to eliminate Manny. The police need to uncover who wanted to rub out Manny."

"Maybe they all planned it," Shelby said.

"It's possible," Ben said, as he scratched the back of his hand. "Maybe it was a mob execution."

"Come on, Ben," Mark said. "This isn't Chicago. Mob hits don't happen in Boulder."

"Oh, yeah?" Ben's eyes flashed. "Remember that Asian gang that raped that C.U. coed? Wake up. We have gangs, thieves and murderers here. They may be disguised in designer jeans and jogging suits, but there's no lack of criminals in this community."

"Ben should know," Woody jumped in. "He has the opportunity to represent some of them."

"I stick to the minor violations, but we could give Washington, D.C., a run for it with the number of crimes per capita committed here."

"And to think that I moved here for the peace and quiet," Woody said with a sigh.

"Boulder appears to be this safe, upper-middle-class, professional community, but it has a serious drug trade and more than its fair share of crime," Ben continued.

"Must be what's in that good glacier water the Chamber of Commerce always promotes," Shelby said. "In any case, I think those guys worked together."

"I could see the four of them plotting the murder," Woody said.

"But all considered, I don't think that's what happened," Ben said. "They seemed pretty argumentative when the police arrived. The four suspects kept blaming each other. No cooperation among that crowd."

"I think they play platform tennis because on the small court they can drive the ball into someone's stomach," Woody added. "They like taking their frustrations out by damaging their opponents."

"There must have been some evidence at the scene of the crime," Shelby said.

"The crime scene investigators collected blood spatter," Ben said. "But the suspects were bunched so close together that they all had evidence of blood on their clothes. Probably nothing conclusive."

Mark listened, squirming in his seat and tapping his fingers on his thighs. If he could only find a way to mobilize his friends.

"I hope the police solve the case quickly," Shelby said.

"Not much chance of that," Ben said. "I called a friend in the DA's office this morning, and the police still have no clue which of the four did it."

"Manny's owed justice," Mark said, pounding his fist on the yellow, circular table and jolting his companions. "His murderer shouldn't be roaming free. We need to do something."

"What do you have in mind?" Woody asked.

"We have connections in this community," Mark said. "We could do our own investigation and speed things up."

"I thought you needed to take it easy after your surgery," Shelby said as he pointed a finger at Mark.

"If I've recovered enough to play platform tennis, I can tackle an investigation. We need to pool our resources to try to help. It seems to me that if we each took one of the four suspects and did our own background check, we might be able to find out who the murderer is."

"And use Vic's as our headquarters?" Shelby asked.

"Why not? We can meet here before our Tuesday evening games and after our Thursday noon and Saturday morning games. Woody, use your engineer's mind to work at solving this problem. Ben maintains excellent connections with the local police. Shelby can probably marshal a group of students to help him. I have contacts in the business community to follow up with. What do you say?"

"I'm in," Woody answered.

Shelby thought for a moment. "Okay, but I can't put too much time into this."

"The police don't appreciate amateur detectives messing with their investigations," Ben said. "What makes you think we can do more than they can?"

Mark paused as the aroma of mint tea wafted from the next table. "I'm not saying we're better than the police. We just might have some different perspectives and take some new approaches to the problem."

Woody nodded. "I agree. If we reach a dead end, it will only cost us the time invested. If we discover something, it might speed up bringing the perpetrator to justice."

Ben pulled at his chin. "In some states, you'd have a real problem doing what you suggest. At least in Colorado, no laws require any examination or certification to become a private investigator. Anyone can investigate. Still doesn't mean the police like it."

"Besides, we're not asking to be paid investigators," Mark said. "I think we can do something constructive. Why not give it a try, Ben?"

Ben looked around the table. "If the two of you have lost your senses enough to go along with Mark's crazy scheme, what the hell." Ben shrugged.

"You could say that with a little more conviction," Mark said, patting him on the back. "Now, here's how we divide up the four suspects, with Ben and Shelby reporting back on Saturday."

CHAPTER 4

Sophie greeted Mark when he arrived home. "Good game?"

"Less eventful today. No murders."

Her smile disappeared. "That's not funny."

"You're right. In fact we decided to do something."

"Oh?"

"The boys and I plan to help track down Manny's killer."

"That's ridiculous." Her eyes flared. "You don't know anything about investigating a murder. What are you trying to prove?"

"This will give me some focus before I return to consulting."

"And you talked Ben, Woody and Shelby into this crazy scheme?"

"Manny played platform tennis with us. He convinced me to visit the doctor, otherwise the cancer wouldn't have been diagnosed so early. Then he covered for me during my surgery. I feel an obligation to help find his murderer."

Sophie slammed her book down. "No. You have an obligation to not end up like Manny. I don't want you associating with murderers." She stalked out of the room.

Shaking his head, Mark navigated his way through knee-deep stacks of manila folders to the desk in his home office. He opened the blinds, enjoying the view that overlooked the greenbelt and the National Center for Atmospheric Research perched on the hill beyond. Sunlight from a bright afternoon sky above the Flatirons, the iconic local rock formation, flooded the room.

A few keystrokes brought up the Google search engine on the Internet. His assignment: research Jacob Fish.

After a few misleading trails, Mark narrowed in on a two-month-old article from the *Denver Post*. This profiled several Colorado Front Range entrepreneurs who had started software businesses. Jacob Fish, a graduate of MIT and now thirty-five, had once been married but now divorced. No children. Jacob made his first million before the age of twenty-five as a programmer at a successful start-up company in Silicon Valley. He moved to Boulder and started his own company, Creo Tech, three years ago.

Mark snapped his fingers and dialed Al Lawson, his longtime friend and the editor of the business section of the *Denver Post*.

"Al, it's Mark Yeager. I need a favor."

"What's in it for me?" Al replied, with an audible yawn.

"I need you to do a little research. You might uncover something interesting concerning a local company."

"Exclusive story?"

"Maybe. Check a guy named Jacob Fish and a company called Creo Tech."

"Can't do it until tomorrow morning. You still at the same number?"

After hanging up, Mark returned to the Internet. He was ready to give up when one new article on Creo Tech caught his attention.

CHAPTER 5

Mark was cleaning out the garage on Friday when Sophie told him he had a call.

Mark picked up the phone to hear Al Lawson on the line. "I found a little info for you regarding Jacob Fish and Creo Tech."

"I'm all ears."

"But before I divulge anything, I want to know why you're so interested in Fish and his company."

Mark sighed. "Jacob Fish is a suspect in a murder investigation that involves the death of a friend of mine named Manny Grimes."

"That's interesting."

"How so?"

"One of the tidbits I uncovered indicates that this Manny Grimes invested in Creo Tech."

On Saturday morning Mark, Ben and Woody all arrived within five minutes of each other at the North Boulder Rec Center. No Shelby. The net on the south court was missing a strap, so they decided to play on the north court.

Mark dropped his equipment bag on the deck, one-third the size of a tennis court.

Ben looked carefully at Mark.

"Do I detect a new haircut?"

Mark ran his fingers through his hair. "Yes, I had it clipped yesterday."

"You obviously went to a clip joint," Woody said.

Mark groaned.

"Don't encourage any of his awful puns," Ben said. "But, Mark, your hair does appear a little uneven. Did you have it cut with a lawnmower?"

Woody rejoined the conversation. "No, but he does save money by going to the barber college. Right, Mark?"

Mark scowled. "I've done that for years. Helps the students train."

"Right," Ben replied with a laugh. "Just the ticket for the world's cheapest ex-entrepreneur."

"I'm merely being thrifty," Mark said. "That's how my startup company succeeded. We spent frugally and conserved cash."

After a lengthy warm-up, they saw Shelby sauntering up the walkway.

"Don't hurry," Woody shouted. "You might strain yourself."

"I'm getting there. Hold your water."

Mark flinched at the expression. That phrase had often been on his mind after his prostate surgery.

Shelby threw his equipment bag down inside the court and slammed the door.

That sound reminded Mark of the night of the murder. They now stood on the very same court where Manny had died! Mark looked at the court surface, expecting to see bloodstains, but the court appeared clear except for a few mud clods, probably tossed inside by neighborhood kids. He recollected the scene he had viewed from the adjoining court: Manny's body slumped over.

"Do you want to stand around all day or consider playing a game or two?" Shelby nudged Mark.

Mark sighed and looked at his companions. "I'm ready. Let's start the match."

He walked to the baseline, touching the perforations in the

paddle with gloved fingers, then swung back and forth, letting the air swish through the eighty-six holes. Of course slicing the paddle straight down onto someone's head would also cut down air resistance. How could someone so brutally misuse such a carefully crafted piece of sports equipment? He swatted his palm with the flat of the paddle.

Mark tried to free his mind for the game, taking the ad court while his partner, Woody, took the deuce court. Ben served to Woody and the ball hit the net.

"Love-fifteen," Ben said. "Damn fault. I wish I had two serves like in tennis instead of only one."

"You need to serve softer," Shelby coached his partner. "Woody doesn't hit it back that hard anyway."

Mark positioned himself to receive the next serve. As his left hand touched the sixteen-gauge wire side screen, he readied himself to hit a strong forehand drive off almost any serve. Only a serve hit perfectly on the outside line would force him to return a weaker backhand shot.

Ben launched a solid serve down the middle.

Mark scooted over and drove back a hard forehand.

Ben volleyed a defensive shot, deep and toward the middle of the court.

Mark played it off the fence and launched a high, deep lob that forced Ben back.

Ben reached up and retrieved the ball, but hit it short. Woody stepped in and drove the ball between Ben and Shelby.

Seeing their opponents retreat to chase down the careening shot off the back screen, Mark and Woody charged the net to gain the offense.

Shelby, scrambling in the back court, finally reached the ball and hit a weak lob to Mark.

Mark, his paddle poised in mid-air, hit a soft overhead to Ben's backhand.

Ben back-pedaled and could only poke at the ball, sending it short to Woody.

Woody gleefully smashed the ball causing it to ricochet off the side screen behind Shelby, who couldn't reach it.

Mark and Woody gave each other a high five. "Way to make the old professor move," Mark said.

"Love-thirty," Ben announced, preparing to serve to Woody. Mark positioned himself behind the baseline. In tennis, a player would stand near the service line when his partner received serve, but in platform tennis he needed to stay back.

Mark watched Woody set his feet in preparation to receive the serve. He thought of Woody as Mr. Methodical, the consummate engineer playing conservatively and waiting for his opening.

Woody hit a lob off a good serve, and Shelby sent the ball spinning deep to Mark's backhand. Mark launched another lob but miss-hit it, sending the ball too short, barely clearing the net on Shelby's side.

Shelby tapped the ball cross-court toward Mark's alley.

Mark had just enough warning of the drop shot to charge toward the net as the ball skimmed over, bounced on the line and ricocheted off the side screen. Mark felt a rush of adrenaline as he lunged. Within inches of the court surface, the final thrust of his paddle made contact, sending the ball shooting alongside the net post into the opposing alley and outside Ben's reach.

"What a shot!" Woody shouted.

Mark felt his heart racing with the exultation of a perfect winner.

"Wait a Goddamn minute," Ben protested. "The ball didn't go over the net."

"That doesn't matter," Woody gloated. "Mark can hit around the net post as long as the ball lands inside the lines on your side of the court. In fact, he could cross or reach over the net.

As long as he doesn't touch the net or put his foot within the lines on your side. You lose the argument, counselor."

Ben shook his head in disgust, looking toward Shelby for an appeal.

"He's right," Shelby said with a nod. "Mark won the point fair and square."

As Mark and Woody returned to the baseline, Mark whispered in Woody's ear. "Play the ball to Ben. He's mad and apt to make a mistake."

Mark looked up and saw a woman in a blue ski jacket and matching hat standing right outside the fence. A panting golden retriever sat next to her.

"What's this sport called?" she asked.

"Platform tennis," Mark answered.

"How's it played?"

"A lot like tennis except you only have one serve and can play the ball off the screen."

"Can you play singles?"

"Some people do, but we only play doubles. One team on offense and one team on defense. The serving team's at the net and the receiving team stays back and lobs a lot."

"Looks like a hard game to learn."

"Not really," Mark said. "My son picked up the game much quicker than tennis. Once you get used to hitting the ball off the screen, it's pretty easy. It's more forgiving than tennis. If you miss the ball the first time, you might still be able to play it when it bounces off the screen."

"And you play all winter?"

"That's the best part. No matter how cold it is, we bundle up and have fun while exercising. If it snows, we raise the snow boards on the side, shovel the court and can play within an hour."

Ben, waiting to serve, yelled impatiently over to Mark, "Move your butt back for the next point and quit flirting, or I'll tell your wife."

Sheepishly Mark turned back to prepare for the next serve. Trying to show off somewhat for the woman watching, Mark managed to lose the next three points, then noticed that the woman and her dog had departed anyway.

After their match they reconvened at Vic's. The typical fall Saturday crowd of joggers, dog walkers, bicyclists and other assorted young-to-middle-aged athletic wannabes milled around the coffee house. Mark's group sat in the back near a green neon sign displaying the words "Tea Room." Mark inspected the carpet pattern of yellow and red ellipses and kicked aside the remains of a bagel as he slumped into a worn chair.

"Shelby, I see you traded in your old clunker for a newer car," Ben said.

"Yes, in spite of my precarious financial condition, I had to procure a replacement. Found a slightly used Honda Civic that's supposed to consume hardly any gas."

"Is that so?" Ben said, raising his eyebrows.

"Absolutely. I'm going to track it on every tank to see what good mileage I obtain."

Mark tapped his fingers on the table. "Let's return to the matter at hand. Ben and Shelby, what did you learn about the murder suspects?"

"I'll start," Ben said. "I've been digging up dirt on Lee Daggett. He's a real sweetheart. It reminds me of my days dealing with the wise guys back in New York." Ben had been a prosecuting attorney before moving to the quieter life of private practice in Boulder.

"This guy Daggett was arrested, but not prosecuted, ten years ago on gambling charges. He's now state-sanctioned as an investor in one of the casinos up in Black Hawk. The gaming commission owns the responsibility to keep his type out of the state gambling industry, but with the earlier charges dropped, Daggett's now viewed as having a clean bill of health."

Woody jumped in. "If he's making money at it, you might say he has a green hill of wealth."

Everyone groaned, including Ben.

"I've seen Daggett play platform tennis," Shelby said. "Reminds me of a fireplug. He positions himself at the net and doesn't let anything get past him. Fearless. Not concerned when someone drives the ball at him. He stands his ground and makes a drop shot with an unorthodox stroke."

"And his personal life?" Mark asked Ben, ignoring Shelby.

"A bitter divorce involving physical abuse. His ex-wife Melinda still lives in Boulder. Local police keep their eyes on Daggett. He has a reputation for waving around large amounts of cash. Once beat up a 'friend,' but the guy didn't press charges. Daggett seems like a natural to bash one of his buddies with a paddle."

"Any specific link to Manny?" Woody asked.

"A possibility. Daggett's financial status seems to be as smooth as the top of the Rockies. One year he's flush and the next he's scrambling. One of my contacts in the DA's office suspects that he owed money to Manny. Probably no notarized loan agreement. Good motive. Knock off the guy who wants money back." Ben dusted his hands together. "Debt eliminated."

"Lee Daggett stays on the suspect list," Mark said, as if running a business meeting. "Shelby, what did you find out about Ken Idler?"

Shelby took a sip of his latte. "Sorry guys, I don't have much to report. I meant to do my investigating, but with buying the car and getting stuck interviewing three candidates to replace the retiring Dean . . ."

"I thought you were up for consideration," Woody said.

"No. I've made too many enemies along the way. When I thought I could afford to retire four years ago, I told too many colleagues what I really thought of them. Now that I'm broke, they're certainly not going to help me obtain a promotion."

"And I always thought the politics bad in business," Mark responded.

Shelby rolled his eyes. "You haven't seen anything like the politics in academia. We murder each other with subtlety and innuendo, not paddles."

"Don't get us off the track," Mark said, wagging his finger. "You must have discovered something."

"Only that Idler runs an import-export business. I'll have a student contact his company to perform a study project. We'll see what pops up. So Mark, what did you find out?"

Mark studied the other three as their heads turned toward him. "I planned to wait to report until next time, but since Shelby doesn't have much, I'll go now. I found some very interesting things regarding Jacob Fish: genius, ruthless, driven by money and success. In digging into his software business, I came across an article linking his firm to white-collar fraud. Then a contact of mine uncovered that Manny Grimes invested in Jacob's company. What better motive than eliminating someone who may know the details of your slimy business practices?"

"And he cheats," Shelby interjected. Three pairs of eyes turned to Shelby. "He serves before his opponents are ready and calls good shots out. When I watched him play once, he spent the whole time arguing and distracting his opponents."

"Bottom line—at least two of these jerks remain suspects," Ben said, slamming his hand on the table and jostling the cups.

"Can we return to this discussion in a moment?" Shelby asked. "I need to use the restroom."

As soon as he was out of earshot, Ben leaned toward Mark

and Woody. "Shelby's so enthusiastic about the gas mileage he's going to achieve with his new car that I think I'll tweak him with a little prank."

"What do you have in mind?" Ben asked.

"Listen to his gas mileage results over the next few weeks," Ben replied with a twinkle in his eyes.

When Shelby returned, Mark brought the meeting back to order. "Shelby and Woody, report back on Tuesday with your findings. Now, there's another issue we need to discuss." Mark had been thinking over a comment made by Sophie. He leaned toward the others. "This awful murder will impact our ability to play platform tennis."

"How so?" Woody asked.

"The expansion of the North Boulder Recreation Center building starts in three months," Mark answered. "The two platform tennis courts interfere with the planned renovation. They either need to be moved to another part of the outdoor area or demolished. No decision's been made yet."

"I get your drift," Ben said. "The neighbors feel platform tennis disrupts their peaceful neighborhood, and this murder will only give their complaint more credibility."

"Exactly," Mark replied. "I don't want the reputation of our sport ruined by one criminal. No other courts exist in town and if they're voted down, we're done playing. What can we do to convince the parks and recreation board to keep our courts?"

CHAPTER 6

Late Saturday, Mark's fingers ran over the keyboard of his computer.

Sophie came into his office. "Just a reminder that we have the benefit show at the Dairy this evening. One hour warning. There's some soup and salad waiting for you in the kitchen."

Mark looked up. "I'd forgotten. Give me ten minutes. I'll wrap up."

He completed the search he had initiated, wrote a few notes to remind himself when he next continued with his research, and sauntered into the kitchen to have his light meal.

Sophie brought a bowl of split-pea soup over to the kitchen table.

Mark shook some ranch dressing onto his salad. "I hope this isn't a dress-up affair," he said.

"You could wear a tie, but you don't have to."

"I suppose I can't show up in a sweat suit."

"No. But a nice sweater would be okay."

Mark had worn a tie twice in the last three years, both times at weddings. Early in his career he'd worn a suit and tie every workday, but when he started his own company, he let the ties collect dust in his closet. It was one of the advantages of a small, startup company.

Mark grabbed a pair of pants and a shirt and completed dressing in five minutes, only to have to wait in the living room for Sophie to finish primping.

She appeared in a short black dress, laced with shimmering gold thread.

He admired her well-formed legs and whistled. "You look great."

"Thank you, sir. You don't look too bad yourself, for a retired entrepreneur."

After they drove off, Sophie said, "Remember how we had discussed a trip to Maui?"

"Yeah, and then the little distraction of prostate cancer occurred."

Sophie patted his arm. "Now that you're on the mend, we should pick a date and make plans."

"Some time over the holiday season?"

"No. We'll want to either go down to Norm's or have them come up here. And maybe we can convince Audrey to come to Colorado for the holidays."

Mark thought of his two children, grown and off on their own. He felt that longing to see them. Norm lived in Colorado Springs, but Mark hadn't taken a trip down to see him since the surgery. Norm had been up to visit him in the hospital, but that wasn't the right kind of occasion to really catch up on things. Audrey had also flown out at that time. He should visit her in Los Angeles one of these days. "You're right. A Christmas family reunion would be nice."

"But January or February for Maui might work out," Sophie said.

"I wouldn't mind a calm stay on the beach, sunning and snorkeling." Mark thought back to their last vacation, a Caribbean cruise a year ago. Just the two of them. And a few passionate nights when they had contributed to the roll of the ship. He wondered if that would be possible again.

"Well, let's give it some more thought, and I'll start checking out hotels in a few weeks or so."

When they arrived at the Dairy Center for the Performing Arts, no open parking spaces remained in the lot so they had to park two blocks away. Mark put his arm around Sophie as they walked, and she snuggled up close against him.

The exterior of the building consisted of institutional, white-painted brick, complemented by a series of sculptures outside the door: a colorful modern art totem pole, a metal bench adorned with flying dragon fish and a metal wire contraption that looked like a seated person with a pig's head. Mark shook his head. He didn't understand art.

Many years ago this building had been a working dairy plant, putting milk into glass bottles and, at a later date, cartons. When the Watts-Hardy Dairy moved to a more modern facility, the company donated the old building to the city to be converted into an arts center. As funds were raised, more performance spaces had been added to the facility. Tonight, one partially completed area held folding chairs, and a wooden platform had been installed as a stage. Rental sound equipment stood on both sides of the room.

Mark and Sophie left their coats on a rack in the lobby and mingled with the crowd of several hundred people already assembled.

Sophie immediately waved to some friends and joined their group. Mark said hello to some people he vaguely remembered and started looking around frantically for some way to escape. He saw a dessert bar along the back wall of the room, so he excused himself and scampered over to pick out something chocolate.

Ahead of him in line stood a very attractive woman. She looked like a model, probably mid-thirties, flowing blond hair, excellent figure, low-cut dress. She seemed to be alone so Mark struck up a conversation with her.

"Do you come to the Dairy Center often?" he asked.

She turned her head, and her hair flowed like in one of those shampoo commercials. She had full lips, elegant, dark eyes and cleavage that took his breath away.

"Yes. I'm on the Dairy board. My husband and I participated in the planning for the upcoming renovations."

Mark smiled at the lilt of her southern accent. "I've never attended an event here before." He looked around the room. "The place has . . . potential."

She laughed. "That's an understatement. This room lacks any charm, but it will be a world-class performance space when completed."

Mark helped himself to a piece of German chocolate cake. "By the way, let me introduce myself—Mark Yeager."

"Cheryl Idler." She reached out her hand.

Mark resisted the urge to gawk. He grasped her hand. A firm, warm handshake.

"Are you related to Ken Idler?"

"Yes, he's my husband."

"Is he here tonight?"

She shook her head. "No, he's on a business trip to Central America. He'll be back tomorrow. Do you know him?"

Mark's mind raced a mile a minute. "I know of him. I understand he runs a successful import-export business."

Cheryl looked at Mark warily. "Yes, he's very good at what he does."

"Are you involved in the business at all?"

"No. I leave that to Ken. My interests rest with the arts. Like this center."

"I also play platform tennis. I've seen your husband at the courts. It's a shame what happened to Manny Grimes."

Now Cheryl raised her eyebrows. "You knew Manny?"

"Yes. I played platform tennis with him. I'm surprised your

husband can travel out of the country. I thought he was a suspect."

"He had to request special permission from the Boulder police. He has a business to run."

"It still floors me that someone would murder a nice guy like Manny."

"Maybe he wasn't such a nice guy," Cheryl said as her mouth twitched.

"It sounds like your husband might have had some differences with Manny."

Cheryl clenched the plate in her hand. "Manny hid behind his veneer. He fooled a lot of people."

"I certainly didn't pick up on that. Can you be more specific?"

They had come to the end of the dessert buffet. Cheryl picked up a fork and smiled at Mark. "It's been interesting talking with you. I need to rejoin the other board members."

With that she turned away.

Damn attractive woman, Mark thought as he watched her feline grace.

At that moment Sophie appeared.

"Trying to pick up beautiful blondes?"

"You're all the beautiful blonde I can handle."

"And your new friend?"

"You'll never guess who she is."

"I know her. She's an ex–Miss America runner-up."

"Really?" Mark exclaimed, surprised. "She also happens to be the wife of one of the suspects in the Manny Grimes murder."

"Great. In addition to following attractive women, you're still messing around with the murder."

"I'm off-duty now," Mark said, giving Sophie's hand a squeeze. "Let's find a seat."

They enjoyed a program of musical numbers from hit Broadway shows. The entertainment included several Broadway performers who had grown up in Boulder.

On the way home it suddenly hit Mark that Cheryl Idler had hinted at some issue with Manny and then had avoided discussing it further. He had to find out more.

On Monday evening Mark arrived at the public safety building.

The middle-aged, paunchy lobby guard escorted him up to the meeting room.

Opening the door, Mark surveyed the chamber, which reminded him of a padded cell. It smelled like a locker room.

He sat down next to Ben Quentin.

Ben whispered in his ear, "If you want to make a statement, there's a sign-up sheet by the podium."

Mark strode to a wooden table, covered with grooved gashes that looked like an angry detainee had attacked it with a screwdriver. He added his name to the list.

The Parks and Recreation Advisory Board meeting started promptly at six. Mark scanned the agenda and saw that the platform tennis question wasn't scheduled until eight thirty-five. As the meeting droned on, he realized that it would be nine before his topic of interest would be discussed. After a heated debate for an hour on whether to install gravel around the city soccer fields, Mark extended his estimate to the tune of a growling stomach.

With his head nodding, he jolted upright when the moderator announced that the platform tennis topic would be next.

The recreation administrator began by presenting the plans to the board: "The expansion of the North Boulder Recreation Center building will consume the space currently occupied by two platform tennis courts. We have two alternatives to consider: move within the current property or eliminate the courts. We recommend relocation." He showed drawings of the proposed new site along with the accompanying budget quotes. Then the moderator opened the meeting for comments from interested parties.

First, a platform tennis advocate gave a three-minute summary of working with a committee of nearby residents to develop a design that minimized noise and light pollution.

Then a woman in a tie-dye dress and accompanying headband went to the podium. "These people are elitist and are disrupting our neighborhood with their noisy game that sounds like jumping on a metal drum. I can't look out my window without the glare of lights at night, and with the recreation center expansion if the courts are moved, my children won't have park space to play in anymore."

Ben leaned over and whispered to Mark, "Right. That park is heaped so full of dog shit right now that a kid wouldn't dare play in it."

The woman tugged at the hem of her skirt and straightened her headband. "This so-called sport brings troublemakers into our neighborhood. We don't want murderers wandering our streets."

Mark bolted upright in his seat and grabbed Ben's arm. "Of all the nerve! They *are* using the murder against us."

The woman rambled on. "These people should get a life. It's just a sport. Don't let this small group of undesirables destroy our community. I ask the parks board to honor the greater interest of Boulder and remove this disruptive activity."

Shouts of encouragement reverberated from her supporters as she left the podium.

Mark wanted to kick the seat in front of him. When the moderator called his name to make a statement, he took a deep breath. Grabbing the agenda on the back of which he had scribbled some notes, he clambered up to the microphone.

"Thank you. This debate concerns conflicting rights, the rights of the neighbors versus the rights of the community of platform tennis players. We aren't asking for anything new, only the continuation of a resource that many Boulder citizens actively enjoy."

Mark looked at the faces of the parks board members. One man in coat and tie smiled at him. Three other men and two women sat impassively. He grasped the lectern and flinched with pain. He watched a drop of blood fall to the worn wood surface. He looked at his left thumb and saw a large, imbedded splinter. He let out a breath and regained his focus.

"I understand the concern of the neighbors, but the relocated courts, as planned by the recreation center, will be quieter and have less visible light. People living near a recreation center have an advantage and a disadvantage. The advantage being that they have easy access to an outstanding recreation facility. The disadvantage is that other people use it."

Mark scanned the collection of supporting and antagonistic faces in the auditorium. He returned his gaze to the board members.

"Common sense should prevail. Don't take away a valued resource enjoyed by many Boulder citizens. Please keep the courts at the North Boulder Rec Center."

As Mark returned to his seat, he heard a smattering of applause from his supporters and witnessed the glares from the contingent of hostile neighbors. He sat down and sucked on his injured thumb.

The board moderator leaned toward the microphone. "This concludes the public comments. We will decide tonight to recommend for or against the North Boulder location of the platform tennis courts. That recommendation will then be passed on to the Boulder Planning Board for review."

Mark jerked his head toward Ben. "You mean the issue isn't going to be settled tonight?"

"No, it's a three-step process. First, the parks board, then the planning board and finally the city council."

Mark sat up straight. "So we have to keep fighting this battle."

"You got it, soldier."

CHAPTER 7

On Tuesday evening the partners waited for Shelby at Vic's before their platform tennis game. Shelby finally arrived ten minutes late.

"What happened this time?" Mark asked.

"I had to stop to check the pressure in my tires. I want to take all necessary steps to achieve the best mileage with my new car."

"Couldn't you have done that earlier in the day?" Woody asked.

"Oh, I did. But I'm checking each time I drive," Shelby replied, looking smug.

Ben jumped in. "Our man Mark gave a speech at the park board meeting last night."

"So Mark really bored them," Woody said.

"That doesn't even rate a groan, Woody," Shelby said. "I'm sorry I missed it. I was too busy to attend."

"I understand we won the first round," Woody said.

"So far so good," Ben continued. "The board agreed four to two to recommend keeping the courts at North Boulder Rec. One of the members who voted against us said she would fight it at the next level. Good to see such a unified board."

"What's the next step?" Woody asked.

"A week from Thursday there will be a hearing before the planning board," Ben said. "That will be the tough one. They care about land use and will be inclined to accommodate the arguments of the neighbors."

Mark had been listening thoughtfully. He now raised his head. "Enough concerning our civics lesson. Let's take a checkpoint. Woody, what dirt did you uncover on Howard Roscoe?"

Woody ran his right hand through the sparse hair on the side of his head. "Roscoe's an ex-Marine and gun salesman. Not your typical tofu-eating, protect-the-prairie-dogs Boulder resident. I played platform tennis against him once. He peered at me with steely eyes and drilled the ball right into my chest. No remorse. Just an evil grin."

"Even more than Daggett, he's the suspect I'd put my money on," Ben said. "Minutes after he arrives, he starts an argument, so the game stops and they're all close together at the net. Then bang, the lights go out and whack, Manny does a nose dive."

"I've reached the same conclusion," Mark added. "The timing appeared too convenient."

"It's possible," Woody said, scratching his chin. "But the police would have arrested him by now if it were that simple. One other interesting item regarding Howard Roscoe. He may be dealing in illegal arms, and he sold guns from his company, Westerfield Weapons, to Manny Grimes. Maybe Manny knew too much."

"Why did Manny buy weapons from Roscoe?" Mark asked.

"I don't know," Woody replied. "Something we'll have to investigate."

"So Roscoe exhibits the slimy characteristics of the rest of them and has a potential motive to do away with Manny," Mark said. "Shelby, have you found out anything about Ken Idler?"

Shelby smirked. "I'm happy to report that I took the bull by the horns and am now a full-fledged investigator. I had my teaching assistant spend yesterday doing research for me. Here's what I found out." With a flick of the wrist, he plucked some notes out of his sweat-suit pocket. "First, Ken Idler, fifty years old, owns an import-export business called Idler Enterprises. Once divorced and now married to a trophy wife, Cheryl, prominent in the local social scene."

"I met her at a party on Saturday," Mark interrupted. "Very attractive. Sharp. Not a blonde bimbo."

"You're not picking up other people's wives are you, Mark?" Ben said with a wink.

Shelby furrowed his brow. "Will you two let me continue?"

"Sure, Shelby," Ben said. "Wow us with your findings."

"The Federal Trade Commission investigated Idler Enterprises two years ago. Ken even received a subpoena regarding deceptive practices, but the charges were dropped."

"That's a good start," Ben said. "I've watched him play platform tennis. He loves to goad people. Drives Jacob Fish nuts with his harassing comments."

"Ken has nicknames for people," Woody added. "He calls Howard Roscoe 'Howie,' which he hates."

"I remember hearing him refer to Jacob Fish as 'Fishcakes' and Lee Daggett as 'Animal,' " Shelby said.

"Idler plays a decent game but appears much more interested in what happens between points," Ben said. "Usually has one or more of his opponents irate before completing the second game of the first set. Stays cool himself as he dispassionately watches his opponents unravel."

"Any more?" Mark asked, turning back to Shelby.

"I'll say," Shelby said as a smile crept across his face. "I talked to Ken in person this morning."

"What?" Ben shouted.

"Yes, my TA set up an appointment for me at Ken's office on the Pearl Street mall. Small, basement suite."

"What pretext did you use?" Mark asked.

"I said the police had asked me to do some background checks in regards to the Manny Grimes murder."

Ben smacked his forehead with the palm of his hand. "You're going to land us in deep shit with the police as well as with this group of criminals. How could you do something so stupid?"

Shelby pursed his lips. "If we're going to uncover information, we have to investigate."

"Shelby, for a brilliant professor you have the common sense of a four year old," Ben said, spitting out the words with contempt. "We don't want these assholes to know we're investigating them. They're violent and could easily take it out on us."

"Well, it's too late for that," Shelby said as he threw his notes on the table. "Do you want to hear what I found out or not?"

"Might as well," Ben said, shaking his head. "Before the murderer kills all of us."

CHAPTER 8

Shelby's mouth hung open at Ben's comment.

"That's the first time I've ever seen you speechless," Woody said, elbowing Shelby in the ribs.

Shelby picked up his notes, shuffled them and selected one sheet of paper. He scanned it and then said, "In spite of your irritating interruptions, I'll share this one last item with all of you. I specifically asked Ken Idler who he thought committed the murder."

"And he said the butler did it." Woody chortled.

Shelby gave him an indignant stare. "Of course not. He said he suspected Jacob Fish because Jacob wanted to eliminate Manny as an unwanted investor in Jacob's software business."

"I'm sure each of the suspects puts the finger on someone else," Ben said. "What else did you learn in regards to Ken's business?"

"He wouldn't tell me much more. I think it's crooked though. Probably into some kind of smuggling."

"Look at the time, guys," Mark interrupted. "We'd better head over to the rec center before we lose our reservation."

When Mark arrived at the court, he slammed his paddle onto the net cord. He felt like he wanted to use it on Shelby after hearing of the ill-conceived interview with Ken Idler. He expected repercussions from what Shelby had done. How to contain them? He'd need to put more energy into the investigation to quickly reach a resolution. He took a deep breath and stretched to touch his toes. Now he was ready for action, both off and on the court.

Ben strolled over and poked Mark's equipment bag with his paddle. "Look at this duct-tape repair job. Why don't you buy a new bag?"

"It's still in good shape. A mere tear in the lining."

Ben shook his head. "You should be in a commercial for duct tape. Testimonial from Mark Yeager. Duct tape, the all-purpose adhesive. Holds my shoes, equipment bag and life together."

Mark flinched at the memory of the stitches after his surgery.

Mark teamed with Ben and served first.

Woody drove the return hard to Mark's backhand.

Mark hit a crisp volley that careened off the side screen.

Woody retrieved the shot and hit a deep lob over Mark's head.

Never let a lob bounce was the cardinal rule he'd learned when first playing the game. It presented a new way of thinking. On the small court, once at net, you never gave up the offense.

He reached high and hit a looping shot to the middle of the court. It had to be placed just right so Shelby wouldn't step over and drive a forehand. The ball hit two inches inside the line and rebounded off the back screen.

Woody bent low and thrust his paddle under the ball, sending another lob skyward.

Mark played the shot deep cross court, hoping to force a crazy bounce off the corner where the screens converged. Connect right and the ball would rebound as though launched from a slingshot.

Ben hit an overhead, sending Shelby scrambling to retrieve it.

So many options. Play the ball on a volley, on one bounce, off one screen or off two screens.

After winning the point with a well-placed volley, Mark smiled. What a game!

On Wednesday morning Mark and Sophie sat at the breakfast table, a cup of coffee in each of their hands, looking out the window at the hillside.

"You still have a few late-blooming flowers," Mark said.

"They won't last long between the fall weather and the deer."

"Is your nemesis back again?"

"Yes. That one doe particularly likes our yard. I've shooed her away countless times. She even eats the flowers that deer aren't supposed to like."

"She must appreciate your gardening."

"I've half a mind to take up hunting."

Mark laughed. "I can just picture you looking through the sights of a rifle, especially with your dislike of guns."

"It could happen."

"I doubt that. We could adopt a dog."

Sophie shook her head. "No. I don't miss cleaning up after a pet, and all of our neighbors who have dogs still have deer in their yards. I guess it's the price you pay for living next to open space."

"You have to admit it's quite a sight to watch deer out on the hillside."

"As long as they stay there and don't try to eat my flowers."

Later that morning, Mark drove to the Boulder public library to do some further research on Jacob Fish's company, Creo Tech. He wanted to read a six-month-old article that he'd found a reference to on the Internet, but hadn't yet been able to track down the full write-up. He found it in the stack of magazines, lying askew on the shelf.

He selected a seat in the periodicals section, enjoying the

bright sunlight streaming onto the desk. The article described how Creo Tech contracted a portion of its development to a Taiwanese company called Lingan Ling, a company suspected of selling unauthorized copies of Microsoft Word in Taiwan. More questionable business dealings for Creo Tech and Jacob Fish!

He searched for more information about Lingan Ling, but could find nothing. A dead end. He'd have to locate some other sources.

When Mark returned home, he found Sophie in tears. She stood in the living room.

"What have you got us into," she said with a sob.

"What happened?" he asked, approaching to give her a hug.

"Don't touch me!" She flinched. "Look at that." She pointed to the rug.

Mark bent down and picked up a rock amid shards of glass.

"I came home and found our window broken and this attached to the rock." Sophie tossed a crumpled piece of paper at Mark.

He unfolded it, finding a neatly typed message: CUT OUT THE AMATEUR DETECTIVE CRAP IF YOU VALUE YOUR WIFE, LIFE AND HOUSE.

Mark reached out for Sophie's hand, but she smacked his away.

The doorbell rang.

"I called the police," Sophie said, her eyes blazing. "You can take care of it now." She turned and ran upstairs. He waited a moment and heard the bedroom door slam. He sighed and answered the front door.

Detective Peters stood there. "Mr. Yeager. We received a call reporting some vandalism."

Mark handed the note to Peters and showed him into the living room.

"My wife came home to find this." Mark pointed to the broken glass.

Peters inspected the scene. "I'll have the lab analyze the note, but there's probably nothing we'll discover. You seem to have made some enemies, Mr. Yeager."

"I think we've uncovered a nest of rattlesnakes."

"We?"

"Several of us have been looking into the backgrounds of the suspects in the Manny Grimes murder since Manny was a friend of ours."

Peters's head lifted from the notes he jotted on a pad, and met Mark's gaze. "I need to warn you of the inadvisability of involving yourself in a murder investigation. Who else is helping you?"

Mark looked down. "Shelby Prescott, Ben Quentin and Woody Thorp. You interviewed them the night of the murder."

"And why do you suppose you've received a threat at this time?"

Mark gulped. "Unfortunately, Shelby told Ken Idler that he was investigating the murder. I don't know what linked me to it." Then Mark had a disconcerting thought. He had to talk to Shelby.

Peters snapped his notebook shut. "I'll need to speak with each of your co-conspirators."

Sophie had reappeared. "Please talk some sense into my husband."

"This would be a good time to listen to your wife," Peters said. "The police have an investigation to do. You're only adding work for us and endangering your family."

Mark took a deep breath. "I understand, Detective. I feel I owe it to Manny to try to help. Have you made progress in find-

"I can't discuss the details with you. Be assured that we're doing everything possible. Do you have anything else to tell me about the murder suspects?"

"You probably know this, but here's what I've heard. For starters, Ken Idler and Manny Grimes may have been involved together in suspect business dealings. Also, Lee Daggett gambles and may have been in debt to Manny."

Detective Peters stared at Mark. "You and your friends have come up with more information than the casual observer."

"We all want to see Manny's murderer off the street."

"And what conclusions have you reached?"

"I think all the suspects appear capable of murder. I expect they're pointing fingers at each other. Also, since many platform tennis players wear gloves you probably found no fingerprints on the murder weapon."

Detective Peters chuckled. "You've obviously been mulling this over. One error in your analysis. Fingerprints did appear on the murder weapon. And only one of the people on that court was not using gloves. The problem is that the fingerprints on the paddle used as a bludgeon match the victim's, and the victim was the person without gloves. The murderer used a spare paddle grabbed from Manny's equipment bag."

Mark looked hard at Peters. "I'd be willing to help in any way possible."

"Thanks, but let us take care of it. The rock through your window should convince you to back off."

Peters paused and Mark nodded. "Got it."

"But if your interference turns up anything interesting, please call me. You have the number." Peters winked and headed for the door.

After Peters left, Sophie disappeared upstairs again. Mark called Shelby at his office on the University of Colorado

61

campus. "Shelby, when you spoke with Ken Idler yesterday did you happen to mention my name?"

"Yes, I said we had an investigative team that included you, Ben and Woody."

Mark clenched his fist and said in a strained voice, "Shelby, you'd better go home and check to see if Ken Idler and company left you a love note."

Sophie appeared with a suitcase. "I've called Norm. I'm going to stay with him while you're preoccupied with this ridiculous diversion. I can see by the way you spoke with the policeman that you're only giving lip service to quitting this absurd adventure."

Mark cupped his hand over the phone. "I need to see it through. I owe it to Manny."

"You don't owe anything to Manny. I never liked him. As I've told you, he never seemed on the level to me. In any case, Norm is expecting me. Call me when you come to your senses."

"I will. I need some time to see what I can uncover."

Sophie paused halfway out the door. "How will you stay safe?"

"I'll be careful. I'll be checking in with Ben, Shelby and Woody."

Sophie looked at him in disbelief. "This leads the list of the dumbest things you've ever done."

CHAPTER 9

The Thursday lunchtime platform tennis game generated as much enthusiasm as a steak at a vegetarian convention. Mark resisted the urge to serve the ball into the back of Shelby's shaggy white head when they teamed together, but it was too late to try to knock some sense into him. Afterward, the foursome sat in silence at Vic's.

Mark scanned the room, noting a collection of casually dressed coffee and tea devotees. Then his gaze returned to his companions. "Don't everyone speak at once."

Ben cleared his throat. "I'd like to put my hands around the throat of the bastard who threw that rock through my window. That really pissed me off."

"Did you call the police?" Shelby asked.

"Yeah, a lot of good it will do. And the rest of you?"

"I took a rock as well," Woody said. "I called the police so they'd have it on record." He paused, his eyes darting from side to side. "I don't know if we should continue the investigation," He rested his chin on his hands. "This matter should be left for the professionals. That Detective Peters read me the riot act yesterday. I'll need to think over whether I should stay involved or not."

"What do you have to say, Shelby?" Mark asked.

"This is all my fault." He hung his head for a moment and then looked up. "But it's not possible for me to keep investigating. I can't afford to replace broken windows all the time. My financial situation remains too precarious right now."

"Ben?" Mark fixed him with a steely stare.

"There's a risk if we keep making inquiries into the dealings of these crooks. I've been around enough of them to understand how they operate. They'll only increase their pressure on us. Still, I want to see the bastard nailed who killed Manny."

Mark watched each of them in turn before he spoke. "I understand your concerns. I've thought it over and against my better judgment and the wishes of Sophie, I'm going to continue. Manny helped me, and I want to do what I can to solve this murder."

Ben raised his eyebrows. "I think it's more than that." He wagged a finger at Mark. "You're trying to prove something to yourself."

Mark sighed. "Maybe you're right. This could be my way of coming back from cancer, but I have to see this through."

"There's one viewpoint I'll mention after thinking over what all of you have reported," Ben said. "Ken Idler's now in first place in the suspect beauty pageant. I'm certain that his import-export business involves smuggling. Maybe Manny had some dirt on Idler, so Idler wasted him."

Mark still feared Sophie's reaction to his continued involvement. As he sat in his car outside Vic's, he watched bicyclists in their padded helmets and colorful windbreakers navigate the parking lot. He reached for his cell phone and called his son's law office in Colorado Springs.

"What's up, Dad?"

"Thanks for letting your mother visit, Norm. Did she give you any hint of what I'm doing?"

"Only a comment that you had become too carried away with some project."

"I'm involved in a murder investigation."

There was a pause on the line. "That's not exactly your specialty, Dad. Maybe looking into a new high-tech business but not a murder."

"I know, but the murdered man was a platform tennis friend, and I'm committed to doing what I can to help find the killer."

"What's happened so far?"

"I'm right in the middle of it and trying to piece it together. The biggest surprise so far concerns the murder victim. I've always thought of him as an honest businessman, but I've discovered that he had some pretty dicey dealings with the suspects. They all had reasons to kill him."

"Anything I can do to help?"

Mark thought for a moment. "Actually, you could chase down one thing for me. One of the suspects, Ken Idler, owns a company called Idler Enterprises. I'd like to find out if any legal action has been brought against the company."

"Sure, Dad. I can check that out next week. I'll give you a call when I've had a chance to look into it."

"That'd be helpful."

"But, Dad, I thought you needed to be taking it easy after your cancer surgery."

"Don't start sounding like your mother."

CHAPTER 10

When Mark returned to his home office, he focused on the bookshelf stuffed with the best-selling business books of the last decade. Too bad all that reading hadn't prepared him for the criminal mind. Then he regarded the oil painting of a mountain scene in Alaska. So peaceful. He wouldn't mind being out in the wilderness. He drummed a pencil against his teeth. He had to do something constructive here. Picking up the phone, he punched in the number for Al Lawson at the *Denver Post.*

"Al, have you come across anything else on Jacob Fish or Creo Tech?"

"Yeah, one item came up. Give me a moment to find my notes."

Mark rifled through a few pages of the latest *Business Week* while he waited. He considered starting to read an article on exciting new technologies being tracked by business analysts when Al came back on the line.

"Here it is. Creo Tech recently issued a press release that one of its co-founders, David Randolf, has left the company for personal reasons. Translation—he argued with Jacob Fish and lost."

"Thanks, I'll follow up on that with Randolf. I have something else for you to check out, regarding two other companies that I'm looking into. Do you have any information on either Idler Enterprises or Westerfield Weapons?"

"Never heard of Westerfield Weapons, but Idler Enterprises

sounds familiar . . . Yes, an import-export business based in Boulder. Let me check my computer. I seem to remember an interview I did a while back on that one. Here we go. I interviewed Ken Idler. Kind of a sleazy guy."

"That's the one. What did he have to say?"

"Idler came across as arrogant, bragging how rapidly he had grown his business. Then he turned defensive when I mentioned his smuggling charge a year earlier."

"What kind of smuggling charge?"

"One of his employees was arrested. Here's a direct quote from the smooth-talking Idler: 'That was obviously the work of one individual and not sanctioned by Idler Enterprises. I fired him on the spot and turned him over to the police. I still think one of my competitors paid him to give me a black eye.' Idler's denial doesn't convince me."

"Anything else on Idler?"

"I'll email you my notes. When will I be given something exclusive for all this work I'm doing for you, or do you intend to use up any remaining credibility you still have left?" Al chuckled.

"When I piece this all together, you'll be the first to receive a full report."

"Why am I doubtful that it will be worth anything?"

"You have my word of honor that you'll be the first to know."

"This coming from an ex-entrepreneur?"

After hanging up, Mark tracked down a phone number for a David Randolf. He listened to a voice-mail recording before slamming down the receiver. Back on his computer he did an online search and tried to find the earlier article referencing the smuggling charge, but the *Denver Post* site didn't have that article in their online archive. He'd have to check it out at the library.

Next, he performed a search for Westerfield Weapons. The

web site gave him background on the company: manufactured and sold handguns and rifles. He saw a logo that looked like two crossed rifles and found a listing for a regional office with address and phone number in Denver. Probably the office Howard Roscoe reported into. Mark punched in the number.

"I'm located in Boulder and would like to speak to someone who represents your line of handguns," Mark explained to the woman who answered the phone.

"I can have someone call you," she said very businesslike.

"I'm hard to reach. Can you give me a name and number so I can follow up?"

"One moment, please. Yes, here it is. You can reach our sales representative, Howard Roscoe," she said, and gave Mark the phone number.

Mark ruminated on how far he'd progressed with the investigation. A few unexciting leads to follow up on, but nothing concrete on any of them: Lee Daggett with his gambling connections and possibly illicit financial dealings with Manny; Howard Roscoe, the gun dealer, who supposedly had sold weapons to Manny and who had arrived with perfect timing at the court, right before the lights went out; Jacob Fish of the suspect software business that Manny apparently had invested in. But of them all, Ken Idler currently seemed like *the* prime suspect. Also, Shelby had talked to Idler, and they had all received threatening notes attached to rocks thrown through their windows. Mark decided he'd go to the library the next day to find the article reporting suspected smuggling by Idler's firm.

On Friday Mark turned off Broadway onto Arapahoe and stopped as several scantily clad college girls strolled across the crosswalk from Alfalfa market on this Indian-summer day. He wondered when a sight like that would arouse him as it once had. Parking in the only spot he could find under a now-leafless tree, he looked askance at the crows sitting in the branches, ready to desecrate his freshly washed car.

Inside the library, he located the article he wanted and read: "Inept Criminal or Setup? Raul Hernandez was arrested in Denver after attempting to claim an Italian marble table. Customs officials became suspicious when the long-haired, unshaven and poorly dressed Hernandez arrived to take delivery of the table valued at over ten thousand dollars. They told him that there had been damage in transit and asked him to return the next day. The table was x-rayed, revealing a hidden compartment underneath that contained an estimated fifty thousand dollars of hashish in five packets. When arrested, Hernandez claimed he was acting on behalf of his employer, Idler Enterprises, in Boulder, but the manifest indicated only Hernandez's name. A spokesman for Idler Enterprises denied any knowledge of the shipment."

Mark scanned though later articles to determine that a jury found Hernandez guilty and the judge sentenced him to five to ten years in the Canon City prison.

Mark took out his cell phone to call information and waited to be connected to the prison in Canon City.

"I'm trying to locate a prisoner named Raul Hernandez."

"One moment and I'll connect you with our records department."

After a pause, a man with a slight Spanish accent answered, "Records."

Repeating his request, Mark was told to wait.

The voice came back on the line: "Raul Hernandez was transferred six months ago to a halfway house in Boulder."

"Any reason for the move?"

"Overcrowding. We've moved a number of less violent prisoners to local facilities and he was near the end of his sentence."

Mark next tracked down the number of the halfway house and called. He learned that visiting hours were over, but he could request a meeting the following Monday morning. Mark sat down on a bench outside the library in the now-cooler air, and zipped up his sweatshirt. He thought of the various threads he still had to pursue. Then he opened his notebook and called David Randolf's number again. On the third ring, the ex–Creo Tech employee answered the phone.

CHAPTER 11

During the short phone conversation with David Randolf, Mark set up a lunch meeting for Monday and then drove home in the twilight, squinting at the oncoming headlights. He slumped down at the kitchen table and pushed aside a package of crackers he had left there earlier, struggling to put the pieces together. The doorbell rang. Mark groaned, raised himself and trudged to the door to open it. Two figures with grotesque faces stood there pointing guns at him.

Mark flinched and his heart beat double-time.

"Trick or treat."

He let out his breath, realizing that he had been holding it. He had forgotten it was Halloween. With Sophie gone, he had no idea where she stored the candy.

"Just a minute."

He raced into the kitchen and threw open cupboards until he found bags of Snickers and Three Musketeers. He tore open one of the bags, grabbed a handful of wrapped candy, dashed back to the front door and deposited treats in each outstretched pillowcase.

"Thanks, mister," one of them said as they hustled away.

A steady stream of ghosts, goblins, pirates, princesses and vampires rang the doorbell. Once the trick-or-treaters seemed to be gone for the night, Mark called Sophie at their son's house in Colorado Springs.

"Mark, have you come to your senses yet?" she asked.

"I know you disapprove of what I'm doing. Please give me a little time to see what I can accomplish."

There was a pregnant pause on the line.

Mark heard a sigh.

"If you're going to continue this ridiculous activity, I hope you're taking good care of yourself."

"I'm eating TV dinners, sleeping enough but making very slow progress on the investigation. How is Norm?"

"He's doing amazingly well. I'm so glad he found Dawn. He also seems to be enjoying his law practice. Remember a time when we never would have expected this?"

Mark involuntarily nodded and thought back to Norm's turbulent high-school years. He had always been bright, but as a sophomore he ran with a bad crowd. As hard as Mark and Sophie tried, they couldn't pull him away from this self-destructive group that quickly bypassed alcohol and pot and moved into cocaine. They almost lost Norm in his junior year to an overdose, and it was only after another boy in his group committed suicide that they convinced Norm to join a rehab program. He had stayed clean, finished high school with passable grades, excelled in college, met Dawn and ranked near the top of his class in law school. Now he was married and a successful contract lawyer.

Mark had blamed himself for much of the trouble. He had been too involved at work and had been an absentee father right when he was needed most. Their daughter, Audrey, a year younger than Norm, had experienced her own crisis, having become pregnant at the time Norm was recovering. She gave up the baby for adoption, finished high school and college, and now was a self-assured young woman, working for an insurance company in Los Angeles.

Things he would do over if he had the chance. Sophie had

borne the brunt of their kids' teenage years. One memorable evening she screamed at Mark to quit traveling so much and threw a Spode china plate against the dining-room wall. It was this outburst that had awakened him to his responsibility. Since then he had put his family first . . . up until now.

"Are you still there?" Sophie said.

Mark shook himself out of his recollection. "I'm sorry. I started thinking over the old days. Yes, it's great news how well Norm has been doing."

"For a moment I thought I'd been trapped in one of those television commercials where the cell-phone coverage disappears."

When Mark woke up Saturday morning, he gazed out the window to see snow falling. Checking the outside thermometer, he found the temperature hovered around freezing, accounting for only a thin layer of snow stuck to the ground. He fixed a piece of toast, packed his equipment bag and headed to the North Boulder Recreation Center. As he drove, his mind mulled over things he had learned regarding Manny.

The courts at slightly lower altitude than his home showed some moisture but no accumulated snow.

Ben and Woody stood there smacking balls back and forth to warm up.

"Say, guys," Mark said, "what do either of you really know about Manny Grimes?"

"One of the friendliest players around," Woody answered, bouncing the ball on his paddle. "Always willing to sub for you when you were out of commission. A good sport."

"He played a reasonable game," Ben added. "Manny could hit a powerful forehand, but a crappy lob."

Mark frowned. "Not his platform tennis game. What did you know of him off the court?"

"I met his wife once," Woody said, wiping sleet from his glasses with a towel. "She helped with a fund-raiser for foreign students. Name's Barbara. Kind of a mousy woman."

Their eyes all shifted to the sight of Shelby puffing up the stairs. "Say, we better start," he said, opening the door. "I need to leave by eleven."

"Then how come you're the last one here?" Ben asked.

Shelby ignored him and set his equipment bag down on the deck right inside the door. Then looking up with a huge smile, he said, "By the way, I want to report that my car achieved thirty-five miles to the gallon on the first tank of gas."

"I hope it doesn't drop off," Ben said, winking at Mark. "Some cars quickly change into gas guzzlers."

Woody retrieved a new ball from his sweat-suit pocket. "I love that we can play this game in any weather. With tennis you couldn't play in wet conditions like this."

Mark and Shelby teamed together in the first set. In the middle of the sixth game, Ben hit a high lob to Mark.

"Ken Idler has been on my mind," Shelby said as the ball floated down.

Mark hit a cross-court shot and said through clenched teeth, "Wait until we finish the game."

While changing sides after they won that game, Mark wiped his face. "Okay, Shelby. Now let's discuss Ken Idler."

"I think he's the prime suspect after all. You realize this isn't official since I'm off the case."

Mark rolled his eyes. "None of it's official. You just don't have as much opportunity to put your foot in it anymore."

Shelby took a swig of water from his thermos and wrinkled his forehead. "Do you want to hear my opinion or not?"

"Sure, fire away," Mark said, shrugging.

"As an unofficial observer, I've been thinking. Idler has a very suspicious import/export business and Manny knew this.

Maybe Manny was blackmailing Idler."

"I don't think Manny would do something like that, but you've given me an idea." Mark took his notebook and pen out of his equipment bag and jotted down some notes.

"Are you two going to stall all day?" Ben shouted. "We're ready to finish whipping your butts."

Mark dropped the pad and pen back in his bag. "You, Woody and who else?"

On the next point Mark prepared to return serve.

"One more thing," Shelby said.

Mark's eyes flared at Shelby. "Don't distract me in the middle of the game."

"I'll bet Ken spends a lot of money supporting his wife," Shelby said, ignoring Mark's comment. "Probably can't afford her and paying off Manny. One had to go."

"Who says Manny blackmailed anyone?" Mark hit his paddle against his thigh. "I appreciate your insights, but we're behind in this set."

"It's only a game."

Mark looked at Shelby with disgust. "You sound like some of the neighbors who'd like to rid the city of the platform tennis courts."

The set reached six-all so they decided to play a tiebreaker. Woody prepared to serve, and he stepped over to the deuce side of the court.

"Wait a minute," Shelby called. "You need to serve from the ad court."

Woody grinned. "I always forget the tiebreaker starts on the other side, not like tennis."

He scooted over and served to Mark, who hit a lob back to Ben.

Ben drew his paddle way back and smashed the ball, sending

it bouncing over the fence.

"Damn, bouncy ball," Ben said, kicking the net. "I hate the rule that you lose the point when you hit the ball out of the court."

"We wouldn't have such good rallies if you could always win a point by smacking the ball over the fence," Shelby said, then went out to retrieve the ball.

A few points later Mark played the ball off two screens as Ben kept him pinned back. Five, ten, fifteen rallies. Mark launched yet another lob, feeling a twinge in his sore elbow. He resisted the urge to rub it as he waited for his opponents to hit a short shot so he could drive the ball again. He found beauty in this aspect of the game. Precision and long rallies. Patience. Waiting for the opponents to let down, so he could take the initiative.

Finally, Ben hit a short shot and Mark leaned into it and drove the ball hard enough that Woody missed a volley.

Mark leaned over to catch his breath. Much more finesse than tennis. And besides, at the end of each point he didn't have to waste time retrieving the ball, unless Ben hit it over the fence.

Mark's breathing had returned to normal when a car alarm sounded in the parking lot.

"That God-awful sound coming from any of your cars?" Ben asked.

"Hey, that could me mine," Mark said. "I better go check." After dropping his paddle and opening the court door, he charged down the stairs and jogged along the walkway. As he approached his car, the sound became louder. Pulling his keys out of his sweat-suit pocket, he deactivated the alarm. He reached to open the door but found someone had shattered the window on the passenger side. He looked inside. A wrench lay on the seat amid shards of glass. His stomach tightened, and he looked wildly around the wet parking lot. He could see no one else there. He sat on the curb with his feet in a puddle and rested his head in his hands. It would be a cold and wet drive to Vic's. What pile of muck had he dropped himself into?

Mark, Ben and Woody sat at a table in Vic's and sipped various forms of steaming coffee amid the noise and confusion of a Saturday-morning crowd.

"You sure you want to keep up this investigation?" Ben asked Mark. "Someone has sent you another pretty clear message."

Mark pursed his lips. "I can't give in to intimidation. We need to figure this out. Maybe the murderer will start making careless mistakes."

"Don't be in the line of fire when the asshole makes a mistake," Ben said as he rolled up a napkin and threw it at Mark.

Mark ducked and the napkin landed on the next table, drawing a glare from a young woman in a purple jogging suit.

"I still think you should have reported the broken window to the police," Woody said.

"What good would that have done? I'd only end up receiving another lecture from Detective Peters to stay out of the investigation. Speaking of which, anything new on your suspects?"

"I've run into a dead end," Woody said. "Can't find out anything else concerning Howard Roscoe."

"I'm having a similar problem with that scumbag Lee Daggett," Ben replied, answering Mark's question. "Without being like Shelby and actually confronting the prick, which might be suicide, I've hit a brick shit house."

Mark watched both of his companions as he took another swallow of coffee. "Come on, guys. With the Internet and your contacts in the community, there are all kinds of sources. I've barely scratched the surface."

"Maybe you're better at this than we are," Woody said. "I'm tapped out. We need a new approach."

"I agree," Ben said. "We need some way to observe these ass-holes."

"Something like a party," Woody said.

Mark's head jerked up from his cup, and a smile crossed his lips. "Maybe you're on to something. What if we held a platform tennis tournament?"

"A tournament?" Ben said.

"Yeah. We could pick a Saturday and invite a group of play-ers, including the four suspects. It'd be a perfect way to mingle without raising any suspicion with them."

Ben scratched his chin. "It might work."

"It's worth a try," Woody said. "We need to figure out how to encourage them to come."

"Make it an event they won't want to miss," Mark said. "Then we have to suck them in. We can make all the arrange-ments, charge a minimal fee and order some sack lunches from Safeway."

"I wouldn't put much stock in that because you'd probably get someone sacked," Woody said.

Mark groaned.

"Don't encourage him by acknowledging his awful puns." Ben glared at Mark. "Ignore him."

Woody sat back with a satisfied grin and took another sip.

"I bet if he doesn't receive his pun fix every hour he'll go into a depression," Ben said. "It's like a drug for him."

"Just don't pull da-rug out from under me," Woody said with a straight face.

"Maybe we should exclude Woody from the tournament," Ben said. "He might piss off the murderer. Then we'd have another dead body on the courts."

"That might be a good way to catch the culprit," Mark said. "Woody, would you be willing to act as a sacrificial lamb?"

"Bah," Woody said. "I'm willing to help pull the wool over someone's eyes." He paused as Mark and Ben looked off in another direction. "We should invite Shelby as well. Then we can each keep an eye on one of the suspects."

"I don't know if we can count on him," Mark said. "Still, we should offer to include him. If we're going to start the tournament at nine, we'll tell Shelby that it starts at eight-thirty. Now let's organize this. Anyone object to the Saturday after next?"

They all shook their heads, so Mark continued. "Woody, you reserve the courts. Ben, make plans to provide refreshments and balls. I'll put a flyer together and send it out to our mailing list, including the suspects."

"What if the four assholes don't show?" Ben asked.

"Worst case, we have a good day of hitting the ball. Best case we uncover some good poop. I think I can make the pitch to pull them in, if they're in town. We need to appeal to their big egos. 'By invitation only. Exclusive for the best players in town. First annual all-Boulder platform tennis championship. Good prizes.' How can they resist?" Mark's intense stare met, in turn, each of his friends' eyes. "Everyone start on this immediately. Let's make it happen."

"You need to fix your car window," Woody said. "Don't forget."

"As if I could." Mark wondered what he would have to deal with next.

CHAPTER 12

After Mark showered, he crafted the message for the invitation, designed an attractive brochure and printed out a draft on his color printer. Scrutinizing the result, he made several minor changes and called Woody.

"Are we lined up with the rec center?" Mark asked.

"All systems go."

"Good. I'm sending out the invitations today to our standard list of players. Anyone else you want to invite?"

"No. That'll be fine. How many teams can we accommodate?"

"I thought we'd limit it to eight teams. That way half of the people can play at any time. I'll accept the first eight teams to sign up for the tournament."

"What if the suspects send in their applications late?"

"Tournament director's prerogative."

Mark reread the brochure. The entry fee of twenty dollars per team seemed very reasonable. Enough to make sure people stayed committed.

He accessed the platform tennis list stored in his computer and reviewed it, verifying the suspects' names and addresses. After deleting Manny's name, he printed mailing labels. Good thing he had label stock in preparation for Christmas letters.

After visiting the post office to mail the invitations, Mark returned home and found the message light on the answering machine flashing. He pushed the PLAY button and heard, "Mom and Dad, this is Audrey. Give me a call as soon as you can."

Mark's heart skipped a beat. His daughter didn't call very often. Was she in some kind of trouble? He thought for a moment and decided her voice on the machine sounded happy, not distressed. He took a deep breath and called her number.

"Dad, thanks for calling back," Audrey said. "I'm sorry I haven't called lately, but I've been really busy."

"I'm delighted to hear from you. You still keeping the insurance industry running in Los Angeles?"

"Absolutely. I even received a promotion and a pay increase."

"Good for you. Is that why you called?"

"Not only that. I need to speak with both you and Mom. Can you ask her to come to the phone?"

"Actually, she's down in Colorado Springs visiting Norm right now."

"Will she be back soon?"

"It could be a few days to a few weeks."

"Oh." There was a pause on the line. "I wanted to speak to both of you at the same time, but I'll give Mom a call right after you and I talk, and let both her and Norm know."

"It sounds like you have some news."

"I do." Another pause on the line.

"Don't keep your old dad in suspense."

"Well . . . I'm engaged."

Mark almost dropped the phone. "Is this the boyfriend you've mentioned over the last year?"

"Yup. Adam proposed to me last night and I accepted."

Mark pictured his daughter in a white gown, holding a bouquet of flowers. "That's great news. Have you set a date yet?"

"No. That's something I need to discuss with Mom."

"She'll be delighted to hear the news. When will we have a

chance to meet Adam?"

"I want to talk to both of you to finalize a visit. Adam and I have arranged some vacation time in a little over three weeks. We plan to come see you."

Mark's excitement for his daughter gave way to concern. What if he hadn't resolved the Manny Grimes murder by then? What if Sophie didn't come back from Norm's?

"Why don't you call your mother, and then we can see what works."

"Okay, Dad. I'm looking forward to seeing you."

"Likewise and thanks for calling with the exciting news. I love you."

"Love you, Dad."

After Mark hung up, he sat there stunned. His little girl was getting married. After all the turmoil of the teenage years, his kids had turned out all right. All the credit to Sophie. And how did he thank her? Sending her off to exile in Colorado Springs.

He had to wrap up this investigation quickly. He sat down at his computer to resume research. He tapped his fingers on the edge of the keyboard, trying to decide what to do next. A fleeting thought of taking a nap fluttered through his brain. No, he had to crank up his activity to complete his sleuthing before his daughter came to visit. Then he remembered the broken car window. A vein in his neck started pulsing. He couldn't give in to threats. He pounded his fist on the desk. He had to find the killer. Maybe by understanding Manny, he'd find some clues pointing to the motive for the murder.

Ten minutes later he had only come up with an Internet reference to an art exhibit. It indicated that Mr. and Mrs. Manny Grimes had loaned a painting by Courbet to a gallery in Denver. The article also included an attached image of the painting and an interview describing furniture, art objects and paintings the Grimeses had collected.

Mark realized he should contact Manny's widow. He had addresses and phone numbers on his platform tennis list but had deleted Manny's entry. Too bad he hadn't kept a backup copy. He retrieved the ancient phone book, grateful that he had squirreled it away in his home office, and found a phone number for Manifred and Barbara Grimes on Bluebell east of the Chautauqua auditorium. He punched in the number, and after four rings a woman's quivering voice answered, "Yes?"

"May I speak to Barbara Grimes, please?" Mark asked.

"That's me."

"Ms. Grimes, my name is Mark Yaeger. I used to play platform tennis with your husband."

There was a pause. "Yes, he mentioned your name to me. He also said he filled in for you when you couldn't play."

"Yes, Manny very kindly took my place while I recuperated from cancer surgery."

Mark thought back to when he prepared to go under the knife.

"I hope you're doing better now."

"I've recovered," Mark said, wishing he could believe it. "I'm calling because of some investigative work regarding the murder of your husband and would appreciate a few minutes of your time."

"My sister has been staying with me, but she's out shopping. I suppose I'm available now." Mark heard a sniffling sound and thought she might burst into tears at any moment.

"Excellent," he said quickly. "I'll be at your house in fifteen minutes."

Barbara Grimes lived in an old, two-story, stone house that looked like it belonged on the Boulder Preservation Society's registry of historical homes. A large, well-manicured lawn sloped up from the sidewalk to a solid oak front door.

Mark pressed the doorbell and heard chimes play one of the few classical tunes he recognized from Beethoven's Fifth. He waited for several minutes before the door slowly opened.

An attractive redhead in her early forties stood before him. She wore a red knit top, a black jacket, black skirt and a gold necklace with embedded rubies.

Mark stared at her, and she averted her eyes. Still not looking at him, she invited him in and pointed to a chair in the living room.

"May I offer you some coffee?"

"Yes, thank you. Black."

When she scurried into the kitchen, Mark looked around. The matching Louis XIV furniture he had read about rested on a lush, Persian carpet that covered most of the floor, with one section of polished, grained wood showing. The walls displayed a collection of paintings and a large gilded mirror. A fire burned in a fireplace beneath a mantle exhibiting Greek vases. Mark felt like he had entered a museum.

Barbara returned and set a coffee cup and matching flower-patterned china saucer on a doily on the end table next to Mark. She sat down on a couch across from him and smoothed her skirt.

She still didn't make eye contact.

Mark wondered how to induce Barbara to communicate with him. Then with a flash of inspiration he began to talk. "This room is amazing. Did you decorate it?"

She raised her eyes, and a hint of a smile formed on her face. "Yes. I collected all the paintings and vases."

Mark stood and sauntered over to the painting he recognized from the Internet article. "This looks like a Courbet."

"That's right. One of his early works before he became a realist. I bought it at an auction in Paris, five years ago."

Mark strolled around the room and returned to his chair.

"This is quite a treat. I didn't know a collection like this existed in Boulder."

"I inherited some of the paintings, but I've selectively purchased the rest."

She had transformed into a confident woman, and her blue eyes sparkled.

Mark took a breath. "Ms. Grimes, I'm sorry to bother you at this time, but I'd like to ask you a few questions that may help solve your husband's murder."

"You can call me Barbara. I'll try to help in any way I can."

"First, could you fill me in on Manny's earlier life?"

She thought for a moment. "Manny was a self-made man. An orphan at age six, he learned to take care of himself. He was a natural salesman and investor. He had a full scholarship to Penn State and after college pursued a career as a stockbroker. He became independently wealthy by the age of thirty. We met in New York at an art show, married there and moved to Boulder eight years ago."

"Did Manny discuss any business deals he had with Lee Daggett, Howard Roscoe, Ken Idler or Jacob Fish?" Mark asked.

Barbara fidgeted with her hair. "I didn't involve myself in his business activities, so I don't really know."

"There may be something useful in his files. Did he have an outside office or one at home?"

"He converted our den into a home office. I stayed out of the office. That was his personal space."

"What have the police done with Manny's records?" Mark asked.

"They spent an hour going through his office the morning after he died. Later that day I went to stay with my sister Millie in Detroit . . ." She snuffled and wiped her eyes with a tissue clutched in her hand. "I couldn't stay in this house by myself. She came back with me yesterday and will be here a while. She should be back soon."

"Have you started sorting Manny's papers?"

She frowned. "I don't know what to do or where to start."

"Did he have any business partners who can help you?"

She wrung her hands. "No. He worked alone."

Mark decided to take a gamble. "You're going to need to organize all his things, and I know that can be a daunting task. I had to do that when my dad died five years ago. I'd be willing to help."

"Really?" She looked up at Mark, her lip quivering. "It would be such a relief to have someone take care of that." Tears formed again in her eyes. "I dread having to even go into that office. I don't know who to turn to. I'm not even sure where he kept his will."

"If it's okay with you, I could go through his files and look for the records you'll need. And besides, we may find some new clues pointing to the murderer."

Barbara directed Mark to Manny's office, a spacious room containing a large mahogany desk, separate computer table and two four-drawer file cabinets. A neat stack of paper on the desk rested between the phone and a picture of Barbara on a sailboat.

Mark sat down in the leather swivel chair and opened the third drawer of the first file cabinet. He found it crammed full of unlabeled, bulging manila folders. He opened the other three drawers and saw more of the same. Then Mark picked up the papers on the top of the desk. He found bills from Qwest, Comcast, Xcel, Western Disposal, YourStore Self Storage, the Daily Camera, a Merrill Lynch account summary and several letters requesting charitable contributions.

Mark started leafing through the folders. After scanning a few of them, he discovered that although no labels appeared on the tabs, when he opened them, he often found an identifier written in pencil inside the manila jacket. More than an hour later and in the middle of the fourth drawer, a folded sheet of paper tucked between the pages of a stapled document in a folder with no written identifier caught his eye.

CHAPTER 13

Mark's heart beat faster as he reread the handwritten letter. It said very simply: "I've made the last payment you'll ever see. You've extracted your pound of flesh. Keep this up, you're a dead man." Mark shook his head in amazement that the police hadn't removed this, but apparently they hadn't searched the file cabinet thoroughly. No signature appeared, but the police would be able to trace the handwriting. Mark set the letter aside and continued his search.

After another half hour rifling through pointless papers, he heard Barbara call from the hallway. "If you're hungry, I can make some sandwiches."

"That would be great, but don't go out of your way."

"I'll make something simple."

He continued systematically leafing through the contents of the manila folders in the second file cabinet, but nothing else shed light on the murder.

Barbara arrived with a plate of sandwiches. She had removed the crusts and cut them into neat squares. She darted back out of the room like a scared rabbit.

Mark ate a square of tuna. His tongue savored the sweet-sour taste of pickle relish mixed with mayonnaise. He felt like he had been invited to a tea party. After a few more bites, he resumed surveying the files.

Halfway through the next drawer, Mark found a folder that had information related to suspect Jacob Fish. He skimmed through it. It included a photocopy of a stock certificate. Manny held shares in Jacob's company, Creo Tech. Next appeared a copy of a letter to Jacob Fish introducing him to the principals of Lingan Ling in Taiwan and a letter to a Mr. L. Ling suggesting that Creo Tech would be a good company to work with in the United States. Finally, he found a note: "I want you out of my company. You can either sell back your shares or tear them up." Mark compared the handwriting to the death-threat message, but this handwriting had large loops compared to the constricted writing of the first note. He set this folder on the desk.

Did he really want to know all of this? Was he running a risk of further infuriating the murderer? His stomach churned as he looked out the window and saw a group of children in bright colored jackets walking up the street toward Chautauqua. He sighed, remembering his own children years ago in their ski jackets. Then his thoughts flashed to Sophie visiting their son down in Colorado Springs.

He had to stay focused. Back to the files.

After searching through all eight drawers of the two file cabinets, Mark had four additional manila folders stacked on the desk. One referenced Westerfield Weapons. It contained a copy of an invoice for twenty AR-15 rifles. A letter from Howard Roscoe reminded Manny of being sixty days overdue in paying the bill for his "special" order. This signature differed from the script on the threatening letter. Mark wondered if this special order had anything to do with the purported illegal weapons dealings. He wrote down the type of rifle in his notebook for future research.

Another folder had "Lee Daggett" written in pencil inside the jacket. A ledger had dates and amounts of money—always twenty thousand dollars. Mark looked for a pattern of dates. For six months Manny posted entries around the twentieth of

the month. Then sporadically; some months had no listings.
Nothing appeared for the last two months. Ben had mentioned
a suspicion that Manny had lent money to Lee. Could this be
the record of repayments?

The final folder had some perplexing information citing Idler
Enterprises. It included a handwritten list titled "shipments"
that had specific dates going back several years. At the bottom a
note indicated "consulting opportunity" with a double under-
line.

Mark picked up the material he had set aside and strode into
the living room, where Barbara sat talking with a woman he as-
sumed to be her sister.

He cleared his throat, and Barbara jumped.

"I didn't mean to startle you, but I've found some files that
the police should review if they didn't see them during their
previous visit. I'll call Detective Peters."

Barbara's head jerked. "Yes, please do that . . . Oh, meet my
sister, Millie."

The woman, who appeared to be a well-preserved but older
version of Barbara, raised her eyebrows and said a curt, "Hello."

Mark introduced himself and then asked Barbara if he could
use her phone. He took the detective's card out of his wallet,
placed a call and then said to Barbara, "I've found something
else that will be of use to you." He handed her a manila folder.
"It contains a lockbox key and number at World Savings. I
expect you'll find a copy of Manny's will there."

"I'll go there Monday."

"And you'll need to start assembling Manny's estate information."

A look of panic crossed Barbara's face. "What for?"

"Manny's will should name an executor. You'll need to work
with that person on settling Manny's financial affairs."

"I don't know the first thing about his business dealings."

She turned to her sister. "Millie and I don't have any financial background."

Mark watched her wring her hands again. "You should start with a good accountant," he said. "Do you know who helped Manny with his taxes?"

"I never paid any attention to who worked with him."

"You must have heard a name mentioned."

She put her finger to her cheek and wrinkled her brow. "Wait a minute. I heard a name. Something like Caulder or Coleman."

"Reagan Caldwell?" Mark asked.

"That's it." Her eyes lit up, and she smiled. "That's the name."

"I know him. A very reputable accountant. He'll help you."

Then the smile disappeared from Barbara's face. "But I don't know what to do first."

Mark thought for a moment. "Since I know Reagan and have dealt with numerous financial issues, I'd be willing to assist you in starting the process."

"Would you really?" Her eyes pleaded with him.

"Sure. Give Reagan a call. Tell him that you've authorized me to help with Manny's estate, and I'll give it a shot."

Mark returned to Manny's office and rooted around the desk, finally finding a business card with Reagan's phone number. He wrote it on two slips of paper, put one in his pocket and handed the other to Barbara. "Leave him a message on his voice mail today. I'll follow up tomorrow."

"I don't know how to thank you," Barbara said, her blue eyes still surrounded by streaks of red.

"Don't worry. Manny did me a big favor once, so I'm happy to do anything I can to help. Now I have one difficult question to ask you. Who do you suspect killed Manny?"

She looked like she might cry again. "I overheard Manny

screaming at Ken Idler over the phone the day before he died. I think some problem existed between them."

CHAPTER 14

On Monday morning, as Mark drove up Canyon Boulevard to the halfway house, he thought over what Barbara had said. She'd heard Manny swear at Ken Idler. She claimed this was not characteristic of him. But what had made Manny so mad at Idler? And how did it relate to the murder?

As he entered the modified apartment complex, his thoughts turned to Raul Hernandez, ex-convict and ex-employee of Idler enterprises, who out of boredom or curiosity had agreed to this appointment.

After signing in, Mark followed the receptionist to a room off the lobby. Moments later Mark and Raul sat facing each other across a card table. Raul had long, jet-black hair that fell down his back, a small goatee, gaunt, pockmarked cheeks and darting eyes. Looked to be in his early thirties.

"You wanted to talk to me?" Raul asked, his feet tapping on the floor.

"Yes, I'm investigating Idler Enterprises. I'd appreciate it if you could share with me the events leading up to your arrest."

Raul's gaze bored in on him before he displayed a slight upturn at the side of his mouth.

"Maybe you believe my story and not theirs?"

Mark opened his hands. "I don't know, but I'd like to hear your version."

"It's like this. That asshole Ken Idler paid me to go pick up his smuggled dope. I didn't know that only my name showed and not the company name. When it went down, the feds arrested me."

"Had you done this before for Idler?"

"Yeah, he had told me to pick up two other deliveries." Raul's eyes smoldered.

"Didn't the authorities investigate the company's activity?"

"No one found anything to link Idler. He's smart and let me take the fall." Raul clenched the table as if he wanted to crush it.

"Have you had any contact with Ken Idler since your arrest?"

"No, and I never want to see him again."

"Do you consider Idler capable of murdering someone?"

Raul laughed, showing yellowing teeth. "That bastard would rape and kill his own mother if he could make money from it."

After Mark left the halfway house, he sat in his car, his stomach churning. Pieces started to come together. Manny had an argument with Ken Idler, and, according to Raul Hernandez, Idler had nefarious business dealings. Manny may have been doing some consulting for Idler. Could these links have led to Idler killing Manny? He definitely needed to learn more concerning Manny's relationship with Ken Idler. With Shelby out of the investigation, Idler became his responsibility now anyway. He'd start on that right away. In fact, his promise to Barbara Grimes might help turn up some new information.

He extracted the piece of paper with Reagan's phone number from his pocket, picked up his cell phone and pushed the numbers.

"Reagan, this is Mark Yeager."

"Mark, I had a confused message from Barbara Grimes that you'd be contacting me. Something regarding Manny's estate."

"Yeah. I stopped by her house over the weekend, and she

kind of panicked when confronted with taking care of financial matters after Manny's death. I said I'd talk to you and help out in any way I could."

"You, Barbara and I have our work cut out for us. Manny's estate will be very complicated to sort out."

"How so?"

"He had so many different business dealings. His taxes always presented me with one of my biggest challenges. It took me several weeks, but he always paid the fee promptly."

"Did Manny keep good records?"

"Yes and no. Those he maintained appeared very comprehensive. But periodically I had to handle an undocumented transaction. That always posed problems."

"Why don't we set up an appointment at your office? We can go through what needs to be done. I'll ask Barbara to begin collecting the appropriate material."

"Works for me. How's Wednesday afternoon? Say, two o'clock."

As Mark clicked off his cell phone, he spotted a platform tennis ball on the floor of the car and remembered an action item for the tournament. He punched in Ben's phone number.

When Ben answered, Mark said, "I want to discuss the tournament, but first let me tell you what I learned during my visit to Manny's house over the weekend."

"Hold on. Before you launch into anything concerning the investigation, I have some bad news for you."

"Oh?"

"I want to see Manny's murderer arrested as much as you do, but I have to pull out of the investigation."

There was a long pause on the line as if Ben couldn't find the next thing to say. Mark kept quiet, waiting for Ben to continue.

"My partner agreed to represent a new client today who has

a legal claim against the Manny Grimes estate. Going forward I shouldn't be involved in anything that smacks of a conflict of interest. Sorry."

Mark sighed. "I could use your assistance on this, but understand your problem."

"We'll see each other three times a week when we play, if the courts remain at the rec center," Ben said. "But no more pow-wows at Vic's for me."

Mark felt his stomach tighten. First Shelby and now Ben. He'd have to do more of the fact-finding himself. He decided to discuss the tournament another time.

Mark thought he should chuck the whole investigation. But he couldn't admit defeat. In addition to solving the murder, he now felt a further compunction to help Barbara Grimes. He set his jaw. Her husband's murderer should not be roaming free.

Mark arrived for his lunch meeting at the Boulder Cork ten minutes ahead of schedule so he could be sure of being seated in the corner of the room. He asked the hostess to direct his guest to the table.

Mark's stomach rumbled. He hadn't been eating well with Sophie gone, mainly grabbing a sandwich here and there. He inspected the menu. Time to feast, he told himself. He decided he would order a spinach salad and Maryland-style crab cakes served with coleslaw and rice. Maybe even have mud pie for dessert. Saliva formed in his mouth.

Right on time, a man in his late twenties, well groomed, thick glasses and a firm, serious expression on his face, appeared. David Randolf, the ex-Creo Tech employee, sat down facing Mark.

"I'm doing some investigation of Creo Tech and Jacob Fish," Mark began.

"If there's anything I can do to hurt Jacob, I'm your man."

Mark could almost picture a twenty-pound chip on David's

shoulder. "What makes you so bitter?"

"The guy's turned into a crook. I knew him as a brilliant software engineer when we started Creo Tech together. Along the way something happened. He hooked up with this other loser named Manny Grimes and, suddenly, things changed."

Mark sat forward in his chair. "How so?"

"Instead of developing our own products, we began dealing with a suspicious company in Taiwan. I became more and more concerned. When I voiced my objections to Jacob, he fired me."

"Did you ever find out more information regarding the Taiwanese company?"

"No. Jacob threw me out, flat on my ass. He didn't even give me time to clear out my personal belongings. Illegal activity's going on. I hope you nail him."

"By calling attention to this, aren't you worried that you'll hurt the value of any remaining stock you own?"

"I made nothing on my stock. Jacob set up Creo Tech as an S Corp. The covenants said I had to sell the stock back at the current valuation. Jacob keeps the valuation artificially low for just such an eventuality. He'll end up with ninety percent of the stock and sell it at a huge profit."

"Why didn't you have someone investigate this suspicious company in Taiwan?"

"I should have, but Jacob canned me too fast. Now I only want to distance myself from him and all he stands for."

Mark looked at this beaten man. "Do you think Jacob could kill someone?"

David did a double take. "What makes you ask that?"

"He's a suspect in a murder."

"He's definitely ruthless enough to kill someone. I wouldn't put it past him."

★ ★ ★ ★ ★

When Mark returned home, a message awaited him on his answering machine asking him to call Woody. He dialed immediately.

"I have a problem," Woody said.

"Yes?"

"My project at work reached a critical stage this week, and my boss wants me to put in extra hours."

"So?"

"It means I won't have much time for anything else. Something has to go. I have to choose between giving up platform tennis or the investigation."

"And I know you're not going to forgo our regular game."

"Exactly. I don't want to let you down, but I guess you'll have to find Manny's murderer without me. I'll be willing to discuss it, but not put in the extra time to meet at Vic's and do the leg work."

"All right. Why don't you bring all your notes on Tuesday and give them to me? I've already done a little research on Westerfield Weapons, so I'll take over Howard Roscoe."

Of the four who had agreed to help find Manny's killer, Mark now retained sole responsibility for the investigation. Since the police hadn't solved the crime yet, he felt an obligation to keep trying. He tried to assess his progress so far. Jacob Fish and Ken Idler headed the list of prime slime, having flunked the smell test. He needed to delve deeper into Lee Daggett and Howard Roscoe. First, Daggett.

Mark called Ben. "What's the name of the casino that Lee Daggett invested in?"

"Hold on a moment. I'll find my notes."

Mark looked out the window while he waited.

"Here it is. It's called the Taj Mahal."

Next, Mark picked up the phone and called the state gaming commission to investigate the Taj Mahal and its investors. A bored voice read a short bio on Daggett that indicated a position of president of Daggett, Inc., a Colorado company described as providing gaming consultation.

A search of the Colorado Secretary of State's web site indicated two directors for the company: Leland R. Daggett and Melinda S. Daggett. Mark remembered Ben describing a messy divorce. Maybe the ex-wife would be a good source. He found a listing and punched in the digits.

CHAPTER 15

Mark met Melinda Daggett for breakfast the following morning at Turley's Restaurant.

In stark contrast to Lee Daggett's bull-necked, husky bulk, a diminutive, slender brunette greeted Mark. Up close, Daggett's ex-wife appeared early forties, but could have passed across a table for early thirties just as well.

Mark made a snap assessment and decided to jump right in. "I'm trying to obtain the background of the suspects in the Manny Grimes murder."

"Are you a private investigator or plain nosy?" she said, staring directly into his eyes.

Mark gave a nervous laugh. "You don't beat around the bush. I'm an unsanctioned, unofficial snoop."

She continued to stare at him. "In that case, I'll consider talking to you under one condition."

"Which is?"

"First, you tell me what you've learned so far. Then I'll decide if I'll answer your questions."

Mark felt a bead of sweat running down his cheek as he realized she enjoyed testing him.

"Fair enough," he said. "I've learned of Jacob Fish's involvement in illegal software dealings and Ken Idler's in drug smuggling. I recently discovered that Lee invested in a casino and you used to be part of his corporation."

"And you think Lee might be involved in similar illegal activi-

100

ties, same as Ken and Jacob?"

"It's possible. He seemed to be in debt to Manny Grimes."

"Quite a group, aren't they?" She smiled for the first time.

Mark gave a sigh of relief. "I'm trying to piece together the backgrounds of the suspects and their possible motives. Would you be willing to share a little about Lee?"

"Lee has nothing little associated with him. He does everything big. Big deals. Big fights. Big affairs. That's what ended our marriage."

"Let's start with his business. What is Daggett, Inc.?"

"That's Lee, period. He set up his own corporation so he could do whatever he wanted. It's supposed to be a gaming consulting business, but it's the shell for Lee's gambling activity. Lee's a world-class poker player. He's won and lost millions. Sometimes he's in the chips and sometimes he's on the dole."

"And the relationship between Lee and Manny Grimes?"

Melinda gave a bitter laugh. "It takes a crook to know a crook. They both came from the same mold. I would never have married Lee if I'd known his similarity to Manny."

Mark raised his eyebrows. "Obviously your experience with Manny differed from mine."

"To put it bluntly, Manny was a con artist. He had most people snowed."

Mark felt his cheeks turn warm. "I don't understand. I've played platform tennis with Manny. He always seemed like a perfect gentleman."

"He came across that way," Melinda said. "He put up a front, hiding a complete fraud. Most people had the same opinion you did. He even made a play for me, but I couldn't stand the slimeball. His mousy little wife probably didn't know the real Manny, who was great on outer appearances, but underneath, no good."

Mark took a bite of his California omelet and watched nearby

Mike Befeler

diners for a few moments. He made a mental note to do some further research into Manny's background. "Now, back to Lee."

"He had a real aura that attracted me," Melinda said. "Slip in judgment, I guess."

"Did you know that he owed money to Manny?"

"Only that they always had some deal cooking."

"Any specifics you can share?"

"No. Lee kept his business dealings to himself. But I overheard bits of conversations when they conspired together."

"What happened between you and Lee?"

She bit her lip, then let out a deep sigh. "Lee's a study in contrasts. When we first married, he treated me wonderfully. He had a sense of humor and a love of life. He did little things that I loved. He was a sucker when Girl Scouts came to the door selling cookies. He'd throw away twenty-dollar bills on cookies just as he did when he played roulette. We had boxes of girl-scout cookies stashed all over the house." A faraway look shown in her eyes.

"But that didn't last?"

"No. He has a dark side. He could just as easily put a box of those cookies on the floor and stomp them into powder. The worst of him came out when he started chasing other women."

"Do you think Lee could have killed Manny?"

Melinda paused for a moment. Then she parted her full head of hair with her right hand to reveal a scar hidden high on her forehead. "Lee possesses a violent streak. He was a frustrated lineman cut from the squad at Florida State because he punched out the coach. After a year of marriage, when I told him to give up his outside dalliances, he beat me up and almost killed me. He's knocked out countless men in bar brawls. He easily could have committed a murder."

102

★ ★ ★ ★ ★

Later that morning, Mark had an appointment that he dreaded. He needed to see Dr. Gallagher at the Boulder Medical Center for his next checkup.

As he drove to the appointment, he pushed aside images of the violent Lee Daggett and recalled the whole sequence of events after Manny's insistence that he have a checkup. First the suspicious lump in his prostate. Then the lab test indicating an astronomical PSA. He had immediately scheduled an appointment to see the specialist, Dr. Gallagher, who confirmed the diagnosis. Then the knife.

When Mark arrived at the clinic, he sat down and paged through a medical journal. He had always skipped stories in magazines describing people recovering from heart attacks, strokes and cancer, viewing them as remote fiction, not applicable to him. Now these articles meant something. They portrayed him. He had transformed into a victim, trying to figure out his options—a patient at the mercy of the experts. His body had been invaded by an uncontrolled growth, and now he wondered if that growth had been completely eliminated.

He threw the magazine down and looked up at the abstract art blobs on the wall of the clinic, thinking of growing cancer cells, until a nurse led him into an examination room. Then he stared at a scalpel on the table until Dr. Gallagher finally arrived, dashing in with a manila folder in his hand. He sat down at a laptop computer and tapped away at the keyboard before looking up at Mark over the top of his reading glasses.

"How have you been feeling?"

"As well as can be expected. I hope you cut out all the cancer."

"The radical prostatectomy removed all the cancerous tissue." Dr. Gallagher looked at the screen of the laptop. "I see you suffered no incontinence right after surgery. Has this still been the case?"

"Yes, I've been able to hold my water." Mark thought back to the weakness he had experienced during the three months of recuperation. "Doctor, do you think the cancer has been eliminated?"

"To answer that I'm going to have you come back tomorrow morning for a blood test before you've eaten anything. Go right to the lab on the first floor. They open at seven o'clock." He scribbled instructions on a pad, tore off the sheet and handed it to Mark. "I'll have the results back within two weeks."

"What do you expect the tests to show?"

"Any indications that the cancer has spread. It's something we'll have to check every six months. And you need to pay attention to your diet."

"I know. I used to eat too many cheeseburgers. Much like my dad and uncle who also suffered from prostate cancer."

"With your family history and previous diet, we'll have to keep a close watch."

"What about my side effect," Mark asked as his cheeks flushed.

"As I told you before, it may take time. Nothing indicates a permanent loss of erectile function. Often trauma from the surgery takes months to heal. I've seen function return as long as two years after surgery. We'll have to wait and see."

It had been four months since the surgery. Would he be able to have a normal sexual relationship with Sophie again? Their lovemaking remained in limbo, and he had seen no hopeful signs yet.

Mark left the office with mixed feelings. He appreciated that everything looked good so far. Still, he had two weeks to wait for the results of a blood test that might show further signs of cancer. He needed to stay focused and keep a positive attitude.

That afternoon Mark made plans to check out the final suspect, Howard Roscoe. He had no indirect links to try so he went for the direct approach by calling Roscoe.

"I'd like to talk to you about handguns, and your Denver office gave me this number."

"Sure, why don't we meet tomorrow morning? If you want to come to my place, I can show you the complete line. Also, if you're interested, I own quite a collection of antique weapons."

Mark agreed to be at Roscoe's house at nine the next morning.

That evening Mark made the trek to the courts for the regular Thursday evening game, arriving at nearly the same time as Ben and Woody. The three of them had a good ten-minute warm-up of hitting ground strokes and volleys before Shelby sauntered up the path.

"What kept you, professor?" Ben asked.

"I'm still not used to being off daylight savings time," Shelby answered, rubbing his beard.

"If that's the case then you should be an hour early, since we set the clocks back, not forward," Woody said.

Shelby looked blank.

"Don't confuse him with facts." Ben stuck his paddle under his arm and rubbed his hands together. "Let's start. I'm ready to whip some butt tonight."

Mark teamed up with Woody for the first set. While at net and receiving lobs, he practiced returning a soft, deep, arching shot. This worked until he hit one that was too much of a puff, and Shelby rushed in to hit it in the air, driving the ball between Mark and Woody.

Mark pulled Woody aside after losing that point. "Let me know if he runs in like that again."

"I'll shout 'coming in,'" Woody replied.

Two games later, Mark received a high lob and prepared to hit the arched shot.

"Coming in," Woody shouted.

Mark adjusted his return and hit an angled shot into Shelby's alley.

With a thundering charge, Shelby continued toward the net as the ball whizzed by him for a winner.

"That shows the old goat," Woody said as he touched paddles with Mark.

Mark was in a mood to try some new shots, so he placed more spin on some of his serves. Although he made a few more faults than usual, he succeeded in catching Ben unaware with a spin serve that caused Ben to miss-hit the return.

Then, after a heated rally, one of Shelby's shots clipped the net and dribbled over. Mark raced to the net and dove for the ball. His outstretched paddle couldn't reach the ball before it bounced twice as his body skipped along the court. When he picked himself up he noticed a tear in his left glove and the right leg of his sweat suit.

"A noble effort, but not good enough," Ben said.

Mark dusted himself off, checking to see if he'd lost any skin. The glove had taken the brunt of the rough court but he did find a strawberry on his right knee. The slight injury only steeled his resolve, and Mark drove winners on the next two shots.

Not having heard from Sophie, Mark decided to call her that night when he returned from the game. To begin on a positive note, he said, "Isn't that something? That daughter of ours getting engaged."

"Oh, Mark, I'm so excited for her."

"Did you two discuss a wedding date?"

"She wants to hold the ceremony and reception in Boulder.

We thought next June would be a good time."

"I'll have the checkbook ready." With the uncertainty of his medical situation still on his mind, Mark then changed the subject. "I saw Dr. Gallagher."

"What did he have to say?"

"He thinks I'm recovering well. I have a blood test scheduled in the morning and will have the results back in two weeks."

Mark listened to momentary silence on the phone line before Sophie said, "I've been thinking of you a lot. I'm convinced that you no longer have any cancer."

Mark smiled. "Thanks for the vote of confidence. I wish I could share your optimism. I feel fine, but I'm still worried. I keep wondering if some of the nasty stuff is still there."

"Just stay away from the fatty cheeseburgers."

"I've been good. I'm living off the stack of Lean Cuisine in our freezer."

"Good. By the way, Dawn sends her love and Norm wants to talk to you. Here he is."

"Hi, Dad."

"Good to hear your voice, son. Any luck in tracking down more information on Idler Enterprises?"

"Work continues to be crazy, but I hope to free up some time in the next few days. I haven't forgotten."

"I'm still looking for any clues, so give me a call when you find something."

"You bet. Mom wants to talk to you again."

Mark heard muffled sounds. Then Sophie's businesslike voice came on the line. "Mark, I've been enjoying my visit with Norm and Dawn, but I'm worried about you. When are you going to wrap up this diversion?"

"I'm making slow progress. Shelby, Woody and Ben have dropped out."

"That shows good judgment on their part. Why don't you

follow their lead?"

"I've considered it, but I still think I can help solve this case."

She sighed. "I know how stubborn you can be when you get your teeth into a project. That's your best and worst trait."

"I'll keep at it for the time being." Mark paused, remembering the earlier conversation with Sophie. "I have learned that Manny wasn't the blameless character I thought. Your intuition proved correct."

"I won't say 'I told you so.' But I can't continue to impose on Norm and Dawn forever."

"I think it's still safest for you to be there. I miss you, but I'd be worrying all the time if you came back here. I'm finding that these suspects are pretty unsavory characters."

"That doesn't make me feel very comfortable regarding your safety."

"I'm being careful. I can keep my back covered, but I can't do it while looking around to see if they might do something to you. Be patient."

He heard her sigh again. "I'm learning to be patient."

Mark realized how much Sophie had dealt with through his surgery and now this time of being apart. She could have made his life miserable, but she had chosen to give him some space in his tilting at windmills. Maybe he needed to give up this charade of investigation. How much had he really helped? Why not let Detective Peters carry on? No, he had uncovered the materials at Barbara Grimes's house that the police had overlooked. He would see it out a little longer. Maybe he'd make a breakthrough with Howard Roscoe in the morning. But he had depleted his treasure chest of ideas to pursue. A few more days and he'd take a checkpoint.

"I'll try to wrap this up quickly," he said.

"You better. With Audrey and Adam coming to visit, I need

to return home."

"I'll get cranking."

Roscoe lived in the Wonderland Lake residential area. The hillside above his large, ranch-style home still bore black scars from a fire—a number of summers before—that had sent flames shooting into the night sky.

Mark felt dizzy as he pulled up in front of the house with its well-maintained rock garden. He should have had something to eat after his blood test.

At the door, Roscoe's hand shot out like a cobra to grasp Mark's hand with a firm grip. He ushered Mark into his den, where the wall displayed a variety of firearms. His crisp, dark-blue sports shirt, open at the collar, guarded a late-fifties square jaw beneath a balding head.

"I'm glad we could meet today," Roscoe said. "I have to go out of town tomorrow. Here, take a look at some of my weapons."

"Quite a collection," Mark noted, trying to fake enthusiasm since he couldn't tell a Luger from a Glock.

"Yup. I've collected these since my tour in the Gulf War. Can I offer you coffee, tea or a beer?" Roscoe grinned.

"No, thanks. How long have you been with Westerfield Weapons?"

"Three years in February. Great company and excellent products, as you can see." Howard waved his hand toward the gun collection. "I know my weapons, and Westerfield makes the best."

Not wanting to be sucked into a detailed discussion on guns, Mark decided to change the subject. "Where did you work before Westerfield?"

"Spent five years at Marston Electronics. Another good company. Westerfield recruited me away."

Mark smiled. "I met Norborne Marston, the CEO, a few

years ago. Good man. Took a struggling family-owned business and grew it into an industry leader."

Roscoe's upper lip twitched.

Mark detected a bead of sweat on Roscoe's forehead.

"Yeah. I sold for Marston. Made good money, but Westerfield made it more lucrative."

"Seems like it would be quite a change from electronic surveillance equipment to selling weapons," Mark said.

"Not really. Similar types of customers. Local government agencies like sheriffs' departments and police and then security firms. So tell me what kind of weapons you're looking for."

"I'm starting to familiarize myself with the leading manufacturers and their products. Westerfield's one of the companies I want to explore further."

"So who directed you to me?"

Mark hesitated a moment. "I understand you did business with a mutual acquaintance, Manny Grimes."

Roscoe froze and gave Mark a withering stare.

"We worked a deal or two. How did you know Manny?"

Mark took a deep breath. "I've played platform tennis with him."

Roscoe's eyes flared. "That's what it is. I thought you looked familiar. You're one of the snooping assholes that Ken Idler mentioned. Meeting over. Get the hell out of my house."

With that Roscoe grabbed Mark by the shoulder and shoved him toward the front door.

"Hold it." Mark brushed Roscoe's arm away. "I'll leave on my own. But answer one question: Who do you think killed Manny Grimes?"

"I think a meteorite hit him on the head. Now move your ass out of here."

CHAPTER 16

As Mark drove away, he slammed his palm against the dashboard. He'd sure blown that one. He had only confirmed that the suspects all exhibited violent behavior and that each of them had a motive. As he came to a stop sign, his scowl turned to a smile. He had uncovered one new piece of information.

Ken Idler, having learned of the amateur investigation when interviewed by Shelby, had appeared previously as public enemy number one on the list of most likely candidates to have thrown the rock through his living-room window and broken his car window. But since Howard indicated that Ken had talked to the other suspects about Shelby, any of those creeps could have been the source of the intimidation.

When Mark reached home, he called Marston Electronics in Denver and reached Norborne Marston's administrative assistant.

"Just a minute, Mr. Yeager."

After a momentary pause, a booming voice came on the line. "Mark Yeager. How the hell are you? You still taking over the networking market?"

"Actually, I'm semi-retired. Since we last spoke a year ago, I sold my company to Cisco and plan to do some consulting soon."

"You're too young to retire. Can't see you sitting around on your butt as a consultant."

"I had a little bout with cancer that slowed me down for a while."

"Sorry to hear that. How're you doing now?"

"I'm bouncing back." Mark took a deep breath. "I'm calling because I ran into someone who used to work for you. A man named Howard Roscoe."

"Roscoe, huh?" Norborne's tone sounded cold. "We let him go. Aggressive salesman, but trouble."

"Can you share any particulars?"

Norborne gave a deep sigh. "Best hear it from my VP of sales, Chip Deever. Why are you asking?"

Mark braced himself and then decided to be direct since Norborne didn't like beating around the bush. "Howard Roscoe is a suspect in a murder. I'm checking out his background."

"Doesn't surprise me. The guy had a violent temper. I'll tell Chip to speak openly with you. Give him a call tomorrow."

That afternoon Mark pulled into the parking structure on Walnut and walked the block to Reagan Caldwell's second-floor office.

A tanned arm poking out of a polo shirt shot out to welcome Mark. "Haven't seen you at any of the Chamber of Commerce luncheons in the last year."

"No. With selling my company and then dealing with prostate cancer, I've been inactive."

Reagan furled his brow. "Sorry to hear you had cancer."

"I've recovered," Mark said, hoping he spoke the truth. "So, let's discuss Manny."

"Since we last talked, there has been one further development. Barbara Grimes called again, said she found his will. I'm executor."

"That will simplify things since Barbara doesn't have a clue on how to proceed."

"How much do you know about Manny's business?" Reagan asked.

"Not very much. I knew him through platform tennis. When I visited Barbara this last weekend, she let me go through some of the files in his home office."

"Manny could be rated as one of my more unusual clients. You couldn't classify him as a traditional investor. He ran his own business, didn't have any associates but participated in a diverse range of financial activities."

"I understand he had some sort of business relationship with Ken Idler of Idler Enterprises."

Reagan frowned. "One of those undocumented transactions I mentioned to you. Manny never showed me any contract that defined the terms and conditions of their agreement."

"What I saw hinted at some sort of a consulting relationship."

"I never learned a great deal, but it involved significant payments on an irregular basis."

"How much?"

"Fifty thousand dollars at a time."

Mark whistled. "What could he have done for Idler worth that kind of money?"

"That's what I can't figure out."

"And Manny never mentioned any details to you?"

Reagan shook his head. "I asked him, but he didn't want to discuss it."

If he were a betting man, Mark thought, he'd place his money on blackmail. He'd have to find some specific evidence.

"I understand Manny also invested in Jacob Fish's company, Creo Tech," Mark said.

"Yes. Manny kept good records on that deal. He received a profit distribution at the end of last year from Creo Tech."

"Did you have any indication that Jacob Fish put pressure on

Manny to pull out of Creo?"

Reagan pursed his lips. "No. Why would he?"

"There seemed to be a growing conflict between Manny and Fish. Regarding another project, I also found evidence that Manny bought and sold rifles, his source of supply being a company called Westerfield Weapons."

Reagan looked surprised. "That's a new one to me. It must be an additional sideline. I'm not aware of any business expenses associated with a Westerfield Weapons from last fiscal year."

"Another file I found indicated financial transactions between Manny and Lee Daggett."

"I'm aware of that. Interest payments on a loan that Manny made to Daggett."

"How long had that been going on?"

"Manny made the loan over a year ago."

"It must have been sizeable."

"Yes," Reagan replied. "One point two million dollars."

Mark gasped. "Why did Manny loan that kind of money to Daggett?"

"I questioned him," Reagan said. "He only laughed and said he earned a fantastic interest rate."

"It may have been, but that seems like an awfully risky loan."

"My take as well."

"From what I saw in the files, Daggett didn't make the interest payments consistently," Mark said.

"That's correct. For whatever reason, Manny didn't seem concerned."

"Have you ever seen the loan agreement?"

"No," Reagan replied.

"What would prevent Lee from defaulting and sticking Manny with the remainder of the loan?"

"I don't know."

Ben had speculated about an undocumented loan, Mark

recalled. Maybe Lee had eliminated the financial exposure of repaying Manny.

Thursday morning Mark called Chip Deever.

"Norborne told me you wanted to talk regarding Howard Roscoe," Deever said.

"Yes. I'm trying to track down some information and would like to speak with you."

"I'd prefer not to discuss it over the phone. I'm going out of town this afternoon and will be gone the rest of the week, but could meet you for lunch on Monday. Would noon at the Brown Palace work for you?"

"That's fine."

"Good. I'll have my admin make a reservation for us."

At dusk, Mark sat staring out his window at two deer grazing in the greenbelt. One ducked to eat the brown grass, while the other peered ahead with its ears perked up.

These deer always need to be looking out for mountain lions, Mark thought. Just as he would have to watch out for one of the suspects who might take the next step beyond making threats. If he could only determine which of the four to focus on. It was still an open playing field.

He looked again as the sky continued to darken, wishing more daylight remained. He detested one thing about this time of year—losing the hour of evening light now that they had gone off daylight savings time. He had no objection to the darkness in the morning, but he didn't like the daylight ending so early in the late afternoon.

He wiggled a pen between his thumb and index finger and tried to decide what to do next in the investigation. His game at lunch time had been disappointing. Shelby had arrived twenty minutes late, setting a record even for him.

Mark's friends had razzed him regarding the duct tape he had placed on his torn glove and sweat-suit pants.

"Do you want us to take up a collection so you can buy some new togs?" Ben had asked, laughing loudly.

"Maybe a trip to the Salvation Army store if you're too cheap to buy something new," Woody had suggested.

Mark had played badly, and Woody had to leave early so, all in all, a frustrating outing.

He considered taking a brief walk or catching a short catnap so he'd be prepared for a long night session meeting with the planning board to fight for the platform tennis courts. The ring of the telephone interrupted his stalled decision process. He sighed and picked up the phone to hear his son, Norm, on the line.

"Dad, I tracked down that Idler Enterprises info for you."

"What'd you find?"

"Did you know that Idler was under investigation by the FTC?"

"My tennis buddy, Shelby, uncovered that information before he and the others dropped out of the investigation, but he didn't have any details."

"Ken Idler received a subpoena to testify and turned over a slew of records. They charged him with two counts of deceptive practices under the Federal Trade Commission act. Seems he imported antique vases from China, but some customers claimed they were imitations made in Taiwan. Idler settled by reimbursing his clients and claiming that someone tampered with his shipment. The FTC dropped the case for lack of further evidence."

"The Taiwan connection's interesting. What happened there?"

"Again, nothing conclusive. But the record shows that Idler Enterprises did import vases from a company called Lingan Ling."

Mark jumped up, bashing his knee on his desk. "That's the company Jacob Fish dealt with. These guys all seem linked together. Woody speculated that they all plotted Manny's murder. Maybe a conspiracy among the suspects isn't too farfetched."

"Do you want me to do some checking on Lingan Ling?"

"Yes, please. See if you can find anything further that ties them to either Idler Enterprises or Creo Tech." Mark rubbed his knee and sat down again.

"Okay, I'll see what I can do. By the way, Mom's worried."

"I know, but I'm taking care of myself. It's good she's safe with you for a while. I hope it's not causing you any inconvenience."

"No. It's working out fine. Dawn and Mom have been shopping and playing tourists. It's good for Dawn as well. She's taking a break before resuming her job search."

"I thought she had found something."

"She had an offer, but after meeting more of the people and thinking it over she decided to turn it down. It offered low pay, and the products they manufactured didn't excite her."

"And the name of the company?"

"Westerfield Weapons."

CHAPTER 17

After Mark had leaped up, bashing his knee a second time, he asked Norm to put Dawn on the line.

"I understand you spent some time looking into Westerfield Weapons."

"Yes. I had a series of interviews with them."

"Did you ever hear the name of Howard Roscoe mentioned?" Mark asked.

"No. That doesn't ring a bell."

"Norm says the company didn't impress you."

"That's an understatement. I'd say I found the outfit downright sleazy."

Mark laughed. "Okay. Thanks for the update."

After saying good-bye, Mark sat there, tapping his right foot as he stared at the wall, and tried to collect his thoughts and focus back on the murder investigation. Instead, his mind spun off on its own agenda: cancer.

Mark had his own little murderer inside his body. Rather than using a paddle or bullet, it had turned good cells into bad. He pictured a meat grinder churning steak into hamburger. Meat and muscles being ground into mush.

Did the surgeon cut away all of the malignancy? He pictured cancer cells still chewing up his insides.

And Sophie had stood by him. How did he thank her? By bogging down in this crazy investigation and causing a threat to his family, so she had to run off to their son's house.

118

He pressed his fingers against his temples, trying to stem the unwanted memories, while struggling to regulate his breathing. *Regain control.*

He sighed, flicked a paper clip at the wall and then looked at his watch. Time to prepare himself to go fight for the platform tennis courts again. He couldn't even play his beloved sport without a hassle.

Round two to save the courts started promptly at six P.M. in the auditorium also used by the city council. Enough topics appeared on the planning board agenda to choke a Rocky Mountain elk. Mark gasped when he saw how far down the list the platform tennis topic appeared and left the chamber to go buy some dinner.

When he returned at eight, the board had hardly made a dent in the topic list. He dropped into a seat next to Ben.

"What's the process this time?" Mark asked.

"Similar to the previous hearing: an introduction by city staff, public comment, then board discussion and voting on the topic."

"Then why go through this all again?" Mark asked.

"This board has a different emphasis. They don't care how many people play or what a great sport it is. They make their decision based on factors that impact the recreation-center site and the surrounding area."

"So, what do we need to do to convince them to keep the courts?"

"Answer questions like: Will there be enough parking? How will a decision affect nearby property? What alternative sites exist?"

Mark yawned. "That shouldn't be a problem."

"It's not that simple. They'll treat this like a new application—as an amendment to the original rec-center expansion

119

plan, which they've already approved. Too bad the planners didn't include the relocated platform tennis courts when submitting the original plans."

"What a screw up," Mark said, flicking a speck of lint off his pants.

"Yeah. If we had only known at that time, we could have prevented this whole battle. Now it may be too late."

"You don't sound optimistic."

"It's the nature of these boards," Ben said. "They have their agenda and may overlook the points we consider important."

"It could be a long evening."

"While we're waiting, there's something I've been meaning to ask you," Ben said.

"Fire away."

"You mentioned that you visited Manny's house."

"Yeah. I talked to his wife and looked through his files."

"As you know, my partner has a client with a claim against Manny's estate. It's for a collection of antique paperweights. He paid Manny half the fee, but he never received delivery of the goods."

"And you're trying to find the collection."

"Either that or request a refund. I thought you might have seen something."

"No. But if I come across anything I'll let you know."

Mark listened to an hour-long debate on the design of a new building. Then the board voted to send the architect back for another revision and to report again in one month.

"All talk and no decision," Mark said, shaking his head in disbelief. "If I'd run my company this way, it would have gone bankrupt in two months."

"Welcome to the wonderful world of city government."

★ ★ ★ ★ ★

Finally the platform tennis topic opened for public comment.

The first several statements repeated points made at the previous hearing. Then to Mark's surprise he saw Howard Roscoe, the suspicious gun dealer, go to the podium. Mark had an uneasy feeling in his stomach.

"You're dealing with a damn simple problem here." Roscoe faced the board. "A group of malcontents intends to prevent us from playing our sport. If they don't like it, why don't they move? This board needs to act like adults and not buy this childish crap."

"He's doing us more harm than good," Mark whispered to Ben.

As Roscoe gazed toward the audience, his eyes met Mark's. Roscoe raised his right hand to make a fist, watching with a smirk on his face to ensure that Mark saw him. Then he sauntered to the back of the room.

One of the neighbors went on the offensive during his allotted three minutes: "I request that you mitigate the impact this sport has on our otherwise quiet neighborhood. Please don't subject us to the extensive light and noise pollution. Also keep a small park for our children to play in."

"He makes it sound like we're crashing cymbals together in his backyard and shining searchlights in his windows," Mark said to Ben.

"You wouldn't want a nuclear power plant next door," Ben replied with a twinkle in his eyes as he faced Mark. "These people don't want us disrupting their lives."

"At least no one threw the murder in our faces tonight."

"They don't think they need to."

The final vote came at eleven thirty. Four votes against and two in favor of keeping the platform tennis courts at the North

Boulder Recreation Center.

Mark shook his head in disgust as he gathered in the parking lot with a group of the faithful, fortunately excluding Howard Roscoe. The long day stretched his post-cancer stamina, but he wanted to find out what the next step would be.

"Time to call up the issue before the city council," Ben announced. "With an obvious split between the parks board and the planning board, we need the attention of the higher authority."

"Let's aim for next Tuesday," one of the people said.

"We have to be prepared to address the topics of noise, open space and lights," Ben said.

Just then it struck Mark. He raised his head as a smile spread across his face. "Ben, you're a genius. I'll have to check it out tomorrow."

"What?"

"Lights. That's what I had forgotten."

CHAPTER 18

On the drive home, Mark had the distinct impression of a car following him. He turned off Broadway, and the car stayed on his tail. Rather than going right home, Mark took a side street. He saw a pair of lights still in his rearview mirror. Finally, after another turn the car went a different direction.

I'm becoming paranoid. Still, Mark watched in his rearview mirror for the rest of the drive home.

He woke up the following morning tired and depressed. After breakfast, he headed to the recreation center to continue his investigation. He found out that Julia Ruthers had been the attendant the night of the murder, but she wouldn't be on duty until the afternoon.

Mark returned later in the day to find Julia on a break.

"Where can I find her?" Mark asked the attendant on duty.

"She's in the gym watching a pickup basketball game. She should be there for another ten minutes or so."

Mark strolled into the gym and found an early-twenties woman in shorts and T-shirt sitting on a chair by herself on the sidelines. He pulled up another folding chair and sat beside her.

"Are you Julia Ruthers?"

Her unwavering, wide brown eyes and dimpled smile enhanced her nod.

"I'd like to ask you a few questions regarding the night of the murder on the platform tennis court," he said.

Her smile faded. "Do I have to go over that again?"

"I'd very much appreciate it if you could answer a few questions. I won't take up much of your time."

"I can only spare a few minutes." She peeked at her watch. "Then I have to cover the front desk."

Mark pressed on. "I played on the adjoining court that night. When I arrived, one of the lights was out in the parking lot. Do you know what happened to it?"

"We received a complaint that a vagrant threw rocks at the light. I went out to check, but he ran away."

"Did you see him clearly?"

"Not then, but I think the same man came inside later."

Mark's heart beat faster. "What happened?"

"This street guy sneaked in when I wasn't looking and turned off the platform tennis court lights."

"How'd he do that?"

"There's a switch behind the counter. While I retrieved a towel for someone else, he apparently walked behind the desk. The lights make a clicking sound when turned on or off. I heard the noise and saw him sneaking away from the switch."

Mark watched the pickup basketball game end and the group of players head toward the locker room. "Did you get a good look at him then?"

"Yeah. When I turned around, I surprised him as much as he surprised me."

"Did anyone else spot him?"

"I don't think so. I shouted, 'Hey,' when I saw him, and he ran outside. I went to the door, but he had disappeared by then."

Mark tried to picture in his mind the scene Julia described and then returned his attention to her. "Do me a favor. Close your eyes and try to remember exactly what this man looked like."

She pushed a strand of hair back from her forehead and narrowed her gaze at Mark. "Are you kidding me? I told you I need to return to work."

His eyes met hers. "Humor me. Just try it."

She shrugged and closed her eyes.

"Put yourself back to that night," Mark said in a soothing voice.

She opened her eyes, blinked and closed them again.

He waited a moment for her to stop fidgeting. Then he continued. "You turn and see this man behind you."

Her shoulders visibly relaxed.

"Describe him."

"An old guy, skinny, gray mustache, gray goatee, long gray hair, pockmarked leathery face."

"Do you notice any unique characteristics?" Mark asked.

"Just an old vagrant. Dirty, wild-eyed." She wrinkled her nose. "Smelled like garbage."

"Any distinguishing clothes?"

"No, only worn jeans and a dirty, black sweatshirt. I don't remember any writing on the sweatshirt."

"You see him clearly now. You notice something distinctive. Describe it."

"Nothing . . . wait . . . it's shiny . . . that's it. He had an earring. A silver cross." She opened her eyes wide in surprise.

"Did you tell all this to the police?"

"All except the silver cross earring. I didn't recall that until now."

"You've been a big help. Thanks. I won't keep you any longer."

Mark sat outside on a cement bench, watching the sun disappear behind the foothills. He had to locate this street person.

If he didn't have a home, where would he hang out? He'd choose the Pearl Street Mall. Full of homeless people and panhandlers. Since winter hadn't set in, they hadn't moved south yet.

As Mark pulled out of the parking lot, he remembered the feeling of being followed the night before. He looked in his mirror and saw numerous cars behind him on the busy street.

CHAPTER 19

As he drove, Mark once again had the feeling of being followed. Too many cars on Broadway to make any clear identification. Was his paranoia acting up again?

He locked his car and made his way out of the parking structure on the east end of the outdoor downtown mall. A group of children climbed sculptured animals and jumped into the sand in a play area. Amid the shouts of "Quit pushing" and "Leave my truck alone," Mark remembered his own children playing here when they were young. He jogged across Fourteenth Street to avoid a speeding car and then slowed down as he saw a crowd of street people sitting on the courthouse lawn. He sauntered up to the group.

"Any of you seen a guy with gray hair and goatee who has a silver cross earring?" Mark asked.

"Maybe," one man in a torn, brown, bomber jacket said, looking up. "Got some change?"

Mark dug into his pocket and came up with all his loose coins. Three hands shot out.

He dispensed the money as if feeding parking meters.

"Now what can you tell me?" Mark asked.

The faces went blank.

"Who has seen a man with a cross earring?"

"Don't know anyone like that," the man in the bomber jacket answered, before he closed his eyes and leaned back on the brown grass.

All the others turned away as well.

Realizing he had struck out on any useful information here, Mark turned west and continued to negotiate his way along the mall. A group of people stood on the other side of Thirteenth Street, watching a street performer who could locate any town in the United States by zip code. Another group of street people sprawled against the side of a red brick building. Mark approached them.

"I'm looking for a man: gray hair, a goatee and a pockmarked face. Wears a silver cross earring. Anyone seen him?"

"Sounds like Old Mel," a man in a colorful African robe said.

Mark felt his eyes open wider. "Is he around today?"

"Nah, haven't seen him this week. But he usually turns up on Friday and Saturday nights. Likes to sit in front of Peppercorn. Got a quarter?"

With all of his change gone, Mark pulled out his wallet and found a dollar bill and a twenty. He gave the man the dollar.

"Where does Old Mel sleep?"

"Probably by the railroad tracks out east near Boulder Creek. Nice wooded area to camp out."

Mark found no one in front of Peppercorn, so he meandered two more blocks and ordered a pepperoni pizza and beer at Old Chicago. By the time he started back, darkness had descended. Mark camped out on a wooden bench with a view of the entrance to Peppercorn. He watched the collection of college students, families, teenagers and street people stroll by for two hours. As the autumn evening turned cooler, he gave up and navigated back toward the parking structure. Two doors past the Cheesecake Factory, he cut through an alley. A form caught his attention. He stared. A man lay stretched out along the wall of one building.

As Mark approached, he saw a wine bottle sticking out of a brown paper bag, torn jeans and a black sweatshirt. The man faced the wall.

Mark cleared his throat.

The man remained motionless.

Mark looked around and saw no one else in sight. Gritting his teeth, he shook the man.

A hand fluttered and a drunken voice said, "Go 'way."

Then slowly the man's head turned. A gray goatee, pockmarks and a silver cross earring.

Mark's hand now clamped onto the man's shoulder. "Are you Mel?"

"What's it to you?"

"Thought you might like some wine money in exchange for answering some questions."

The gray-haired head poked up. "Yeah?"

Mark reached in his wallet, took out the twenty-dollar bill and waved it in front of Old Mel like tempting a bull with a red flag.

Mel made an inept grab for the money.

Mark pulled it back out of his reach. "Something for you . . . after we've had a little chat." He noticed an empty chain dangling from Mel's other ear. "Where's your other earring?"

"Lost it."

"Why don't you tell me what you did the night you turned out the lights at the North Boulder Rec Center?"

"Why should I?"

"I thought you might like this twenty-dollar bill."

Mel grabbed again, but missed by six inches and flopped over onto the ground.

Mark waited for Mel to right himself. "Answer my question. Tell me what happened the night you went to the rec center."

The man scratched his leg. "I remember that."

"First, who asked you to turn off the lights?"

"Some guy gave me fifty bucks. Said he'd give me another

fifty after I did it."

"What'd he look like?"

"Never saw him clearly. Too dark. He only said his name was Manny."

Mark gave a start. "That doesn't make any sense. It couldn't have been Manny."

"What're you talking about, man?"

"You're sure that's the name he used?"

"Gave me money and said someone would give me a ride over there. Told me to knock out the light in the parking lot and when I saw a fifth guy walk into the court to go inside and turn out the lights."

Mark heard a noise behind him. He turned as a fist crashed into the side of his face. He fell as a shoe lashed out at his stomach. Not his groin. Anything but that. Mark curled up in a ball as another kick glanced off his back. Then something hit his head.

CHAPTER 20

Mark awoke in a daze. He thought he might have to throw up. His head hurt. Where was he? He felt something unfamiliar in his hand. In the dim light he saw a handgun. Still disoriented, with his ears ringing, he sat up. The smell of smoke made him cough. As his eyes adjusted, he discovered a body sprawled out in front of him. Blood seeped from the forehead below gray hair. Mark remembered. Old Mel.

Mark heard the sound of footsteps behind him. He turned to find a policeman pointing a pistol at him. "Put that gun down. Carefully."

Mark's confusion increased. "I don't know where this gun came from."

"Drop it right now."

Mark opened his hand and the gun clattered to the pavement.

The officer kicked the gun out of Mark's reach. "That's better." He got on his cell phone and called for backup and the EMTs.

Mark put his hand to his forehead and felt a gash. He lowered his hand to his cheek and winced at finding a tender spot. He stared at his hand—covered with blood.

"You have the right to remain silent—"

"Wait a minute. You don't think I did this?"

"Anything you say—"

"Something's wrong here."

"You have the right—"

"I was talking to Old Mel, and someone hit me."

"If you cannot afford—"

"I've been set up," Mark roared. "Look, someone hit me. I'm bleeding."

"I've called to have the EMTs come check you. You can decide at any time—"

"Enough reading rights. Contact Detective Carl Peters. He knows me. Tell him to come speak with Mark Yeager."

Mark's head buzzed. He couldn't get through to this square-jawed fanatic with protruding brow ridges.

"Before I search you, I must advise you of your rights under the Fourth Amendment to the Constitution," the policeman continued with a level gaze at Mark. "You have the right to refuse to permit me to search you. If you voluntarily permit me to search you, any incriminating evidence that I find may be used against you in court, or other proceedings."

"You can search me. Just call Detective Peters."

"Please place your hands against the wall."

Mark felt two hands pat his back and waist.

"Now put your hands behind your back."

Mark complied.

He heard two clicks as the handcuffs closed around his wrists.

Another policeman arrived and began putting yellow tape in a perimeter around Old Mel's body. He opened a satchel and took out a swab that he ran over Mark's handcuffed hands.

Then the first policeman took Mark's arm and led him down the alley. "This way."

Mark stumbled and then regained his balance. As the officer propelled him along, he staggered toward the street.

"What about medical attention?"

"It's coming, sir. Right now I need you to stay in a safe location."

Mark ducked his head and dropped onto the hard plastic backseat of the police car. He watched car lights coming toward him as his head cleared. He squirmed unsuccessfully, trying to find some comfortable position in the cramped quarters.

Shortly, an ambulance screeched to a stop, and two men got out. They spoke with the police officer, who then opened the back door of his car. One of the EMTs cleaned Mark's forehead. He then cleansed the bruise on his cheek. Finally, he slapped bandages on his forehead and cheek. "Do you feel nauseous, sir?"

"No. But my head hurts."

He flashed a light in Mark's eyes. "Are you dizzy?"

"Not now."

"We can take you to the hospital."

Mark remembered when he had been in the hospital for his prostate cancer surgery. He didn't want to be anywhere near a hospital. "I don't need that."

At the county jail the policeman removed the handcuffs. Mark took out his wallet to show his driver's license and then watched as each inked finger made a mark on a card. After one more fruitless request to see Detective Peters, he was led to a holding cell and locked in with two other men.

An unshaven, skinny detainee with a plaid shirt sat on a wooden chair. His companion, appearing to have a similar build to Mark's and sporting an unkempt beard and tattoo of a snake on his forearm, sprawled out on a cot. Both stared at Mark as the door closed.

The man in the chair laughed. "Welcome to the Boulder Ritz. You look like you got in a fight."

"Something like that." Mark sat down on another wooden chair and placed his head in his hands.

"Name's Hansen," the man in the chair said.

Mark looked up. "What are you in for?"

Hansen laughed again. "I tried to rob a Brinks armored truck. Screwed up and got caught."

In spite of the situation, Mark remained curious. "What went wrong?"

"I'd been tracking the pickup and delivery routes between the Worlds Savings branches here in Boulder. Very predictable route. Earlier today I made my move. One of the guards hopped out with a sack. I jumped him and made off with the loot."

Mark pictured Hansen sprinting away with a bag of money in his hand.

"Didn't get very far. Cops stopped me two blocks away. Wouldn't have made any difference anyway. Turns out the armored-truck guard was only delivering lunch to a friend. Inside the bag, the police found a roast beef sandwich. The story of my life. One to ten for stealing a roast beef sandwich." Hansen shook his head. "Didn't even have a chance to take a bite before a cop had handcuffs on me. Roddy here didn't do much better." Hansen pointed at the man on the cot. "Tell Newbie how you robbed a store."

Roddy yawned and sat up, rubbing the side of his face.

"I set up the perfect crime. My girlfriend works at a convenience store. She showed me how to avoid being seen clearly in the cameras. Then one night, I came to the store and threatened her with a fake gun. She gave me all the cash in the register and told the cops she'd been robbed by a guy who looked like Elvis." He scratched his stomach. "I planned to stay low for a while but met this other chick, and we skipped off to Colorado Springs. My girlfriend got pissed and told the police what had happened. Imagine that. Turning herself in just to get back at me. Never trust a broad."

Hansen eyed Mark. "So, what brings you here, sweetheart?"

Mark leveled his gaze at Hansen. "Murder."

After a night of fitful sleep, Mark was escorted by a guard to a room and allowed to make a phone call. His head and cheek still hurt, but he decided he would live.

"Ben, I need your legal services. I've been arrested. Come to the county jail to bail me out. Also, contact Detective Carl Peters. I've been trying to find him, but no one here will give him my message."

"I'll be right there."

While Mark waited, he reviewed the events of the night before. He had found Old Mel, and then someone snuck up on him, punched him in the face and hit him in the head with something. From the wound, it could have been a baseball bat, or as they always said on the crime shows, a blunt object. Had one of the suspects been following him?

When Ben arrived, the desk sergeant led the two of them to a room for a private conversation. Ben wore his sweats, ready for their platform tennis game.

"You look like you're auditioning for the mummy. What happened to you?"

"One of the suspects punched my cheek and hit me on the head."

"Do you need to go to the hospital?"

"No way. My face and head hurt, but I have a hard skull. I've had enough of hospitals to last me for a lifetime. I just want to get out of here."

Ben's eyes widened. "Did you see who hit you?"

"Nope. Are you going to get me released?"

"I had to argue with the sergeant to be allowed to use this room by ourselves," Ben explained. "They haven't set bail yet."

"Have you contacted Peters?" Mark asked.

"I reached him. He'll be here shortly. Maybe he can help speed along the process."

"I'm sure ready to leave this place. I'd rather be playing platform tennis than spending my time with felons."

"I wouldn't care if I left you here, but we'd never find a replacement player for you at this late date," Ben said with a chuckle.

Mark gave him a dirty look.

Peters arrived and asked Ben to wait outside the room. He whistled as he looked at Mark, sitting there. "You don't look so hot. You have some serious bandages. What happened to your face?"

"I was attacked in an alley."

"Do you need to go to the hospital?"

"No. I went through that with the EMTs last night. I have some bruises, but don't need any further medical attention. I would be doing much better if someone had reached you last night."

"I understand you're involved with another murder."

"I didn't do it." Mark glared at Peters.

"I know that."

"What? Then why'd I spend the night here?"

"I only received notification this morning. I checked into the situation and came as soon as I could."

"So, how do you know I'm innocent?"

"They tested you for gunpowder residue and found minute amounts on your hand, providing enough evidence to hold you. But we know you didn't fire the murder weapon. A witness saw another man club you and fire the gun. Then the shooter placed the gun in your hand, accounting for the trace of gunpowder residue left on you. Unfortunately, the witness was too far away to describe the murderer."

"And that whole routine with the police officer reading me my rights?"

Peters shrugged. "He's a new cop—been on the beat on his own for two weeks. He didn't want to take any chance that something you said would be thrown out in court."

"So, am I free to leave?"

"I can have you released in a few minutes, but first you need to answer some questions."

Mark sighed. "Okay. I'll cooperate."

"First, what do you know concerning this latest murder victim?"

"People called him Old Mel. A man hired him to turn out the lights at the rec center. Mel told me he never caught a good glimpse of the guy, who said his name was Manny."

Peters's face revealed nothing. "Anything else?"

Mark considered mentioning that Old Mel camped out in the woods near Boulder Creek on the east end of town, but decided to keep that to himself for the moment. "Only that he received a ride to the rec center. The attack came before I could find out anything else."

"And the attacker?"

"I didn't see him. When I woke up I had the gun in my hand." Mark paused to think. "Has the gun given you any leads?"

Wrinkles formed on Peters's forehead and he tapped his fingers on his knee. "Actually, it has. But I can't discuss it with you."

"Well, at least you know it doesn't belong to me."

"What do you make of the vagrant's statement that a man named Manny paid him to turn off the lights at the rec center?"

"I'm puzzled by that. Manny wouldn't set up his own murder. Someone pretended to be Manny. I haven't been able to make much sense of this whole situation. All four of the suspects have motives, and they all seem capable of having killed Manny and Old Mel."

"So you think one of the suspects in the Manny Grimes murder tried to pin this latest murder on you? Why would someone want to do that?"

Mark looked sheepishly at Peters. "They know I'm still snooping around. I even talked directly with Howard Roscoe."

"Mr. Yeager, leave the investigation to us from now on. As you've discovered, you're dealing with one violent person. Or more. You'll only put yourself, your family and your friends at risk."

Guilty and furious, Mark said, "I hope you're closer to solving this case than the Jon Benet Ramsey murder. Any progress?"

Peters frowned. "I can't share those particulars with you."

"Did you find out who wrote that threatening note to Manny that I left for you on the desk in his house?"

"Yes, but I can't comment further at this time."

"I know the note didn't come from Howard Roscoe or Jacob Fish, so that leaves Lee Daggett or Ken Idler."

"Although I appreciate what you helped uncover in the Grimes files, we'll take it from here."

"But you still haven't arrested anyone."

"Not yet."

"In that case I'll keep snooping. Other than receiving a knock on the head, what damage have I done?"

Peters stood and stared Mark in the eyes. "The coroner has the body of one dead street person who might still be alive if you hadn't been questioning him."

CHAPTER 21

In addition to his cheek and head, Mark felt like he'd been punched in the stomach. He sat in the chair in silence. The detective had nailed the situation accurately. Mark had only accomplished endangering his own life and contributing to the murder of Old Mel. Like his platform tennis partners, he should have butted out of the investigation.

"Can I leave now?" Mark asked.

"Sure. Come with me. We have some paperwork to process. Also, stick around town for the next week in case we have further questions. And I'd suggest getting your head looked at."

"I can manage."

After completing the bureaucratic requirements, Mark rode with Ben to the mall to retrieve his car.

"Ben, I know you can't officially do anything regarding the Manny Grimes murder, but please look into one thing for me."

"What do you have in mind?"

"Check with your contacts in the police department. See if you can find out anything that indicates ownership of the gun they found in my hand. I have a sneaking suspicion it belongs to Howard Roscoe."

Ben pulled to the curb by the parking structure and turned toward Mark. "What makes you think that?"

"I recently visited Howard Roscoe, and the gun looked like one made by his company." Mark opened the door and staggered out of the car. "Thanks, Ben. I'll see you on the court as soon as I can return home, change and grab my stuff."

When Mark pulled in at the North Boulder rec parking lot, he spotted the other three already warming up. He jogged up the stairs to the court, the adrenaline from an anticipated game overcoming the lingering pain in his head.

Woody winced. "You sure you're up to playing? Ben mentioned you had a little problem last night."

Shelby picked up a ball on the court. "It's about time you got here. It seems like we're always waiting for you." He finally looked at Mark. "Whoa. What happened to you? Are you auditioning for a gauze commercial?"

Mark threw his equipment bag onto the court. "I'm fine. This has to be the first time you've arrived before me."

Ben turned to Shelby. "By the way, how's the gas mileage on your car?"

Shelby furrowed his brow. "Second tank of gas didn't do quite as well. This time only twenty-five miles to the gallon."

"Either you've developed a lead foot or that car has problems," Ben said.

"It isn't that bad," Shelby replied, then pursed his lips. "Down from thirty-five miles per gallon to twenty-five."

"Sounds like it's headed to the scrap heap," Ben said, giving Woody a wink.

Mark picked up his paddle. "Let's start the match. I don't need to warm up."

After a bad first set, Mark's adrenaline kicked in again. He hit a winning shot that landed in the corner out of Woody's reach. He pushed aside his bad experience and focused on the strategy of play. The right amount of power. Too weak a shot and the opponents would step in to drive the ball. Too much power and the ball would shoot off the screen and set up the opponents to drive the ball into his body. The golden mean. Just like the investigation. He'd have to walk that middle ground between threat and withdrawal.

After a late afternoon rain shower that didn't quite convince itself to become snow, Mark drove east on Arapahoe, turned left on 48th, parked at the end of the street and stepped out of his car. He staggered momentarily and leaned against the door, his head still throbbing from the assault. Four damp sand volleyball courts and a fence separated the business buildings from the wooded, open space. Mark crossed, leaving footprints in the moist sand. He found an opening in the fence and trudged toward the railroad tracks fifty yards away. The large oak trees had recently been trimmed. The brush within ten yards of the fence had also been cleared, but closer to the railroad tracks the leafless undergrowth thickened. As the branches overhead cut out more of the light of dusk, Mark squinted and finally spotted a lean-to built of sticks and rotten wood. A man sat on a rock in front of it, smoking a cigarette. He wore a black overcoat with the collar turned up in the cool of early evening and a dirty, white Denver Broncos cap. His dull eyes above a white beard stared into the distance.

"Mind if I sit down with you?" Mark asked.

"I don't own any of the rocks here." The man finally looked at Mark. "What happened to you?"

"A minor accident." Mark lowered his sore body to ground level and sat on another rock. "You a friend of Old Mel?" Mark asked.

"Yeah. We share this mansion." Dirty Cap waved his cigarette at the lean-to.

"When did you last see him?"

"Two days ago."

Mark took a deep breath before proceeding. "He was

murdered last night."

The man threw his cigarette onto the ground. "Shit. He owed me five bucks. Well, I guess I'll keep his stuff."

Mark flinched. Not much sorrow here.

"I'm trying to find out who might have murdered him."

"Don't look at me. I didn't do nothin'."

"I know you . . . didn't do nothin' . . . but I have a question. A couple of weeks ago a man paid Mel fifty dollars. Did he mention that to you?"

"Damn right. We had a celebration that night."

"What did he say?"

"Just that this dude gave him money to go turn out some lights at the rec center. He hit payday again after he did it. We celebrated twice."

"Did he tell you how he got over to the rec center to turn off the lights?"

"This classy broad picked him up and drove him over there."

"Did you see her?"

"Damn straight. Blond hair, young, thin, sexy. Looked like a model. Drove a black Jaguar."

Mark thought over what he had heard. There couldn't be that many good looking blondes driving black Jaguars. He should be able to track her down.

"Did it look like a new or old car?"

"Seemed new to me."

"Any identification on the car, dealer plates or license that you noticed?"

"Are you kidding me? Shit. It was a black Jaguar, man. That's all I remember."

As Mark returned to the parking lot, he crossed the volleyball court, retracing his footprints in the sand. Halfway across he noticed additional footprints. Someone had walked part way out and then back. His heart beat faster. He scanned the parking lot, but saw no other cars nearby. He raced to his car, jumped in and locked the doors. He felt a drop of sweat form on his forehead. As he drove away he glanced in his rearview mirror to see if anyone followed him. No lights.

The next day Mark slept late, but still had to down two Advil to settle the lingering headache attributed to the incident at the mall. In the afternoon, he decided to take a break and explore the mountains. He drove up Boulder Canyon and then took the dirt road to Caribou. Old mines dotted the hillside like a pockmarked face. It only made him think of Old Mel. After a short hike, he stopped for dinner in Nederland before returning home after dark.

As Mark pulled into his driveway after stopping at the supermarket, he noticed a dark shape on his porch. He didn't remember leaving anything there. After parking his car in the garage, he walked around to the front of his house. In the darkness he could see a large form. He raced back and entered the house through the garage. Once inside he turned on the front porch light, unlocked the door and stepped out. The vacant eyes of a dead deer reflected in the porch light. Mark bent over. Its throat had been slit, and someone had stuck a yellow, Wilson platform tennis ball in its mouth. A puddle of blood had dried under the deer's neck. A large Bowie knife lay next to the deer. Off to the side, Mark saw, against the white background of the porch, blood-smeared block letters: QUIT.

Sick to his stomach, Mark turned, stumbled into the house, closed the door and staggered to the phone to call Detective Peters.

★ ★ ★ ★ ★

When Peters arrived, he surveyed the scene and shook his head. "I'll have a crime scene investigator come out. Let's sit and talk."

Mark fixed two cups of coffee while Peters placed a call, and then they took seats in Mark's living room.

"Regarding the animal killing," Peters said, "when did you find it?"

"Just before I phoned you. Right when I returned home this evening."

"Where were you?"

"I took a hike and ran an errand. With my wife out of town, it's up to me to keep everything under control."

"Have you noticed anyone suspicious around your house lately?"

"No. But I've been gone a lot. Another thing, though. That unusual knife left on my porch. I bet you'll find it belongs to Howard Roscoe."

"What makes you think that?"

"Roscoe is a weapons guy. It wouldn't surprise me if he had large hunting knives."

"I'll check it out tomorrow. Look, Mr. Yeager. I appreciate the information you're providing, but you seem to have become a target. It would be best if you backed off and let us work the investigation."

Mark took a deep breath. "Everyone is encouraging me to quit, including whoever left the dead deer. I started this thing because of the brutal murder of my friend Manny. Since then, I've discovered that he wasn't a very reputable person. But finding the killer has become a personal issue." Mark's hands turned into fists. "Someone has threatened my family and me. I can't sit and let that happen. I have to do everything possible to help get this criminal off the streets."

"A noble speech," Peters said, staring evenly at Mark. "I admire your commitment, but if you keep this up we'll probably have another murder on our hands. I can't spare anyone to watch you and your house right now. You'd be best served by taking a vacation."

Mark sighed. "I'll take my chances."

"Just remember," Peters said with a withering stare. "Don't think of this as some sort of game."

"I'm very much aware of that. I consider the threat very serious."

The doorbell rang, and Mark opened the door to find the crime-scene investigator, a young man in his twenties, bundled up in a ski jacket and ski cap.

Peters directed him to the deer. Then Peters put on rubber gloves and carefully deposited the Bowie knife in a paper bag.

"What will be done with the carcass?" Mark asked.

"I'll have someone from animal control remove it in the morning," Peters said.

CHAPTER 22

Mark watched as the two men returned to their cars and drove away. He thought of his earlier conversation with Sophie regarding deer in their yard. Clearly, better ways existed to solve deer eating her flowers. With Sophie on his mind, Mark picked up the telephone.

"I haven't heard from you in a few days," she said.

Mark felt daggers of ice travel through the phone line.

"I had a little accident, but everything's fine now."

"How come when I hear 'little accident' I think it's more than that?"

Mark sighed. "There was another murder. A homeless man at the mall. The murderer also hit me over the head."

"Mark, when are you going to come to your senses?" Sophie's voice had a sharp edge to it.

Mark decided not to tell her that he had spent a night in jail. "I know you're concerned. I'll be more careful."

"Did you go to the doctor for a checkup after your 'little accident'?"

"I didn't need to. I suffered only a lingering headache. We played platform tennis the next day and I was none the worse."

"I wish you'd show the judgment of your buddies and give up on this crazy investigation. As much as I enjoy visiting Norm, I'd like to be home."

"I wish you were here as well. It's just not safe right now."

"But don't you realize how that makes me feel? I'm down

146

here worrying about what you're going to do next. That's the situation you've put me in. You should be able to identify with that. Remember your concern when you were on that business trip to Europe right before Norm was born?"

Mark thought back to the helpless feeling. He had sat in a hotel room in Paris, anxious over his wife home alone, expecting a baby within weeks, and he couldn't help in any way. "You're right. I have put you in an untenable position."

"How will this all end, Mark? You need to set your priorities straight. There's only so long that I can go on like this."

Mark wiped a drop of sweat off his forehead, not knowing what to say.

"I've put up with all I can of your little project," she said.

"You've been very reasonable."

"Time to wrap it up. You have two weeks."

Mark didn't want to ask what the consequences would be after two weeks.

"Two weeks," he repeated.

"Think of it as a business deadline. Audrey and her fiancé will be coming to visit and I want to be back and ready for them. You've got two weeks to complete the deal or give it up. End of story."

Mark considered Sophie's statement. She knew how to send a message that his logical thought process would take in. He now had to balance safety and speed. Achieve results and complete this investigation quickly.

"You know me so well," he said.

"I thought I did, but I never expected anything like this latest little escapade of yours. I'm only giving you a green card for one midlife crisis, but no more. Two weeks."

If Mark were in the military, he would have saluted the phone. Sophie had defined his objective, clearly and succinctly.

"I love you, Sophie."

"I love you, too, Mark, although you make it very difficult at times."

After Mark hung up, he put on his jacket, cap and gloves and walked outside. The temperature had dropped and a light snowfall shimmered in the street lights. He could always give up the investigation. But the murderer who threatened him wouldn't know that. He couldn't put an advertisement in the newspaper saying, "I quit. You win. I'm no longer investigating." No, he had to continue. He would crack this puzzle, much like solving many of the business dilemmas he had excelled at. Determination, hard work and brain power. Two weeks.

Mark slept fitfully—dream images swirling in his brain of deer being bashed with platform tennis paddles, leaving puddles of blood on the court. He thrashed and turned, finally dragging himself out of bed at seven. A bandaged face with dark circles under his eyes greeted him in the mirror. He decided to remove the bandages. His cheek retained a purple tint, but didn't look too bad. After experimenting, he discovered if he combed his hair forward, it would cover the wound on his forehead. If anyone asked, he would say he fell off an ATV over the weekend.

Later, he looked out the window to see snow falling and decided to leave half an hour early to drive into Denver for the lunch he'd set up with Chip Deever, the Marston Electronics vice president of sales. He checked the tires on his BMW and decided that the all-year radials would suffice for one more winter.

After pulling into the valet parking at the Brown Palace, he stood on the curb and watched as a stranger drove his car away. He looked up at the red stone building that formed a triangle bounded by Tremont, Seventeenth and Broadway, and admired the archway where stained glass depicted two colorful dragons with tongues of fire blazing at each other. Images flashed through his mind of the dragon he needed to slay.

Glass partitions encased the center of the lobby and polished hardwood tables displayed china and crystal. A group of women, drinking tea and eating cakes, sat primly in stiff-backed chairs. He smiled remembering Sophie and his daughter, Audrey, once going to such an event. He looked down at the carpet, a dark background with a pattern of gray, rust and green intertwined vines. He thought of his entanglement.

Strolling toward the Palace Arms Restaurant, he waited in the entryway as the maitre d' welcomed guests ahead of him. The small foyer displayed Napoleonic era memorabilia on the walls. Mark inspected a gold frame with a velvet-lined picture of a general mounted on a white steed with foreleg strutting high. Then he admired a cabinet filled with sparkling, crystal vases and Chinese dishes. A general's headdress guarded the top of the doorway.

As Mark followed a waiter to his table, he entered nineteenth-century France. Pictures of Napoleonic infantry covered the wall, and a glass case displayed a pair of dueling pistols.

"Those guns belonged to Napoleon and Josephine," the waiter explained.

"Why the flags?" Mark asked as he looked around the room.

"We have twenty-two flags here, representing the period of the exploration of America and the revolutionary era. Replicas but quite authentic."

Mark sipped water from a crystal glass set among shining silverware on a crisp white tablecloth. The carpet had a fleur-de-lis pattern. He picked up the menu, and his gaze riveted on the sesame-crusted pork tenderloin with guava sauce and lotus-root fries. Twenty-nine dollars. Definitely not your fast-food type of lunch.

Moments later Chip Deever arrived.

He gave Mark's hand a firm shake and dropped into a chair.

"I normally wouldn't have this type of conversation, but our CEO, Norborne Marston, asked me to meet with you."

Mark took note of Chip's closely cropped hair above an aging fraternity face. Business casual attire that still smacked of an upscale men's store. At least he was polite enough not to ask about his bruised face.

"We try to forget ex-employees like Howard Roscoe." Chip snapped out his napkin.

"A bad experience with Roscoe?"

"Not just bad, fucking disastrous."

Chip took a sip of water, obviously debating how much to say.

Mark waited with his hands in his lap.

"He interviewed as slick as a mud wrestler," Chip continued. "My staff and I were all psyched with his sales ability, drive and insight into our customer base. The first six months he beat his numbers, increased our revenue at two key accounts and added a new major customer. Then the shit hit the fan."

Chip paused as the waiter came to take their orders. Mark selected a shaved prime rib sandwich, roasted tomato saffron soup and iced tea. Licking his lips, he figured he needed lots of nutrition to deal with the likes of Howard Roscoe.

"I started receiving complaints about Roscoe," Chip said. "Small things at first—missed meetings, late turning in expense reports, inappropriate jokes in front of women. Then the purchasing manager at one of Roscoe's accounts called to terminate business with us. I nearly crapped in my pants, because the account had seemed to be doing so well. I met with the guy and heard him recount a litany of questionable business practices that Roscoe had been involved in."

"Questionable business practices?"

"Procuring women for executives, attempted blackmail with pictures from said sexual encounters and physical threats."

Chip wiped his forehead with his napkin.

"I called Roscoe into my office and repeated the charges. The bastard didn't deny them, only laughed and said that he did what it took to win a client's business. I pointed out that he had now lost the business because of his asshole actions and fired him on the spot."

"How'd he react to that news?" Mark asked.

"Roscoe changed his tone immediately, grabbed me by the collar, told me I would regret firing him and knocked me to the floor. He stomped out of the office. The next day I received a threatening letter. It read: 'Reinstate me if you value your life.' "

Mark flinched. "That's very similar to a threatening note I received."

"I don't picture Roscoe as someone who rides off into the sunset peacefully. The note also included a compromising photograph. We considered going to the police, but Roscoe received a job offer at Westerfield Weapons. They hired him without talking to anyone at Marston. Apparently, Roscoe manipulated it to appear as if Westerfield hired him away from us. Fortunately, once he started the job, he didn't follow up on the threat, so we let it drop. It took me a year to win back the goddamn account he screwed up."

"His behavior doesn't surprise me," Mark said. "Howard Roscoe is a suspect in a murder case."

Chip's eyes widened. "No shit. That fits. The guy's a thug. I thought he would kill me when he attacked me in my office. I should have sued his ass, but I didn't want to risk it with the photograph he had." Chip gave a wan smile. "I learned my lesson to never drink too much at sales conferences."

"Have you heard anything more from Roscoe since he joined Westerfield?"

"Only a rumor that the asshole's converting semi-automatic weapons to automatic and selling them illegally."

★ ★ ★ ★ ★

After lunch Mark checked his watch and decided he had time to stop to see his reporter friend, Al Lawson, at the *Denver Post.*

When Mark called from the lobby, Al came down to accompany Mark back upstairs.

"You look like crap, Mark."

"A little recreational accident over the weekend. You've helped me, so let me tell you more details of this white-collar crime spree in Boulder."

"Peaceful Boulder," Al replied with a laugh. "Crime capital of the Front Range."

Mark recounted what he had learned of the four suspects and their nefarious business dealings.

"Sounds like you've uncovered a den of vipers."

"I'm amazed at the dealings of those four. Still, the police haven't arrested anyone. You'd think enough evidence could be accumulated to nail them on other charges, irrespective of the murder."

"May fit into an article I'm working on. I'll plant a few seeds and see what sprouts."

"Keep my name out of it," Mark said. "I'm having enough problems with these guys."

"You can be my unnamed source."

When Mark returned home, he had another task to take care of. Having thought over what Old Mel's hut mate had told him, he jotted down some notes and searched the Internet for Jaguar dealers. He found one in Broomfield, called the number and asked for the manager.

After a long pause, a man named Seth Pinter identified himself.

Mark went into his rehearsed spiel. "Mr. Pinter, your dealership has been recommended to me. I'm filming a movie in

Boulder and I'm trying to locate a new, black Jaguar to use. I thought you might be able to direct me to some recent purchasers in this area whom I could contact."

"We don't give out names of our customers."

"I understand. But we would be willing to mention your dealership in the movie. You'd receive free publicity in exchange for your assistance."

During a momentary silence on the line, Mark hoped he had tweaked Pinter with enough thought of greed to cloud asking pointed questions.

"We'd let you borrow one, but we don't have anything black in stock right now."

"I need to find a black Jag, right away," Mark said with an edge to his voice.

"Sorry, but I can't give you any names."

Mark hung up in disgust. How else could he track down a black Jaguar? Then an idea struck him. In addition to the Jaguar, Old Mel's buddy had also mentioned a classy blonde.

CHAPTER 23

I must be nuts. Mark knew he should turn around, but instead continued to drive to the home of Ken and Cheryl Idler at dusk to see if they sported a black Jaguar. The vagrant's description of a blonde had triggered his own recollection of how striking Cheryl Idler appeared when he had met her at the Dairy Center benefit. Was his intuition on track or was he deluding himself?

As he found the correct address, he admired the Idlers' large, renovated, turn-of-the-twentieth-century mansion. Ken Idler's smuggling business obviously paid well.

The last time he had been on this street, a month earlier at the peak of autumn, the trees had glowed a brilliant yellow and orange. Now the leaves had been swept away or covered by the snow earlier that day.

Mark looked at the driveway. A black Jaguar XK attracted his attention like a magnet.

He pulled to the curb, his heart thumping rapidly. How should he proceed? He didn't know whether to ring the doorbell or try to find some way to meet Cheryl again.

As he sat there, trying to decide what to do, the door to the house opened. Cheryl, the classy blonde, emerged from the house. She wore a coat with a fur collar, and literally flowed along the walkway to the Jaguar.

After slamming the car door, she backed out of the driveway and turned east. Once she headed down a hill, Mark started his car. Why not follow her? Maybe he could learn something.

Eventually, she drove past the North Boulder Rec Center.

That sight reminded Mark that he wouldn't be able to play his regular game of platform tennis the coming Tuesday night because of the city council meeting—the next round in the unending battle to keep the courts.

Cheryl Idler turned right and drove east. As she and Mark progressed, the effects of the snow storm diminished. Apparently, the storm hadn't hit as much to the north.

Although unpracticed at this "vocation," Mark kept a reasonable distance and still followed the correct set of taillights. He almost lost her once when a signal changed and he had to run the light. He looked in his rearview mirror. Fortunately no cops spotted him.

Finally the Jaguar pulled into a parking space on Third Street in Longmont. Mark found another spot half a block away. He watched as Cheryl slithered out of the car and swayed toward a cocktail lounge. After waiting a moment, he followed her.

The place reeked of beer and pretzels—a shadowy room with the typical contingent of early-evening drunks clustered around the bar.

Mark scanned the crowd and spotted Cheryl sitting by herself in a corner booth. He couldn't imagine her coming all this way to drink by herself, so he figured she was waiting for someone. Might as well see who it would be.

He positioned himself at the bar with a view toward her, pulled his Rockies baseball cap down over his eyebrows and ordered a Coors Light. Cheryl opened her purse and took out a mirror and began primping. She brushed her already perfect hair and then tossed her head back.

Ten minutes later, a man joined her, snuggling up close against her in the booth. Mark recognized him immediately. He stood approximately five eleven, had the build of a proverbial brick shit house, sported a slightly gray-tinged, brown beard to match his brown hair, and displayed his sartorial splendor with a bright red and yellow Hawaiian shirt under an open blue ski jacket. None other than bull-necked Lee Daggett.

The plot thickens. Mark ducked down but kept his gaze on them the whole time. Lee had seen him before, but probably wouldn't make the connection. Still, Mark didn't want to risk it.

He needn't have worried. Lee and Cheryl appeared completely absorbed in each other's company. Lee put his arm around her, and she leaned against him. More than a casual friendship, especially since they'd driven all the way to Longmont to a place that Ken Idler would not be expected to frequent.

They had drinks as Mark continued to nurse his beer. Half an hour later Lee threw a bill on the table, as the two of them stood and headed for the door.

Mark waited until they had walked through the doorway before he dropped a five-dollar bill on the counter, jumped off the bar stool, dashed to the door and peeked outside.

Lee and Cheryl stood next to a black Lexus with their backs to him.

Mark darted past them to reach his car.

Once ensconced inside, he peered through his windshield to keep an eye on the lovebirds.

Finally, Lee opened the door for Cheryl and she climbed in.

When they pulled out, Mark followed at a safe distance in the light traffic. After several blocks he merged with other cars so he wouldn't appear obvious.

Mark maintained a safe distance, but kept Daggett's car in sight.

Within two miles, they pulled into a motel on the outskirts of Longmont.

Mark parked on the street so that he had a view of the motel, a nondescript place with part of the lighted sign burned out that read: CANCY.

Lee went into the office and shortly emerged and waved toward his car. Cheryl hopped out and followed him into a room on the first floor.

Mark felt like a Peeping Tom. He turned on the ignition and drove away.

On his way back to Boulder, questions buzzed within his head like a swarm of bees. How did Lee Daggett having an affair with Ken Idler's wife fit into the murder? Why did she take Old Mel to the rec center to turn off the lights? What was the connection here with Manny?

CHAPTER 24

On Tuesday morning Mark called Ben.

"Did you uncover anything about the gun found in my hand last Friday night?" Mark asked.

"I did track down some information from my mole. The murder weapon used on the vagrant also links two of the suspects in the Manny Grimes investigation."

"I'm sure that includes Howard Roscoe."

"Right," Ben said. "He owned the gun, but came up with a solid alibi for the night you received your whack on the head."

"Who's the other suspect associated with the gun?"

"Jacob Fish kept his eye on Roscoe's house and had a key. He let the police into the house, and they found that someone had broken into Roscoe's gun and knife cabinet."

"Any fingerprints?" Mark asked.

"No; the wood and glass had been wiped clean. Whoever stole the gun from Roscoe left no evidence."

"Either that or Roscoe or Fish set it up. I wouldn't put it past either of them."

"Why's that?"

"Each of them had a motive to do away with Manny and may have wanted to eliminate the vagrant who turned off the lights."

"Well, it couldn't have been Roscoe. He had dinner that night with a group of people in Dallas, so he didn't kill Old Mel."

Mark thought for a moment. "I received another threat the

night before last."

"You did? What kind of threat?"

"A dead deer left on my porch. I bet whoever removed the gun from Roscoe's house also filched a Bowie knife that was later left with the carcass on my porch."

"Could be. Apparently the thief took a number of weapons. You need to be careful around these slimebags."

"Ben, another thing I need to mention to you. I want to be at the whole city council meeting tonight, so I'm going to beg off of our game this evening."

"I'll find a replacement for you," Ben said. "And I'll meet you at the city council chamber after we finish the match."

Mark wanted to make a statement to the murderer. He would not succumb to intimidation. Still, he didn't know which of the suspects seemed bent on harassing him. He retrieved his platform tennis list and looked up the phone numbers of each of the suspects. He dialed each of their numbers, heard a recorded voice each time and left the same message: "I will not quit."

In the afternoon, Mark phoned Peters, but the detective remained unavailable, so Mark left a message.

An hour later Peters returned the call.

"Does the Bowie knife belong to Howard Roscoe?" Mark asked.

A pause on the line, and then Peters said, "You know I don't need to share any information with you," his voice cold.

"I understand. But, I'm more than ever convinced of the link between Roscoe and the Manny Grimes murder. The gun found in my hand belonged to Roscoe. Someone stole it from his house."

"You shouldn't know that."

"Maybe so, but I also suspect the same person took a Bowie knife from Roscoe's house. You could save me the step of confirming that as well."

There was another brief silence on the line. "I met with Roscoe yesterday, and he verified that the knife belongs to him," Peters answered in a businesslike tone. "It seems several items have gone missing from his weapons collection."

Mark quickly processed the information. "Since Jacob Fish had a key to Roscoe's house, he could have taken both the gun and knife."

"I'm not going to confirm that."

"And Roscoe could have reported the gun and knife missing, but really hidden them somewhere else."

"Also possible. Or they could have been stolen."

Mark continued to contemplate the possibilities. Lee Daggett or Jacob Fish or Ken Idler, for that matter, could have stolen the gun and knife.

"And I bet only Howard Roscoe's fingerprints appeared on the knife," Mark added.

"You said it, not me."

Tuesday night. Round three with the powers-that-be to keep the platform tennis courts. This meeting convened with the city council to determine if the issue would be called up for an official vote at the following council meeting. A vote to take a vote.

Mark sank into the comfortable but worn cushion of an auditorium chair in the front row of the city council chamber moments before the meeting began at six. This time, the platform tennis issue appeared on the agenda near the beginning of the meeting. After listening to a discussion on street repair, his cell phone suddenly rang. He reached for it.

The moderator glared at him. "Turn off your cell phone or

you'll be escorted out."

"Sorry," Mark mumbled as he pushed the power button. He'd check who called later.

By seven the public statements began.

The park planner again presented the proposal with the background of how relocating the platform tennis courts within the North Boulder Rec Center property had been approved by the parks board but rejected by the planning board. He concluded, "Given this split in opinion, I request that the city council call this issue up for a final vote next Tuesday."

Supporters then described the wonders of platform tennis, while opponents painted the picture of murderers roaming through what would otherwise be a quiet and peaceful neighborhood. The council members gave no hint of supporting or denying the request to keep the courts, but did agree that, given the diversity of viewpoints, it merited city-council attention. By eight thirty they agreed by a vote of six to one to bring the issue up for a final vote at the next meeting.

As Mark prepared to leave, Ben raced into the room and waved his arms like he held semaphore flags.

Mark signaled back in acknowledgement and ambled over to meet Ben by the door.

"We need to talk," Ben said, his eyes darting from side to side. "Outside."

"What's the panic?" Mark asked.

"I can't say anything here."

He pushed Mark toward the door, and they moved into the empty hallway.

Mark looked at his friend closely. "I've never seen you this upset, Ben."

"Upset? I'm more than upset! Someone almost committed another murder at the rec center tonight!"

CHAPTER 25

"What?" Mark grabbed Ben's arm.

"An assailant attacked Paul Crandall," Ben said.

"Slow down. Start at the beginning and tell me exactly what happened."

Ben took a deep breath. "I lined up Paul Crandall to substitute for you. When we finished playing, Ben, Shelby and I had almost reached the parking lot when I noticed Paul had disappeared. I turned around, thinking he must have left something on the courts. I heard a gurgling sound in the bushes off to the side of the walkway. A dark figure was attacking Paul. I shouted and waved my paddle, scaring the attacker away. Paul lay on the ground. He was gagging, with a garrote wrapped around his throat."

Mark felt his head throb. "Is Paul okay?"

"He's in the hospital under observation."

Mark's gut clenched. "Did you spot any distinguishing features of the attacker?"

"No; it all happened in the shadows. Unfortunately, the court lights had already gone out. I only caught a glimpse of a ski mask."

"Why didn't you grab the attacker?"

Ben frowned. "I guess I froze, and then he ran away."

"Any clues?"

"Only the garrote. Clothesline material with handles on each end. Funny thing though. One side looked like the handle of a platform tennis paddle."

"Did the police have anything to say?"

"They checked the scene and took the garrote away. Interviewed all of us. I think it could have been Ken Idler. Shelby thinks the guy had the build of Lee Daggett, and Woody didn't see enough to form an opinion."

"The assailant meant to attack me," Mark said.

"Why do you say that?"

"Paul's my build and when bundled up could be mistaken for me."

"You can't be serious."

"I feel at fault."

Ben looked at Mark carefully. "What makes you blame yourself?"

"My investigation has obviously provoked someone. I'll have to visit Paul tomorrow."

"By the way, how did the meeting go?"

"I don't like the result," Mark said. "Although we 'won' the issue of having a final vote, I'm not certain that the city council will support the courts when they make the decision next Tuesday."

"We have to round up as many people as we can," Ben said. "The city council responds to citizen input, and if they see overwhelming support for our position, it will help. I'm going to put out an email to all the people on my platform tennis list."

As Mark walked toward his car, he remembered he had received a call on his cell phone during the meeting. He turned his phone back on and listened to a message from a credit-card company.

"Shit," he said. He had incurred the wrath of the city council for a cell phone ringing, and it was something he shouldn't have received anyway. He was supposed to be on the telemarketing do-not-call list.

Wednesday morning Mark found an email from Ben. It read: "The future of our platform tennis courts will be decided finally, one way or the other, next Tuesday night. We need to do several things to help our chances of winning. First, send an email message to the city council asking for their support. Second, show up in person next Tuesday night. The city council pays attention to numbers, and the more people there, the more visibility will be given to our position. You can also make a public statement at the meeting if you want to."

Mark immediately composed a message for the city council. It read: "Concerning the platform tennis courts at the North Boulder Recreation Center, I urge you to approve the Parks and Recreation Advisory Board recommendation. My family and I have played here for years, these being the only public courts in Boulder. As a recent cancer survivor, I find this a very important resource to improve the lifestyle that makes Boulder such an outstanding place to live. Please keep this service that adds to the quality of life in our city."

Mark thought back to when he had teamed with Sophie in mixed doubles. They had also taken the kids out to play a number of times—Mark and their daughter, Audrey, taking on Sophie and their son, Norm.

Mark clicked "Send" and his message whizzed off into the electronic mailbox of each city council member.

He stared at the screen a moment, and then one of the things he had written struck him again. Cancer. Without Manny's insistence, he wouldn't have gone for that fateful physical exam. If he had waited another month, it would probably have been too late and the cancer would have spread.

But had the cancer returned?

He needed to gain control of his thoughts. He stood, stretched and paced the room. Memories ricocheted within his skull. The day of his prostate exam when he saw the doctor's worried look. He hadn't realized the implications—that a knife awaited him. The hospital attendant rolling him on the gurney into the operating room and the groggy feeling before he blacked out from the anesthetic dripping into his arm. The uncertainty of what would happen. The disorientation when he woke up. The puking after the surgery. The pain in his groin for days afterward.

This made him think how Paul Crandall had been attacked and almost killed.

Mark reached for the phone.

Paul's wife answered. She said that Paul had returned home from the hospital and taken the day off from work to recuperate.

"Is this a good time to come over to see him?"

"I'm sure he'd like a visitor."

When Mark arrived, he approached Paul, resting in bed, a bandage wrapped around his throat.

"I'm terribly sorry someone attacked you," Mark said, once again taking note of Paul's physical resemblance to his own build.

"I felt completely helpless," Paul said in a gravelly voice. "All at once someone choked me, and I couldn't do anything. I'm glad Ben came back and scared the attacker away."

"Did you notice any unique characteristics of the guy who jumped you?"

Paul shook his head and then groaned. "None whatsoever. He jumped me from behind and knocked me to the ground. I only saw part of a bush and a beat-up shoe."

"It's too bad you ended up in the middle of this. I think the assailant meant to attack me."

Paul's eyes widened. "Why would someone want to kill you?"

"It's a long story. How do you feel now?"

"I'll be fine. But I don't think I'll play platform tennis at night for a while."

That afternoon Mark called Ben.

"Are there any suspects in the attack on Paul last night?" Mark asked.

"Damn right. I've been plying my sources, and have I uncovered some news for you. First, guess whose fingerprints showed up on one of the garrote handles?"

"I can't imagine the attacker not using gloves," Mark said. "So any fingerprints would be from an earlier use of the handle."

"Possibly. Fingerprints belonged to Ken Idler. How does that grab you?"

Mark thought for a moment. "So, either Idler became careless or someone wanted to make it look like Idler."

"And the handle with the fingerprints was the one made from a platform tennis paddle. Do you want to hear another intriguing tidbit from my mole?"

"I'll bet Ken Idler says he has a paddle missing," Mark said.

"How the hell did you know that?"

"Male intuition."

"No, really, how did you know?"

"Ken Idler is too bright a guy to attempt to garrote someone and then leave a clue with his fingerprints. I think one of the other suspects stole Ken's paddle and tried to set him up."

"I don't know. When the police questioned Idler he said he'd lost a paddle. What a sleaze."

Mark's brain sorted all kinds of possibilities. "I wonder if Idler had an alibi for last night."

"What I heard was that his wife told the police he was going to the rec center. Idler says he had gone back to his office, but no one else worked there that late, so no corroboration of his story. Looks awfully suspicious."

"Seems like a big risk for Ken to attack someone at the rec center. None of you saw the attacker, so it could have been any of the suspects or someone hired."

"Come on, Mark. Why the reluctance to accept that Ken murdered Manny and committed the subsequent attack on Paul?"

"It just doesn't feel right. Remember, someone tried to set me up for Old Mel's murder. I think we're dealing with a killer who uses misdirection. I can't believe that Ken would go to all the trouble of an attack and then leave a garrote with his fingerprints at the scene."

"Maybe he panicked when I came back waving my paddle."

"If he knew what a weak forehand you have, he never would have run away."

After Mark hung up the phone, he sat deep in thought. Then an idea occurred to him. Time to revisit Old Mel's ex-roommate in the lean-to near Boulder Creek.

He stopped at Safeway, before parking near the wooded area. The sun had disappeared behind the mountains when Mark arrived in front of the makeshift habitat. Old Mel's ex-roommate sat on a log, carving a stick.

Mark opened the bag he carried and put two wrapped sandwiches and two soft drinks on the ground. Then he hunkered down. "You and I met a few days ago," Mark said.

The man looked at Mark carefully and opened the wrapping around one of the sandwiches. "Yeah, I remember."

"It seems like there's been another incident at the rec center. A man was attacked with a garrote. I thought you might have heard something."

The man clasped his sandwich as if he held a bar of gold. "What makes you think that?"

"Maybe the same person who hired Old Mel also hired someone to do his dirty work again."

"Could be."

"Anything mentioned down on the mall?"

The man continued to munch on the sandwich, swallowed and then regarded Mark. "I heard some rumors. About a guy who gives us a bad name."

"What did you hear?"

"Same as with Old Mel. Guy hired to go to the rec center. This time to do some damage. Didn't see him around today. Good riddance."

Mark took a bite of his sandwich and chewed for a moment. "What's the guy's name?"

"Clyde."

"Any idea where he hangs out?"

"Usually see him on the courthouse lawn during the day. Don't know where he sleeps."

"If Clyde had come into some money, such as pay for doing this little assignment, any special place he might go?"

"Clyde has a serious drug problem. With money, he might go buy some shit."

Mark opened a bag of cookies and put them on the ground. "If he didn't skip town, what's the most likely spot for him to buy drugs?"

"I'm not into that, man, but he'd probably go to the crack house." The man mentioned a street as he reached for a cookie.

Mark felt his eyes widening. "A crack house, right in downtown Boulder?"

"Yeah. Serves a whole community."

"Do you know the address of the house?"

"No. But you can't miss it. It has a black mailbox in front."

Mark dropped a ten-dollar bill on the ground and raised himself up.

Without looking up, the man said, "If you're thinking of stopping by the crack house, you better not look too neat. They'll think you're a cop."

"Thanks for the advice."

Mark turned and headed back to the parking lot.

He drove home and selected old clothes from the closet: worn jeans, tattered boots, an aging flannel shirt and a stained Broncos sweatshirt.

Back in his car, he slowly cruised until he spotted a house with a black mailbox. He pulled up in front of the house in the pitch black and crept up to the front door. Locked. He looked in a window from the porch. There appeared to be no one inside.

Strange for a crack house. For some reason it appeared out of commission this evening.

CHAPTER 26

Later that evening, Mark checked his notes. He needed to find out more regarding the company Howard Roscoe worked for. He accessed the Westerfield Weapons web site to read a catalog describing their product line and background information on the company. Founder Haskell Westerfield, a World War II veteran and outspoken opponent of any gun-control legislation, started the company in 1960. A sidebar indicated Westerfield would be displaying products at the Harvest Gun Show the upcoming weekend, at the Farwest Hotel in Denver. Mark jotted down the hours and address in his notebook.

Next, he took out the box of letters for the platform tennis tournament. He had received entries from ten teams. He addressed two envelopes and inserted the checks to be returned since there would be only eight teams competing. He looked through the others. Lee Daggett and Ken Idler would team. That should be quite a combination. Howard Roscoe sent in a registration to play with Jacob Fish. Mark had decided not to play, but just run the tournament and observe. Ben and Woody formed a team, and Shelby had found another partner. Four other teams rounded out the entries. He filled in a draw sheet making sure the two teams of suspects were in opposite sides of the draw. The format would provide for first-round losers to go into a consolation bracket. That way every team would be assured of playing at least two matches during the day.

Tired, Mark headed off to catch some sleep.

Mark awoke and sat bolt upright in bed. Murky phantoms swirled in his head. His chest tightened. Was he suffering a heart attack? He breathed in gasps. A dream seeped into consciousness. A wisp of a recollection—running, afraid, trying to escape. What chased him? He wracked his brain to recreate the nightmare image. Slowly, a vague picture formed—an arm with a knife? Or a gun? Then something else—a car trying to run him over? A mysterious stalker? He shivered in the cold, early-morning darkness. He looked toward the nightstand. Ten minutes after two. What had caused him to wake up so suddenly at this hour? He turned his head and listened. A floorboard creaked. The faint sound of the heater running. A car in the distance. Then a rustling sound outside. A neighborhood cat? A deer? Or something else? He held his breath, trying to pierce the wall and darkness. Nothing. He let air escape from his lungs, and his chest slumped. After a few quick gasps he brought his breathing back to a steady rhythm. He had to regain control. Not let his mind wander.

Sophie's face flashed into his mind. He felt a pain inside. He missed her. When would it be safe for her to return? When would it be safe for him again? His stomach tensed. Why had he undertaken this lost cause?

He still felt an obligation to Manny, but Manny had turned out to be a sleaze, not the nice guy he knew. Still, Manny had probably saved his life. Could that be reason enough to sustain taking risks with the investigation? Sophie and his friends all thought he was nuts.

Why not let Detective Peters take care of finding the murderer? Peters gave him that message every time they met.

Ben had stated it clearly. He had something to prove. Helping Manny might have been his initial motivation, but he no longer even cared what kind of person Manny had turned out to be. Now he had to solve this puzzle, prove to himself that he could uncover the truth, take the risk and survive. Win again.

It would be a relief to bow out, but he couldn't let go. It reminded him of when his company almost went out of business. There had been a day when he considered chucking it all, closing the doors and admitting failure. But he didn't. He had pressed his investors again. Just one more small round of funding. They had acted reluctant, but his insistence paid off, and he'd had a major order with Cisco pending. He had asked for an additional month of funding, and, finally, they had given it to him. The investors had maintained their skepticism, but Mark had known he could pull it off. And he'd done it. He had won the order, and the follow-on business had taken off like a skyrocket. He had succeeded, and his investors had multiplied their hesitant handout twenty fold.

Maybe now he sought to regain something the surgeon's knife had cut away. A drive to be alive? He shuddered. His heart raced. People had treated him differently right after the surgery. Poor Mark. Vulnerable Mark. No longer the tough entrepreneur. The cancer victim lying in a hospital bed, stumbling around the hospital room with his air-conditioned butt hanging out.

What if the cancer continued growing inside again? What if it was eating away at other organs at this very moment? Did he have a time bomb ticking in his groin? Had his death warrant already been signed? Did it matter if the cancer or the murderer killed him first? He wiped a trickling bead of sweat from his forehead.

He could take a vacation, be with Sophie, play out whatever days remained before the cancer chewed him up.

No, he couldn't. He had made the commitment, not only to Manny but to himself. He couldn't run away. He'd never be able to live with himself if he didn't follow through, no matter how short or long the remaining time would be. Sophie questioned his sanity. But he couldn't look her in the eye if he gave up. It might be quixotic, but that's how he looked at it.

He felt no better, but lay down, eyes wide open, staring into the darkness.

Thursday morning, the world looked better as sunlight streamed in through the gap in the curtains. He shook his head. The demons had vanished, temporarily. He strolled outside to pick up the newspaper and noticed something unfamiliar on his lawn. He sauntered over to look. Someone had burned a pattern in the brown grass. It looked like a skull. Mark clenched his fists. He had to nail this bastard.

Mark debated what to do next in the investigation. He opened the Boulder *Daily Camera* and calmly read until he saw the headline on the first page of the local news section: IDLER ARRESTED IN MURDER OF MANNY GRIMES. Mark's hands tightened on the paper. He read further: "Local businessman Ken Idler was arrested yesterday in connection with the bludgeoning death of Manny Grimes three weeks ago at the North Boulder Recreation Center. A source speaking on condition of anonymity stated that Idler received blackmail threats from Grimes and evidence points to Idler committing a retaliatory murder. Idler remains in the county jail after the judge agreed to no bail. No further information has been released by the police."

Mark had told Peters he'd quit when police made an arrest, but this one didn't smell right.

He hadn't yet confirmed or eliminated any of the other three suspects. He'd have to speed up the investigation to see if he could tie up the loose ends. First, Jacob Fish. Deciding to track down further answers about Jacob's business, Mark called David Randolf, the ex-employee of Creo Tech, and arranged lunch at a sidewalk café on the Pearl Street Mall for noon the following day.

Mark stared out his window. He also needed to understand the connection between Lee Daggett and Cheryl Idler. In addition to their illicit romance, had they cooked up a murder together?

That evening Mark parked again outside the Idler home. He had brought a thermos of coffee and wore a ski jacket in the brisk cold of this November night.

After an hour, his wait was rewarded by the sight of Lee Daggett's Lexus pulling up in front of the house. Lee beeped the horn twice.

Cheryl rushed out and climbed in his car.

Mark followed them as they drove the short distance to Lee's home. Mark stopped a block away and waited for them to go into Lee's house. Then he drove past the house and made a U-turn so that he would be facing toward the exit from the dead-end street when they left.

Mark drank coffee and zipped up his jacket to his chin. Daggett lived in a two-story, Tudor style house with two tall evergreen trees on either side of the front door. Expensive neighborhood. Daggett had won enough gambling to finance this place. And now this relationship with Cheryl Idler. While hubby rotted in jail, they didn't have to be as careful.

Mark planned to sit this one out for as long as he could. He had almost fallen asleep when he heard the sound of breaking glass. He jerked his head up to see the front door of Daggett's house flung open, and Cheryl dashed out. In the reflection of the streetlight he could see a raw bruise on her cheek. Tears streamed from her eyes, and she pivoted her head from side to side frantically as if searching for a knight to rescue her. Mark started his car and pulled up alongside. "Can I give you a ride?"

She grabbed the door handle and jumped in. Moments later Daggett charged out of the house like a mad bull. Mark clicked the doors locked as Lee crashed against the car. Mark's eyes met Daggett's.

Those eyes sent Mark a message of instant death.

Mark punched the accelerator. His car shot ahead, leaving Daggett alone on the sidewalk.

CHAPTER 27

Cheryl Idler continued to cry.

"What did he do to you?" Mark asked, noting that she also sported a black eye.

"He's an animal. He got mad, threw a plate at me and punched me in the face."

"Do you want me to take you to the police or emergency room?"

She abruptly stopped crying. "What for?"

Mark glanced over at her and saw that she'd narrowed her eyes. "Say, don't I know you?" she asked.

"We met at a benefit at the Dairy Center several weeks ago." Mark reached for his cell phone. "Do you want me to call the police to report the attack?"

"No." She grabbed his arm. "I just want to go home. Can you drive me to—"

"I know where you live," he said, hearing the subtle southern drawl in her voice.

She stared at Mark carefully again. "You didn't appear outside Lee's house by chance. What's your involvement here?"

Mark shrugged. "Just an interested party. I also know that the night of the Manny Grimes murder you drove a vagrant named Old Mel to the North Boulder Recreation Center."

"I don't know what you mean."

"That same man was murdered last Friday night. Whoever murdered him also attacked me."

Cheryl sat in silence. She brushed her hair back and put her hand to her bruised cheek.

She had clammed up and wouldn't say anything further, so Mark tried a direct approach. "Who asked you to pick up Old Mel?"

"I told you," she said with a scowl. "I don't know any Old Mel."

They pulled up in front of Cheryl's house. She opened the car door and without so much as a thank you, ran up the walkway, let herself into the house and slammed the door.

Mark sat in his car thinking. Cheryl Idler was obviously lying. With this group of sleazeballs, they all seemed guilty.

He climbed out of his car and circled the black Jaguar parked in the driveway, testing the door and finding it unlocked. Retreating to his own vehicle, he extracted a pen flashlight from his glove compartment. Then he opened the passenger-side door of Cheryl's car and flashed the light around the seat area. Something reflected light back. He bent down and picked up an object from the floor. His hand held a silver cross, the missing part of Old Mel's earring.

After Mark returned to his car, he looked in his rearview mirror. Bright headlights zoomed toward him.

Suddenly, a black Lexus pulled up behind, then rammed his car.

He jolted forward in the seat.

He turned the key and started the engine.

The Lexus rammed him again.

Mark shot forward, and the car followed. He reached the bottom of the hill and turned right in front of a car heading down Broadway. He could see the lights from the Lexus merge in behind.

He made an abrupt left, cutting off an approaching car, and

accelerated down the street. Then he took another quick left. Two more turns and he had lost his pursuer.

Not wanting to return home, he checked into a motel for the night.

A glorious Colorado November day greeted him the next morning—the first warm one in over a week, after nights of subfreezing temperatures. Mark returned to Cheryl's house and knocked on the door. She answered, dressed in jeans and an old sweatshirt. She had tried to hide the bruise with makeup.

"We need to talk," Mark said bluntly.

Cheryl's gaze darted around, and then she focused on Mark. "Why should we?"

"Because you're implicated in the murder of Manny Grimes. Why don't you level with me rather than trying to deny that you drove Old Mel to the rec center."

Mark held up the silver cross. "I found this missing part of Old Mel's earring in your Jaguar. Just tell me what happened."

Cheryl looked angry, but then her face changed as resignation seemed to set in. She sighed. "Why don't you come inside?"

They sat on wooden chairs around a table in her brightly lit kitchen.

"Start at the beginning and tell me who asked you to take Old Mel to the rec center."

Cheryl's wide-eyed gaze met Mark's direct stare. "My husband, Ken. Manny blackmailed him, and Ken wanted me to take that vagrant to the North Boulder Rec Center to help teach Manny a lesson."

"Why did you help?" Mark asked.

"I thought Ken only wanted to scare Manny. I never realized it was more than that. When I found out afterwards what Ken did, I turned to Lee. I can't live with a murderer."

"It seems to me you've traded in one violent man for another."

"Yeah. I seem to attract losers."

"Tell me how Manny blackmailed Ken."

"I came across a whole series of email messages between the two of them," Cheryl said. "Ken usually turns his computer off, but one evening I heard him swearing. He stomped out of the house without shutting it down. Later I went into his office to retrieve a pen and jostled the computer desk. The screen saver disappeared, and I found an email message in front of me."

She paused and walked to the sink to refill her glass with tap water. Mark tried to guess what she would say next, but decided he'd just let her speak.

"That message frightened me. It was from Ken to Manny. Basically, it said, 'You're a dead man. I refuse to pay any more for your blackmail. Kiss your wife one last time, because you're history.' But the saving grace—he hadn't sent it yet. I searched through his email folders and found a whole series of messages describing blackmail, payments and places to meet. It appeared that Ken had been going along with this for over a year."

"What did you do next?"

"When Ken came home that night, I confronted him with what I had accidentally discovered. He became furious. I told him to find some other solution. After arguing for over an hour, he finally agreed to teach Manny a lesson without killing him. Then Ken lined up the vagrant and enlisted me to take the man to the rec center. But Ken really carried out his original intent and murdered Manny. I copied the email messages and turned them over to the police. That's when they arrested him."

"There's still one thing I don't understand. Why would Ken tell Old Mel that his name was Manny?"

She blinked. "I don't know."

When Mark returned home, he paced back and forth in his living room, trying to piece together what he had heard from

Cheryl. At first she didn't want to discuss Old Mel, but then reconsidered and opened up like a boiled clam, laying all the blame on Ken. Why would she do that? Of course. She had already told the police about Ken's activities, leading to his arrest, so she had nothing to lose by divulging the same information to Mark. The phone rang, and he jumped. He picked it up to hear the voice of his son, Norm.

"I have some information for you concerning Lingan Ling."

It took a moment for Mark to remember that he had asked Norm to track down the Taiwanese company linked to Jacob Fish and Creo Tech, as well as Ken Idler and Idler Enterprises. "Thanks for following up, Norm. What did you find?"

"It turns out that both Microsoft and Oracle have filed suits against them for software piracy. Although they've been identified as one of the fastest growing companies in Taiwan, the litigation could put an end to that."

"Anything further that links Jacob Fish?" Mark asked.

"Not Jacob specifically, but Creo Tech is identified as one of eleven companies that have distributed some of the tagged code. Turns out Microsoft has come up with an imbedded identifier. If someone illegally copies their software, the code leaves a unique footprint. Much like dye exploding in a bag of stolen money. Products sold by Creo Tech and the ten other companies have this tag that's been traced to Lingan Ling."

Mark's heart leaped. "This all fits. Jacob Fish is involved in software piracy. Now if I can determine if that link had to do with Jacob Fish wanting to kill Manny Grimes."

"Did it involve blackmail, Dad?"

"That's possible. Ken Idler has been arrested for the murder, and Manny was blackmailing him. I'm not convinced of Idler's guilt. Maybe Manny also blackmailed Jacob Fish."

"Might be worth pursuing that path."

"When I went through Manny's files I found evidence of the

Idler blackmail, but nothing on Jacob Fish," Mark said.

"Was this Manny a friend of yours?"

"Not exactly a friend, but he's the one who insisted I go in for a physical exam that led to the diagnosis of my prostate cancer. I always thought highly of him, but, apparently, he lived a much different life than I would have ever guessed."

"Sounds like you should revisit the Manny side of the puzzle," Norm said. "See if you can find any indication of large payments."

Mark thought back to when he had read through Manny's files. He had found the note from Jacob demanding that Manny give up his investment in Creo Tech but nothing specific hinting at blackmail. Still, he might have missed something. "You make a good point. I'll have to go back and check."

After hanging up, Mark called Barbara Grimes. He wanted to go back to her house to learn more about Manny, as Norm had suggested.

No one answered.

Frustrated, Mark slammed the phone down. He'd have to try again, maybe go over after his lunch appointment.

Mark basked in the sun as he waited at an outside table along the Pearl Street Mall for David Randolf, the ex-Creo Tech employee, to arrive for lunch. He figured he might as well enjoy this sunny day since the weather forecast indicated a drop in temperature again over the weekend. Resting his hands on the round table, separated from the passersby by a metal railing, he watched the collection of people move by: teenagers on skateboards, children chasing each other, shoppers carrying packages, a few business people in casual attire. He looked across the walkway and spotted several people sprawled out on the courthouse lawn, enjoying the sunshine and warmth.

He picked up the menu and realized hunger gnawed at him.

The thought of pasta all'uccelletto made his mouth water.

When David arrived, Mark motioned him to the empty chair. "I'm curious, and there's another item I want your help with. Help me understand how Manny Grimes became an investor in Creo Tech and introduced Jacob to Lingan Ling in Taiwan."

David frowned. "We made a good profit and achieved our financial plan, but Jacob wanted more. One of our products fell behind schedule. Jacob began searching for an income boost that would drive up short-term revenue and profitability. Manny appeared right then with the Taiwanese connection."

"With Jacob's receptivity to Manny's idea, what led to the acrimony between the two of them?"

"Jacob likes to run his own show. Manny began stopping by every day and acting like he ran the company. That infuriated Jacob. They had a confrontation that most of the Boulder-based employees overheard. Then Jacob threw Manny out of his office. Bodily."

Mark remembered how mad he had seen Jacob before and smiled. "I can sure picture that scene."

"Not pretty. Manny's your size. Jacob literally pulled him up, dragged him from the office and pushed him out the door. As Manny stumbled, Jacob yelled, 'You come back here again and I'll kill you.' "

Mark raised his eyebrows. "How many people heard that threat?"

"Probably thirty employees."

"What happened next?"

"Manny didn't come back. Jacob strutted back to his office and slammed the door."

Mark took a sip of iced tea and looked to the side as a group of loud teenagers sauntered by. "Did Jacob mention Manny after the day he threw him out of the office?"

"His name came up in a conversation regarding Lingan Ling.

Jacob said, 'That son of a bitch is history.' "

"No love lost there."

Mark gazed again out toward the mall. The small hairs on the back of his neck stirred.

There stood Jacob Fish with his arms crossed and his eyes blazing murderously.

"What the hell are you two doing together?" Jacob shouted.

"We're enjoying a quiet lunch," Mark answered, facing Jacob as he would when backing away from a bear.

"I bet you two did this." Jacob threw a newspaper over the railing. It landed on the table and knocked over a glass of water.

Mark thrust his chair to the side to avoid ending up with a wet lap. Then he picked up the paper.

An article by Al Lawson in the *Denver Post* business section bore the title "Go Fish." It recounted some of Jacob's illegal business activities.

"David, you signed a confidentiality statement," Jacob shouted. "If I find you've told anything to this snoop, I'm taking you to court."

David's eyes smoldered. "You've already caused me enough problems. Why don't you just continue your walk on the mall?"

Jacob balled his fist and leaned forward.

Without a railing as a barrier, Mark thought Jacob would fly right on top of David.

A policeman stopped to talk to someone three tables away.

Jacob stepped back.

"Don't think either of you can mess with me."

He shook his right index finger at Mark in particular, spun on his heels and stomped away.

"Charming person," Mark said.

David Randolf's face looked white, drained of blood. "He's deranged. I guess I should be glad I'm no longer working for him."

Mark shook his head. He thought of the fine line between genius and insanity. Had Jacob gone over the edge and murdered Manny?

CHAPTER 28

Mark drove to the main Boulder library, navigating through streets peppered with traffic circles and speed bumps. He admired the intent of limiting cars to a safe speed, but these impediments only kept people on the road longer, spewing more pollution into the air. Pollution made him think of the four sleazy suspects.

He spent the rest of the day researching Idler Enterprises. Finally, as dusk approached, he abandoned his futile search and packed up his notes. Outside, he started his car and drove home, still contemplating the latest events. Something didn't feel right. He couldn't see Ken as the murderer in spite of everything Cheryl had said. He didn't trust her—it seemed too convenient that the blackmail led to the murder.

That night Mark put on his grubby clothes and drove by the crack house again, determined to find "Clyde," the man Old Mel's ex-roommate had said was hired to go to the rec center and attack Paul Crandall, the player who had taken Mark's place.

This time Mark's luck improved. Two men sat smoking on the front steps. Mark drove past them and parked on a side street. He waited until he saw no one in sight, hopped out of the car and walked back toward the house. At the same time he mussed his hair.

As he approached the house, he slowed to a shuffle. *Think*

old, down, spent. He only needed to remember prostate cancer to achieve the right frame of mind.

He stumbled up the walkway, and one of the men on the steps shouted, "Where you going?"

Mark scratched his arm. "Lookin' for Clyde. Owes me some money."

The other man, wearing a torn jacket, eyed Mark carefully. "Don't know any Clyde."

"He said he'd be in there." Mark pointed toward the house.

"Guess someone gave you bad information. Beat it."

Mark tried taking a step forward, but one of the men gave him a shove back toward the street. "Get moving, pops."

Mark staggered back the way he had come, and once out of sight of the two men, jogged briskly around the block. He spotted an alley and crept along in the dark until he found the back of the crack house.

He tried the back door, but found it locked. Prowling along the side of the house, he discovered a window with no screen, open a couple of inches. He peeked in, but the room remained in darkness.

Pushing the window up as far as he could reach, he boosted himself up and dove through the opening.

He landed on a hardwood floor.

"Keep it down in there," someone shouted from outside the room.

Mark waited to let his eyes adjust. He saw the faint outline of two men lying on the floor. Neither moved.

He stumbled around the room until he found a doorknob, turned it and peered out into a dimly lit hallway.

He shuffled out, his body sore from landing on the hardwood floor, and found a living room, where he could see some people on the floor, leaning against the walls.

He took a breath and growled, "Where'd goddamn Clyde go?"

"Shaddup, ya jerk," someone slurred. "He's probably up-stairs."

Mark lumbered back into the hall and up the stairs. In the first room he entered he found a man lying on a cot. He went over and shook him.

"Clyde?"

"Get your fuckin' hands off me. No Clyde in here."

He tried two more rooms, garnering equally unreceptive replies.

Opening the last door, he heard a moan, and as his eyes adjusted, he spotted a man in old clothes and worn-out shoes.

"You Clyde?"

"What's it to you?"

"We need to talk."

"Go 'way."

Mark shook him again. "Clyde, I have more money for you."

"Money?"

"I'm going to give you fifty dollars. You don't have to sit up, but you need to answer some questions. Wake up if you want the money."

Clyde's eyes flickered open, his eyelids twitched and then his eyes shut again.

"Clyde, can you hear me?"

"Yeah."

"You remember going to the North Boulder rec center three days ago?"

"I went sometime."

"Who asked you to go there?"

"Some broad."

"What'd she look like?"

"Couldn't tell. All bundled up in a baggy jacket and ski cap."

"What'd she ask you to do?"

"Why should I tell you?"

"You want fifty bucks or not?"

Clyde struggled to sit up, but collapsed back onto the cot.

"Let's see the money."

Mark held out a fifty-dollar bill. "Answer my questions and then you can have the money. What did the woman ask you to do?"

"Shit. She gave me a pair of gloves and a garrote. Told me to work over a guy."

Mark shivered. "Why would you do that?"

"For five hundred bucks, man. I was strapped."

"Who were you supposed to attack?"

He couched. "I've had enough of this."

Mark continued to wave the money. "Fifty bucks, Clyde. Describe the man the woman told you to assault."

"She didn't tell me anything, just gave me an envelope that she said had instructions. I opened it later to find a typed note that said to take out the man who didn't wear glasses and didn't have a white beard. On the funny tennis court."

"And you found him?"

"I caught a bus to the rec center. Saw the guys bouncing around inside this cage. Waited in the shadows . . ." His voice trailed off and he seemed to be falling asleep.

Mark shook him again. "What happened next?"

"It got cold. I waited. They finally quit. The guy I wanted lagged behind the others. I caught him and pulled him into the bushes."

"Did you plan to kill him?"

"I don't know, man. I needed to do something. The broad promised me another five hundred dollars."

"Did you carry out your mission?"

"No . . . never completed . . . guy's friend came back . . .

chased me away."

Mark thought how he could have been the victim. Clyde sprawled powerless now, but he appeared strong and well-built. Whoever had ordered the attack knew what the foursome looked like and that they would be at the courts playing on Tuesday night. Whoever had ordered the attack didn't count on Mark not being there.

"What was the plan for you to receive the additional five hundred bucks?"

"Supposed to be left in a white paper bag in the trash bin on the corner of Pearl and Thirteenth."

"Did you check?"

"Yeah. Nothing there. Say, why you asking all these questions?"

"I'm trying to find out who the woman was."

"Just some bitch."

"Young or old?"

"Young."

"What did she look like?"

"Couldn't see much of her face."

"Any distinctive features?"

"Good skin . . . one small mole on the left side of her neck."

"What did her voice sound like?"

"She tried to speak in a deep voice . . . a little southern accent . . . I need to sleep."

Mark leaned closer. "How did she know to ask you to do this?"

"I'd done it once before. For a guy named Roscoe."

CHAPTER 29

"For Howard Roscoe?" Mark asked as he clutched Clyde's arm.

"Hey, you're hurting my arm." Clyde tried to shake off Mark's grip.

Mark let go. "How do you know Roscoe?"

"We served in the Marines together. Word got out about my background . . ." Clyde stopped with a confused look on his face.

Mark felt like he had to pry every word out of him.

"Your background?"

"I fought in the Gulf War. Trained in hand-to-hand combat. In a fire fight an Iraqi attacked me. I strangled him." He raised his large hands.

"So people heard you had a special skill."

"Yeah. I did it a few times, and people noticed. Then Roscoe paid me to take care of a competitor of his."

Mark shook his head. He didn't know what to make of all this.

"So, you think the woman who approached you learned this from Howard Roscoe?"

"I've had enough of this crap. Leave me alone so I can sleep."

Mark dropped the fifty-dollar bill on the bed. He wondered if he should turn Clyde in to Peters or forget him. Since Peters didn't want him to be investigating, he decided not to risk Peters's wrath.

Leaving the room, Mark raced down the stairs and out the

back door, glad to be outside. As he returned to his car, his stomach tightened as he recalled what Clyde had done. He tried to piece it all together. Maybe Cheryl Idler had paid him. It seemed awfully similar to the setup with Old Mel. And she did have a southern accent. But Howard Roscoe seemed the most likely person to hire Clyde to carry out the attack. Could he have put Cheryl Idler up to it? Or did Roscoe have another woman help him?

More than ever, Mark felt that Ken Idler was *not* the murderer.

He would see if he could uncover any new clues tomorrow—at the platform tennis tournament.

Mark arrived at the courts an hour early. After posting the draw sheet on the outside wall of the rec center facing the courts, he set up a card table and unfolded a chair.

Woody arrived next. He came up to the table to sign in. "Mark, you're wearing the same old gray, University of Colorado sweatshirt. You must have had that shirt for five years."

Mark glared at him. "So what? It's comfortable."

"If you're going to be the tournament director, you should look the part, not like a homeless bum. You should be wearing Armani togs."

The first round had his buddies, Ben and Woody, against two of the suspects, Jacob Fish and Howard Roscoe. That might be informative to see if they gave off any useful signs of their involvement in Manny's death.

Mark had told his other friend Shelby to be there at nine o'clock, so that would give Shelby a buffer of an hour before his scheduled game in the second time slot.

Fifteen minutes before the start, suspect Lee Daggett stomped up to the table where Mark sat. "My asshole partner got himself arrested. I need a new partner."

"Haven't you lined up anyone else?" Mark swallowed a sigh.

"No. I haven't had time."

Mark looked at his watch. He wouldn't be able to track down a replacement.

"Okay," he said. "I'm not scheduled to play. I'll fill in."

A maniacal grin spread over Lee's face. "This should be interesting. You and I have a score to settle anyway from when you interfered with Cheryl in front of my house." He whacked Mark on the back sending him sprawling onto the card table.

Mark wondered what he had set himself up for. Now he'd have a chance to see Lee Daggett in action, up close and personal.

The tournament started calmly. The first four teams warmed up on the two courts. With everything set for the moment, Mark decided to watch Jacob Fish and Howard Roscoe play his friends. He strolled over to the court and looked in the open equipment bags that Fish and Roscoe had left outside the door of the court. Both had a supply of Viking balls.

The game progressed uneventfully until at two-all Jacob called Ben's obvious good shot out.

"That hit in the court by two inches," Ben protested.

"Missed by over a foot," Jacob said with a smirk.

"Howard must have seen it," Ben said. "Didn't you think it was in?"

"I couldn't tell," Howard replied. "Jacob's foot blocked my view."

Ben walked back, shaking his head.

Ten minutes later, Woody hit a lob between Howard and Jacob. They both reached for it and collided as the ball fell in for a winner.

"That was my ball!" Jacob shouted.

"You're out of position," Howard said. "You were supposed to be close to net, not trying to reach for a backhand. My forehand has priority, you jerk."

Jacob gave Howard a shove. Howard slapped Jacob with the back of his hand, sending him reeling.

"Serve and quit the crap." Howard returned to net.

Everyone watched in silence to see what would happen next. Jacob took a step toward Howard, thought better of it and headed back to the baseline.

Ben and Woody won the match in spite of continued bad calls by Jacob Fish. After the last point, Jacob refused to shake hands with anyone and stomped off the court.

Mark sat at the table waiting for Ben to report the score. Lee Daggett reappeared and stood menacingly close to Mark's right shoulder, slapping his paddle against his left hand.

"We won six-four, six-three," Ben said. "Say, Mark, you still planning to attend the city council meeting on Tuesday night?"

"Yes."

"Then we'd better reschedule our Tuesday-night game. We'll need to start at four to be done in time."

"Okay by me. Let Shelby and Woody know."

"Going to be doing your civic duty?" Lee Daggett asked from behind him.

"Yeah. Some of us want to save these courts so we can play in the future. Whereas a group of the neighbors has tried to persuade the city to remove them."

"Someone needs to do a better job of convincing them to change their position," Daggett said. "Grab your paddle, asshole. We're on for the next match."

They both put their equipment bags down on the steps next to the courts. Mark looked in Daggett's bag and noticed that he had a sleeve of Wilson balls.

The first time Lee served, Mark crouched in position at the net. The ball whizzed an inch from his ear.

"Sorry," Lee said with a laugh.

On the following point, Lee charged to the net. As the return came to the middle of the court, Lee lunged for the ball and rammed into Mark, knocking him over.

"Oops." Lee chuckled.

Two games later Lee went back for a high overhead and instead of hitting it over the net, drilled the ball into Mark's back.

Mark staggered from pain but regained his balance. He looked Lee in the eyes. "If you're trying to lose the match, you're doing a good job of it. I can take your shit, but I suggest you try hitting the ball into the court for a change."

"Well, la de da." Lee turned his back on Mark.

Lee sent one more parting shot close to Mark, but kept the ball in play after that. Mark guessed that Lee hated losing more than he wanted to continue his intimidation.

At noon, sandwiches arrived. The players took a break from the scheduled matches so they could have a chance to eat.

Mark motioned Ben, Woody and Shelby to follow him away from the other people. "Any observations regarding the suspects?"

"I think we'll have another murder on our hands if Jacob Fish and Howard Roscoe keep playing together," Ben said. "I don't know why they signed up as a team since they spend more time arguing and fighting than playing."

"Probably couldn't find anyone else willing to be partners," Shelby said.

"How's Lee Daggett doing?" Ben asked Mark.

"He's more focused on harassing me than the opponents. I'd hate to meet him in a dark alley."

Maybe he *had* met Lee in a dark alley the night of Old Mel's murder, Mark thought, as he looked up see a procession proceeding from the parking lot up the walkway. A dozen people, holding signs, marched toward the courts.

The first sign, held by an old man in a ski cap, read: RID OUR NEIGHBORHOOD OF NOISY SPORTS!

Mark recognized the woman who had spoken at the parks board meeting. She had replaced her tie-dye outfit with a pleated, white skirt. In her hands a sign said: MOVE THE COURTS AWAY. FAR AWAY.

A third sign in bright red letters bounced up and down in the hands of a scowling, dark-haired woman. It contained the words: BRING BACK PEACE AND QUIET TO OUR NEIGHBORHOOD!

The dozen or so people stopped right in front of the players, who were gathered on the ground eating lunch. The protesters started chanting, "Drum tennis must go! Drum tennis must go!"

Most of the platform tennis players looked on in amazement, but Jacob Fish, Howard Roscoe and Lee Daggett all jumped to their feet, clenched their fists and moved toward the chanting group.

Jacob pushed a stocky man in front who held a sign that said: OFF THE PLATFORM PIGS!

The man teetered, caught his balance and pushed Jacob back.

Lee Daggett stepped forward and, with a right jab, decked the protester.

A woman slammed her placard down on Daggett's head, tearing a hole in the sign and leaving it strung around his neck.

Daggett roared and catapulted into the crowd, knocking several people over onto the group of platform tennis players, still trying to eat lunch. Pieces of turkey and ham shot skyward.

One man stumbled to the side, landed on the card table and brought it crashing to the ground.

A man shouting obscenities picked up the folding chair and threw it into the mob.

Jacob Fish tackled him.

Two more people fell on top of them with legs splayed in every direction.

Howard Roscoe shoved a woman, who fell against two people behind her.

She kicked, catching him in the ribs.

Roscoe fell over and crushed a bag of cookies, sending crumbs spraying like kernels from a popcorn machine.

Fists and feet shot out from all participants. Someone landed on an orange and a grapefruit, and juice spurted everywhere.

Mark rushed forward to separate the combatants. He reached for a sign being bashed into the crowd and felt a punch hit his shoulder. He staggered and fell to the ground as the woman in the pleated, white skirt landed on top of him. Her crotch nestled tightly against his face.

"Pervert," she yelled and flailed at him with her fists.

Mark covered his face as another falling body knocked him to the side. He smelled a distinctive sour odor as a shoeless foot pressed against his cheek.

He heard curses and shouts above and a jolt as someone else fell on him. He saw an arm reach back to aim a punch at him.

It belonged to Lee Daggett.

Mark held up his arm to ward off the blow. Lee's fist crashed into Mark's right forearm, sending a jolt of pain shooting through his tender elbow.

A whistle blew.

Before Daggett could punch him again, arms began pulling at the pile.

Through a space in the mass of humanity, Mark saw a uniformed policeman grabbing people and flinging them aside.

Mark heard handcuffs clicking into place on his wrist. So much for a peaceful day of platform tennis.

With everyone in handcuffs, the police lined the dozen protesters and sixteen platform tennis players up against the building wall to await a van. It looked like the aftermath of a prison food fight.

Shelby, who was lucky enough to have his hands constrained in front, picked a piece of bread off his forehead, wiped away some mayonnaise with the back of his cuffed hands, then looked at Mark and said, "Does this mean the tournament's over?"

Inside the public-safety building, Mark sat nursing his bruises and sore muscles. "I tried to separate the protesters from three angry players when I got knocked into the melee," he explained to an unsympathetic police officer. "Is Detective Peters on duty? He knows some of the people involved. Please find him."

Five minutes later Peters arrived and shook his head when he saw Mark. "What have you got yourself into this time, Mr. Yeager?"

"Merely a little confrontation between some overly zealous neighbors and three of the murder suspects. Good thing you have Ken Idler locked up or he would have been involved as well."

"One of my fellow officers wants to press charges against you and your friends for disturbing the peace and destruction of public property."

"My only crime involved bringing together three of the suspects again. I think you have an innocent man locked up, or at least he's innocent of murdering Manny Grimes. One of the other three suspects committed the murder. It could be Lee Daggett. I found a Wilson platform tennis ball left in the mouth of the deer on my porch, and Lee Daggett uses Wilson balls."

"That sounds pretty flimsy," Peters said. "We don't have anything on Daggett. All the evidence points to Ken Idler."

Mark looked Peters straight in the eyes. "I've seen some of that evidence. I agree on the surface it looks like Ken Idler had a motive because Manny blackmailed him, but other factors come into play."

"What haven't you told me, Mr. Yeager?"

Mark took a deep breath. "There's something going on between Lee Daggett and Ken Idler's wife, Cheryl. She also drove Old Mel to the rec center to turn off the lights the night of Manny's murder. She professes she did it at the request of Ken, but I think she's in cahoots with Daggett."

"Interesting theory, but it's not supported by the evidence."

Mark realized he had found no conclusive evidence pointing to Daggett as the murderer, but he pressed on. "Lee Daggett and Cheryl Idler are having an affair. They could have planned Manny's murder and probably welcome the fact that Ken Idler is taking the rap and is conveniently out of the way, locked up in jail."

Peters wrote some notes on his pad and then looked up.

Mark took this as a signal to continue. "I haven't found anything to eliminate Jacob Fish or Howard Roscoe. I'm sure you've seen the report regarding the attack on Paul Crandall. The assailant meant that for me. Also, you'll want to bring in a crack user named Clyde, who did a similar job for Howard Roscoe. And while you're at it, there's a downtown crack house for you to clean up."

Peters eyed Mark. "You're a wealth of information."

"I'd especially like to understand Howard Roscoe's dealings with Manny," Mark added.

Peters snapped his notebook closed. "Once again: Leave that to us."

"All right. Now, may I be excused? I'll be happy to pay for any damage done at the rec center. I'll also take responsibility for cleaning up the mess we left by the courts."

After being released, Mark caught a ride back to the rec center. Between the walkway and the building lay broken signs, a caved-in card table, a smashed folding chair and crushed food. He shook his head. Walking inside, he retrieved garbage bags from the receptionist, rolled up his sleeves and began cleaning up the mess. He carted away the bags and broken furniture and tossed the remains into a dumpster.

When he'd finished, the place looked as good as new. Slightly trampled, dried-out grass, but no permanent damage, other than to his pride.

He sat down against the building and stared at the platform tennis courts. What had started as a good idea—to have a Saturday tournament and observe the suspects—had ended in disaster. He had only confirmed the violence of the suspects. He felt convinced that Peters had the wrong man in jail, but had found no way to prove it. So, he would have to follow up on Howard Roscoe tomorrow, either find something or eliminate him in favor of the equally suspicious Lee Daggett.

The neighbors would undoubtedly redouble their effort to rid the city of the platform tennis courts. How could he blame them? It certainly appeared that an unruly crowd had come to the courts. The protesters may have provoked the disturbance with their idiotic signs, but that didn't excuse the melee that ensued.

Idler, Daggett, Roscoe and Fish all deserved to be locked up. And Manny, whom Mark would have earlier considered an innocent bystander, now seemed to be linked to all of the suspects, and embroiled in nefarious dealings.

Mark shook his head again in disgust. How easy to be fooled by people. He considered himself a good judge of character, but he had certainly missed the mark with Manny, who may have brought his death on himself.

Evidence continued to accumulate against all four of the suspects for their various illegal activities, Mark mused, but one of them also needed to be put away permanently for murder.

There had to be some further proof. Maybe he had overlooked something. He would have to call Barbara Grimes and go over to her house to check out Manny's files again.

But not now. Tomorrow.

CHAPTER 30

Back home, an idea occurred to Mark, and he figured he would try one more thing to flush out the guilty party. He had been to Howard Roscoe and Lee Daggett's homes, and now he looked up Jacob Fish's address from the mailing list he had used for the tournament.

Then he carefully composed a note. When satisfied with the result, he printed off four copies, and in large, bold capital letters he carefully printed the name of each of the non-jailed suspects on an envelope before inserting the notes and sealing the envelopes.

After dark Mark loaded three rocks from his garden into his car and drove off to deliver the letters. Outside Lee Daggett's house, he waited a few moments and then sneaked up to the porch to deposit the letter and hold it down with a rock.

No lights shown at Roscoe's house, but as Mark approached the front door, a spotlight flashed on. Mark froze. He looked around, trying to determine whether to proceed or retreat. No one came to the door, and no dogs raced out to tear him apart. He breathed again as he realized an automatic motion detector had turned on the light.

Jacob Fish lived in a large, two-story house with a long driveway.

The house remained dark, but a man with a dog strolled past, so Mark proceeded along the street and parked two houses away. He waited five minutes, exited from the car and returned to Jacob's place to leave the message under a rock.

Back home, his answering machine greeted him with a flashing light. He played the message, and a muffled male voice said slowly, "Your time is up. Drop the investigation. No more warnings."

He couldn't recognize the voice. It could be any of the three suspects not in jail or a man one of them had hired.

How ironic. While he left notes for the suspects, the murderer delivered a message to him.

Mark set the deadbolt and chain for both front and back doors. He wished he had a dog.

He slept fitfully again, his mind racing, his body feeling every single ache and pain from the afternoon's melee. He was glad Sophie couldn't see him.

Once he awoke to listen to a noise outside the house. He staggered to the bedroom window, pushed the curtains aside and peered through the glass.

No one there. Only the wind rattling the gate in his backyard.

On Sunday, Mark drove into Denver with his thoughts focused on the four murder suspects. Still no clear picture. Each had a legitimate motive and clear access. None had expressed any remorse over Manny's death. And they all seemed to have explosive tempers. He remembered Ken Idler throwing a fit at the public-safety building after the murder. The night he gave Cheryl Idler a ride home, Lee Daggett had bashed his body into his car so hard that he left a dent in the door, to say nothing of the scratches caused by Lee ramming his Lexus into the rear bumper of Mark's car. Howard Roscoe had physically thrown Mark out of the house. And Jacob Fish boiled like a volcano ready to erupt during the encounter on the restaurant patio of the Pearl Street Mall.

Now he needed to learn more about Westerfield Weapons and

Howard Roscoe.

Mark pulled his car into a space at the back of an almost full parking lot. He stepped out in front of a telephone pole and noticed a penny stuck in the wood. With his car key he pried the penny out and dropped it in his pocket.

He entered the Farwest Hotel and followed the signs and stream of people flowing toward the convention center. He paid his seven dollars for an admission ticket. As he passed the screener at the door, he shook his head at the question, "Any camera or guns?"

Once inside, a panorama of a military base opened up before him. A room half the size of a football field, full of tables covered with every imaginable weapon, met his startled gaze. A smiling young woman in a cowboy hat handed him a sheet of paper. He looked at it and read that if he filled it out, answering how he'd found out about the show, he'd be entered in a contest to receive a fifteen-dollar gift certificate or two V.I.P. passes to the next show. He considered filling it in and stating that he learned of the show by trying to track down a murderer, but instead threw it in the trash.

He viewed an overhead banner reading BLOWOUT SALE and sauntered by rifles and handguns linked with chains to the tables, as well as a complete array of ammunition, clips and sights. A boy not more than eight years old, dressed in camouflage gear, caressed an AK-47 as his father in jeans, black T-shirt and an NRA cap looked proudly on.

Behind a table a tall, older man with gray hair pulled back in a ponytail and wearing a Harley Davidson jacket spoke to a companion. "This baby can do some serious shit. Fully automatic."

"I thought you couldn't own an automatic weapon," Mark interjected.

"In Colorado you can own a legal automatic weapon. You

can't be a felon, and you have to submit fingerprints and a photo to the Bureau of Alcohol, Tobacco and Firearms. Then with the signature of your local chief of police and a two-hundred-dollar tax payment, you're set."

"Can you change a gun from semi-automatic to automatic?"

"That's different. You can't convert or own a modified weapon. That'll earn you ten years in jail. You can only own a legal, non-converted automatic rifle."

Mark strolled around the convention center. He approached another table covered with American flags. Mark picked up a rifle. The price tag said, "Pre-ban AR-15, $1600."

"What does 'pre-ban' mean?" he asked the bearded man behind the table.

"Means it was manufactured long enough ago that a noise suppressor and bayonet attachment were still legal. The suppressor isn't worth shit. You can hear it a county away. If you're interested I also have a Lightning Link AR-15. Only three thousand dollars."

"Thanks. I'll stick with my bow and arrow," Mark said.

The man turned a cold eye on Mark.

As he walked around the room, he listened to the steady background noise of indistinct conversations and inspected tables covered with camouflage cloth, gingham and more flag patterns. In addition to guns, items for sale included knives, coins and flashlights.

The aroma of hot dogs tickled his nostrils as he approached a refreshment stand in the back of the convention hall. Right beside the food concession, three members of the Colorado Bureau of Investigation manned a table.

Mark stopped. "You here to arrest overzealous gun fanatics?"

An officer, his hair mowed into a crew cut, looked like he had never smiled in his life. He said, "No, sir. Anyone buying a weapon at the show needs to complete a background check with us before they can walk away with their purchase."

"You can do it while they're here?"

"Yes, sir." He tapped the laptop on the desk.

Mark walked on, shaking his head at the wonder of the interaction between computers and guns. All around the convention floor, men strutted with newly purchased rifles. Mark vaguely noted that three-quarters of those in attendance were male.

He looked down at the pattern on the carpet—black with a green, red and brown plant design. It reminded him of the rugs at the Brown Palace, but not as upscale. How different from the ladies having tea and cakes in the lobby of the Brown Palace.

He stopped at a table with a sign reading "Wholesale Ammo." Boxes and boxes of ammunition rested in easy reach of a group of kids playing with a set of Legos. The next table had a sign that said, "AKs, Here. Russian." Behind another sign that read "Buy Sell Trade," a skinny man in a wife beater, highlighting arms covered with tattoos of eagles, juggled three ammo clips, deftly launching the casings into the air and grabbing them on their downward path.

As Mark turned, he saw a man who must have weighed three hundred pounds, plodding along as multiple sets of keys jangled from his bib overalls. He held hunting rifles in each hand as if carrying two toothpicks.

Mark passed a table that advertised legal services. This show covered all the bases. If people ended up in serious trouble, they could find a service to help them get out of it—for a fee.

Finally, he found the Westerfield Weapons exhibit. A flashing sign overhead directed his attention to a large, glass cabinet with a display of guns. Mark looked at the collection, identifying a handgun that resembled the one he had found in his hand after Old Mel's murder.

"Can I answer any questions for you?" an eager young man

in brown and gray camouflage gear asked.

Mark eyed the combat boots and looked up at the man's short-cropped hair.

"What's this handgun?" Mark pointed to the gun he'd recognized.

"One of our most popular models. Small enough to fit in a purse so the little lady can protect herself. Also provides the action and accuracy for a guy like you. Here, let me grab it for you."

He opened the cabinet and extracted the gun.

"Feel how light it is. Contoured grip fits easily in the hand. Safety can be quickly clicked off like this."

Camouflage man's eyes lit up, and Mark could picture a cowboy drawing in a showdown.

"If you place an order right now, I can let you walk away with this baby, and if you want more we can have them delivered to you within one week."

"No. Just looking right now."

Mark sauntered to the next cabinet, which contained a variety of rifles. He took out his notebook and searched through to find the type of weapon mentioned in Manny's file.

"Do you carry AR-15s?" Mark asked.

"Sure do. In addition to weapons we manufacture, we distribute a wide variety of rifles. Third one down on the left side."

Mark looked at the rifle. "Can it be modified into an automatic weapon?"

The man frowned. "It's possible. Some people have done it by machining several parts. Not legal though."

Mark looked around and didn't see Howard. "Who's your toughest competitor here in Colorado?"

"Probably Gentry Guns. See them everywhere."

Mark decided to tackle the subject at hand. "Say, I'm looking for Howard Roscoe."

"I saw him earlier so he must be at the show somewhere. Probably checking out the competition. He has show duty in an hour. You should be able to catch him then."

"Do you work with Howard?"

"I see him at sales meetings and shows. I have the southern Front Range territory, and he has the north. Why do you ask?"

"I'm from Boulder and have run into him a couple of times. How do you rate him as a salesman?"

"Seems to make his numbers. I worked one big deal with him. Colorado Bureau of Investigation. We put a joint proposal together. Won the business and split a good commission."

Mark decided to take a risk. "I've heard that Howard sometimes sells modified weapons."

"Are you crazy?"

Mark winked at camouflage man. "I've heard that you can procure 'special' weapons from Howard. I didn't know if that represented company policy or merely Howard's sideline."

"You some kind of cop?" the man shouted, sending spittle in the air.

"No, only an interested party."

Camouflage man's jovial expression changed to a scowl. "Where'd you hear that?"

"Word has circulated that if you want rifles converted to automatic, see Howard."

"I don't know what you mean. I need to go talk to some real prospects." He turned on his heel and stomped away.

Mark scanned the crowd once again and then explored the exhibits until he found Gentry Guns. "I'd like to speak to your sales rep who handles the Boulder territory."

"That'd be Hal," a young blonde in cowboy boots said. "He's the one in the blue shirt, over there, talking to the man by the counter."

Mark waited until Hal finished his conversation and approached him. "I understand you cover Boulder."

"Yup. Everything north of I-70 in the state."

"Ever run into a rep from Westerfield Weapons named Howard Roscoe."

"Yeah. I know him." Hal's lips curled with disgust.

"What do you think of him?"

"I don't slam my competitors, and Westerfield seems an okay company, but this guy Roscoe is something else. I don't mind good fair competition, but he's underhanded. We both made pitches to the Fort Collins police department a few months back, and he tried to steal my notebook."

"I've heard he deals in special weapons."

Hal looked around, moved closer to Mark and cupped his hand to the side of his mouth. "In this industry you find a few guys who go over the line. And Roscoe didn't just step over the line; he erased it. The guy sells legitimate weapons to the police and modified weapons to the other side."

"You know that for a fact?"

"I saw him make a delivery to a dealer who asked me for modified assault weapons. I refused. Roscoe didn't."

"Why didn't you turn Roscoe in to the authorities?"

"Are you kidding? We're a small industry. It'd be viewed as sour grapes—that I'm trying to smear a competitor. No, thanks. I'll do my business and stay legit. He can do whatever he wants as long as he doesn't steal from me." Hal nodded to a man standing behind Mark. "Excuse me. I need to speak to one of my customers."

Mark left the booth and strolled through the rest of the aisle. After the last table, he spotted a water fountain off in a corner and ambled over to quench his thirst. He bent over, tasted the chlorine-impregnated water and stood. A hand grabbed him, spinning him around and slamming him against the wall. The face thrust two inches from his own belonged to Howard Roscoe.

"What the hell are you doing snooping around here?"

"I'm learning how you sell special weapons to people like Manny Grimes."

Howard thrust him against the wall again. "What's this compulsion you have with Manny?"

Mark pushed Roscoe's arms away and straightened.

"I don't like to see people I play platform tennis with murdered."

Roscoe laughed. "Are you one of those bleeding hearts who considered Manny a nice guy? Well, he wasn't."

"I've learned that Manny had some shady dealings, but that's no reason for someone to kill him. I bet you sold him illegal weapons. Could be a problem during a business transaction. It could even lead to murder."

Roscoe leveled his gaze at Mark. "If you believe that, you're either smoking something or lack brain cells."

"Then why don't you convince me that you didn't kill Manny so I can leave you alone?"

"That's a good joke. I haven't been able to get the cops off my back, either."

"Okay. I'll lay off. But first, answer this: Why did you show up the night of the murder, and why did you arrive after the foursome had already begun playing?"

"Simple. Lee Daggett told me to be there at seven thirty to take his place. When I arrived, he was playing. He said he'd left a message for me that he could play after all. I never received any message."

Mark recalled what he had heard and how it corresponded to Roscoe's comments.

"How'd you and Manny get along?"

"Just fine. Except when he didn't pay his bills."

"Why did Manny order weapons from you?"

"I don't ask my customers what they do with my products. As long as they keep ordering."

"You must have suspected something."

Roscoe shoved Mark again. "Maybe. But even if I did, I wouldn't tell you."

"I thought you wanted to get me off your back."

A glint appeared in Roscoe's eyes. "If you're that persistent, I'm sure that either Jacob Fish or Lee Daggett will be happy to convince you to back off."

"So, you think one of them is the murderer?"

"Yes. Ken or Lee or Jacob. Not me."

"So why'd you send Clyde to try to kill me?" Mark asked.

Howard looked at him and wrinkled his forehead. "What do you mean?"

Mark watched him closely. He was either a good actor or genuinely surprised by the question.

"An old acquaintance of yours named Clyde tried to garrote me at the courts last Tuesday night."

"I've had enough of this shit. I'm going back to my table." Howard poked Mark hard in the chest. "If you know what's good for you, go back to your platform tennis game," he said and left Mark standing there.

If they'd been alone, rather than on a convention floor, would Mark still be alive? One more veiled threat and no substantive proof. With all these guys involved in illegal activities, anything could happen. Maybe some clue remained in Manny's files, a clue Mark had missed before. Time to go look again. He would do a thorough search. The answer was there. It had to be.

CHAPTER 31

Mark pulled out his cell phone and called Barbara Grimes. The same timid voice answered.

"Barbara, this is Mark Yeager. Would it be possible for me to come over and look at Manny's files again?"

Mark heard sobs. "What's the matter?" he asked.

"It's . . . it's . . . someone broke into my house."

"Are you all right?"

"Yes." She paused. "When I came home I heard the back door slam. I looked around and found a file cabinet open in Manny's office and a broken window."

"Did you call the police?"

"No. I don't know what to do. I taped a piece of cardboard over the broken window."

"I'll be there in an hour."

When he pulled up in front of Barbara's house she was sitting on the front steps and shivering, even though she was all bundled up in a white fur coat.

"I couldn't stay in the house any longer," she said, holding the coat closed at her neck as tears ran down her cheeks. "I feel violated."

Mark put an arm around her shoulder. "I understand. Sophie and I felt the same way when someone broke into our first home many years ago. Would it be all right with you if I looked around Manny's office?"

She nodded and gulped down another sob.

Mark escorted her inside and into Manny's office. He scanned the room. Nothing seemed to be disrupted, other than one open file-cabinet drawer.

"Has anyone been through these files since I last visited here?" Mark asked.

Barbara shook her head. "Only the police. They searched the files again and asked my permission to take the note left on the desk. They returned the files you had found. That's all."

Mark kept his gloves on. No sense adding distracting fingerprints. As Barbara made a hasty retreat, Mark leafed through the manila folders in the cabinet. He wanted to check four specific files. After a considerable search, he located the Idler, Roscoe and Fish records and pulled them out. He couldn't find the Daggett file.

He searched again. It had definitely disappeared.

He opened the folder that had writing in pencil inside the jacket. It read: HOWARD ROSCOE AND WESTERFIELD WEAPONS. He found material primarily concerning Lee Daggett, with several letters from Westerfield Weapons.

Mark scratched his head, picked up the three folders and strode into the living room to find Barbara.

"There's something funny here," he said. "The information in the folders seems to be mixed up and one of the files has disappeared."

Barbara's face paled, and she put her hand to her cheek. "Oh, dear. When the police returned the files, I accidentally dropped them on the floor and some papers came out. I threw the sheets back in, any which way, and stuffed the manila folders back in the file cabinet. But everything should be there."

"You're positive the police kept no records from the file cabinet?"

"That's what they told me. Only from the desk."

Mark scanned through the folders. "Most of the Westerfield Weapons information is missing." He looked thoughtfully at Barbara. "Whoever broke in must have taken the folder with Lee Daggett's name inside it, but the contents must have been primarily Westerfield Weapons papers. I wonder if the intruder wanted to steal Daggett or Roscoe documents."

Barbara looked at him blankly.

Mark excused himself and returned to Manny's office. There had to be something else here that would shed light on what had happened. He pulled open the file cabinet and started looking through folders again.

An hour later he had found nothing of significance. What else could he have missed in the office? No papers in the desk drawer. He circled the room and stopped in front of the floor-to-ceiling bookcase. He pulled out a business best-seller from two years ago and blew the dust off. More closely scrutinizing the bookshelf, he realized that every shelf had dust except for one section. He removed a book from this part of the shelf. A small manila envelope peeked out from the open slot. He extracted it from behind the other books, opened it and dumped the contents out on the desk: two folded pieces of paper, an audio tape, a computer memory stick, a key with a piece of paper taped to it and a picture.

He picked up the picture—Ken Idler was leaning over a stack of plastic bags containing a white substance. Two other men Mark didn't recognize stood next to Ken.

Mark unfolded one of the pieces of paper and read an affidavit stating that the inspected batch of twenty AR-15 rifles had been converted to automatic weapons. It listed twenty serial numbers.

The other piece of paper turned out to be an invoice that listed the same twenty serial numbers. A handwritten note read, "Time to pay up," with the signature "Howard Roscoe."

Mark remembered seeing a handheld tape player in one of the desk drawers. He retrieved it, put the tape in and pushed PLAY.

The tape spun for a moment. Then the machine emitted a click followed by the sound of background conversation. After ten seconds a drawling voice said, "She-it, Lee, you can't do that. It's illegal."

Lee's deep voice said, "I don't give a flying fuck. I've set up this gambling operation, and it's going to make a mint."

Mark leaned closer to the tape player.

Drawling Voice said, "But you've already invested in a casino. Why mess with something in Denver?"

"Supply and demand. Not everyone wants to go up to Black Hawk or Central City to gamble. There's a need right here on the flatlands."

"Yeah, but the cops will bust you in under two weeks."

"Not if I watch my clientele. I'm not going to get greedy. Just make my fair share."

A raucous laugh jarred Mark. He had heard enough, so he turned the tape player off. Manny had the goods on Lee. Now on to the memory stick.

He turned on Manny's computer and waited for it to boot up. Fortunately, no message appeared demanding a password.

Not much on security.

Mark inserted the memory stick in the computer's USB port and waited for the icon to appear on the screen. An identifier appeared called "Fishing" on the E drive. He clicked on it and found icons for Word and PDF documents. He selected one called "Fish Facts." On the screen flashed a summary describing Howard Fish's operations at Creo Tech. It highlighted his software piracy operation. Mark closed that document and opened a PDF file named "Fishing Frenzy." Up popped a scanned copy of an invoice from Lingan Ling for ten thousand copies of Microsoft Word at twenty dollars apiece.

No one would legally import copies of Word from Taiwan and clearly not at that price!

Mark removed the memory stick and shut down the computer. Then he carefully replaced the items in the manila envelope and left it on the desk.

Manny had something on every one of the suspects. They all had good reasons to eliminate him. But no one suspect stood out from the others.

Mark picked up the key and removed the strip of paper taped to it. It didn't appear to be a lockbox key. It reminded him of the key to a padlock in his garage. What would it unlock? Obviously, Manny didn't want anyone else to find it or else why would he have hidden it? Then Mark remembered a bill he had seen on the desk during his earlier visit. He grabbed the pile of papers on the desk and thumbed through until he located what he wanted—the bill from YourStore Self Storage. He wrote down the address. Then he looked at the strip of paper. It looked like a security code. Could the key fit a lock for a self-storage bay and the code be used to gain access into the facility? He'd have to check it out. He put the key and slip of paper in his pocket and returned to the living room.

"You need to call the police again," Mark said to Barbara. "In addition to reporting the break-in, there's an envelope on the desk they will want to see. It may help identify Manny's killer. I know it's difficult for you, but hopefully this is the last set of evidence the police will have to collect."

Barbara remained silent.

Mark again admired the furniture and paintings and this time noticed the thick, white shag carpet. "I still think this room belongs in a museum," Mark said, giving his best look of reverence.

"Thank you," Barbara said, fidgeting with the bracelet on her left wrist.

"I'm going to ask you something else," Mark said. "I'm still trying to understand Manny's business dealings, what might have led to his murder and why someone would break in and steal from his office."

"I'll try to answer any questions I can." Barbara's bottom lip quivered.

"This may be difficult for you, but I'm going to bring up a disagreeable subject. I heard from Cheryl Idler that Manny blackmailed her husband. Did you suspect that of Manny?"

Barbara bit her lip. "I've probably been very naïve. Manny once bragged that in high school he had blackmailed a teacher. I don't know if he blackmailed Ken or not."

"And his relationship with Lee Daggett, Jacob Fish and Howard Roscoe? Did you suspect any strange dealings between Manny and any of these three?"

Barbara thought for a moment. "He did say something a few days before he died concerning Jacob. Manny said he planned to take over Creo Tech and kick Jacob out."

"That might be a motive for Jacob to have killed Manny."

Barbara fought back tears. "I can't imagine anyone doing such a horrible thing. Even if problems existed with Manny."

"Is there anything else, any arguments that may point to one of the suspects?"

Barbara put her finger to her chin. "There's one troubling memory that I should mention to you. At a recent party I stood with Manny, Ken and Cheryl Idler, and Lee Daggett. Manny had too much to drink and started an argument with Ken. They began threatening each other." She stopped to catch her breath. "I grabbed Manny's arm and asked him to stop. He brushed me aside, pointed his finger at Ken and said, 'One of these days I'd like to bash your skull in with a paddle.' "

A tear ran down her cheek. "Instead he became a victim that very same way."

Something didn't fit. "Did you report that incident to the police?" Mark asked.

Barbara wiped her tears away with the back of her hand. "Yes. I'm sure that played a part in the arrest of Ken Idler. All those people heard Ken and Manny threatening each other."

Mark tried to put the pieces together. The evidence still led to a jumbled conclusion: Manny's fingerprints on the murder weapon, Old Mel being contacted by a man named Manny, Manny and Ken having argued, Manny threatening to beat Ken's head in with a paddle. If he didn't know better, he'd consider Manny the murderer and not the victim. With Manny dead, the evidence certainly pointed to Ken. But he still couldn't buy that Ken had committed the murder.

Mark replayed the most recent events as he drove away. Was there any significance to some of the Howard Roscoe paper files disappearing from Barbara's house? Howard couldn't have stolen the material since he'd been at the gun show. Had Lee Daggett broken in and retrieved the folder with his name on it? If he did, he would have a rude awakening when he looked at the material referencing Howard Roscoe.

Stopping at McGuckin's hardware store, Mark approached the desk where he had previously had spare keys made.

"You may be able to help me," he said to the clerk. "I found this key and I'm trying to determine what lock it goes to."

The man looked carefully at the key and turned it over. "It belongs with a Master padlock."

"Can you tell what size lock it would fit?"

"Yeah. Approximately an inch square." Scooting around the edge of the counter, he motioned for Mark to follow him into another part of the store.

"That one right there," he said, pointing to a lock on a rack on the wall.

Mark left the store, thinking he'd pay a visit to the storage facility the next day.

Mark spent the evening reviewing the case, making notes and pondering next steps. Eliminating Ken Idler for the moment, Jacob Fish had fallen to the bottom of the suspect list. Howard Roscoe held second place, since he hadn't broken into the Grimes house. That left Lee Daggett who could have ransacked the Grimes files. Furthermore, his affair with Cheryl Idler seemed extremely suspicious, particularly since she had driven Old Mel to the rec center so he could turn out the platform tennis lights.

CHAPTER 32

On Monday morning, Mark called Ben. "You mentioned trying to locate a shipment of antique paperweights owed to your partner's client. I know a possible location where they could have been stored, if you're willing to help me look."

"You bet. I'm available at lunch time."

"Swing by my house and pick me up at eleven-thirty."

When they arrived at the storage facility, the place appeared deserted. Mark gave Ben the access code, and Ben punched it in. When the gate opened, they drove inside.

"We need to find a storage bay that has a keyed Master lock this size," Mark said, forming a square with the thumb and forefinger of both hands. "You start at this end and I'll start at the other. Note wherever you find the right kind of lock."

Mark started his inspection. Almost half the doors had combination locks. In the first row he found no Master locks of the right size. In the next row he found one, but the key didn't fit. After one more futile attempt, he met up with Ben.

"Any luck?" Mark asked.

"I found two. Here, I'll show you."

They made their way back two rows as Ben pointed to a lock.

Mark tried it. The key inserted smoothly, but wouldn't turn.

Then, one row over, Ben showed him another lock on shed number twenty-nine.

Mark inserted the key, turned it, and with a *click* the lock snapped open.

"Jackpot," Mark said as he smiled at Ben. "Let's see what Manny has in his secret stash." He pulled a cord, a light flashed on, and he saw two wooden crates and three cardboard boxes. He stepped over and opened one of the cardboard boxes.

"I've found your paperweights. Let's see what's in the wooden crates."

Mark tugged at a corner, but the crates remained firmly nailed shut.

"I have a screwdriver in the car," Ben said.

He retrieved it and pried one of the boxes open. "Wow. Look at these rifles."

Mark peered inside the box. "I recognize these from the gun show. AR-15s. Manny bought these from Howard Roscoe."

"What did he expect to do with the rifles? Start a war?"

"That's a good question. I assume Manny expected to resell them. He apparently played middleman in a lot of deals."

"Quite an arsenal," Ben said, gawking at the weapons.

"And probably illegally modified from semi-automatic to automatic. A sideline for Howard Roscoe."

Ben replaced the lid and pounded the nails back in with the butt of the screwdriver.

They left the shed and Mark relocked the door. "I'll give the key to Detective Peters. He can follow up on the rifles."

"Once he's officially found the boxes of paperweights, my partner's client will be able to claim them."

"How long do you think that will take?" Mark asked.

"With all the hassle over Manny's estate, as much as six months. But we know they haven't been lost or destroyed."

On Monday night at seven Mark entered Tom's Tavern and positioned himself with a view out a window toward the Pearl

Street Mall. Mark ordered a cheeseburger and a beer. He watched as the time approached, the time he had specified in the notes he'd placed on each of the suspect's porches. None of them approached the large, implanted rock across the street. Mark kept his eyes focused on the boulder. He expected the murderer would show. He waited for another thirty minutes. Still no one. The waitress kept stopping by, so Mark ordered another beer. He soon realized his ploy had failed. He unfolded the copy he had kept: "The murder of Manny Grimes was captured on an infrared photograph. Interested in making a deal? Be at the large rock on the west end of the Pearl Street Mall, 7:30 P.M., this coming Monday."

As he drove home, he realized he had been naïve to think he could flush out the murderer. His amateur attempt probably made the killer laugh.

As Mark pulled into his street, a fireball erupted ahead. He jammed on his brakes and jumped out of his car. Flames shot through a window of his garage.

His next-door neighbor ran out of the house with a cell phone clutched in his hand. Seeing Mark, he shouted, "I'm calling nine-one-one."

Mark's attention focused on a figure running toward the greenbelt, away from the side of his flaming garage. Mark dashed after the disappearing arsonist. By the time he reached the open space, he had lost sight of the person. Rather than randomly charging out into the darkness, he returned to his burning garage.

His mind raced. He thought about hooking up his garden hose, but he had put it away for the winter in the now-burning garage. His jumbled thoughts were interrupted when he heard sirens. A fire engine screeched to a halt in front of his house. Two firemen jumped off the truck and hooked up a hose to the fire hydrant two houses away. Within minutes water poured on the garage roof.

Mark tried to open the garage door with the remote control inside his car, but it wouldn't budge. He used his cell phone to place a call to Detective Peters to notify him of the latest development.

He didn't mind losing the contents in the garage, but he wanted the fire out before the flames reached the walls of his house.

A fireman with an axe broke through the garage door. Water from the hose shot into the garage, dousing the flames that ran from floor to ceiling. Soon the firemen had extinguished the remaining hot spots.

Mark looked at the wall of the garage farthest from the house, a smoldering black surface with all his garden tools destroyed. The fire had burned a hole in the roof. He climbed through the jagged opening in the door and waded through puddles of sooty mess. Wiping his brow, he determined that the fire had not reached the main part of the house.

Good thing neither car was in the garage.

By the time he had completed his visual inspection of the garage, Detective Peters had arrived.

"I saw someone running away from the scene, but I didn't catch a good look," Mark explained. "How do you think he started the fire?"

Peters scanned the scene.

"Broken window. I'd guess a Molotov cocktail. The damage appears contained to one side of the garage. Fortunately, the fire didn't have time to spread and didn't ignite a can of gasoline or a lawn mower full of gas."

"I used to have an extra can of gas on the shelf, but emptied it all when I last mowed in early October. Good thing I also ran the mower dry." Mark looked at the smoldering remains of his five-year-old Toro.

"I'll work with the fire department and have an arson investigator check for glass and other remnants," Peters said.

Mark paused for a moment and then looked Peters in the eyes. "I know you believe Ken Idler murdered Manny Grimes, but I still think you locked up the wrong person. Someone besides Ken Idler started the fire and although it could be someone aiding Idler, it's more likely to be the work of Lee Daggett, Howard Roscoe or Jacob Fish."

The detective's expression didn't change.

"You should nail Idler on drug smuggling charges from what I've seen and heard, but not murder," Mark continued. "You need to investigate the other three. It's obvious they're all involved in illegal activities, but only one is the murderer of Manny Grimes and Old Mel."

"Any other advice for me?" Detective Peters said, sarcastically.

"Yes." Mark reached in his pocket, extracted the padlock key and tossed it to Peters. "Go check out storage shed twenty-nine at the YourStore Self Storage facility on the south side of Arapahoe. Rented by Manny Grimes."

"I should arrest you for tampering with evidence," Peters said with a scowl.

"You should thank me. Your people have been to the Grimes house three times and never found that key."

After Peters left, Mark made a mental note to contact the insurance adjuster in the morning. Right now he wanted to find some place to stay in case the arsonist returned to do more than send a message.

He took out his cell phone and called Ben.

"Could I impose on you and come sleep in your spare bedroom tonight? There's been a little accident at my house."

"What do you mean by 'little accident'?"

"Someone firebombed my garage."

"Mark, I'll be happy to let you stay, but you know you need to lay off this investigation."

"Yes, I know. Everyone tells me the same thing. Obviously, someone thinks I'm getting too close. But, interestingly enough, since Ken Idler has been arrested for the murder, he can't be the one threatening me. It's one of the other three."

"There you go. You're trying to suck me in again."

"No, I'll park it for the night."

"Okay. Besides we need to strategize for the upcoming city council meeting. We can discuss it over breakfast in the morning."

As Mark lay in Ben's guest bedroom, thoughts of murder suspects swirled in his head. Sure, Ken Idler could be sending someone to harass him, but he had larger problems on his hands. Mark's gut said that one of the other three suspects wanted him out of the way. Jacob Fish could easily have stolen the gun and knife from Howard Roscoe's house and committed the Old Mel murder and the deer slashing. The evidence originally weighed toward Howard Roscoe because of the timing of his arrival the night of Manny's murder, but, since then, no evidence directly pointed to Howard. And Lee Daggett with the Cheryl Idler connection bothered Mark. Something Old Mel had said nagged at him, but he couldn't remember what it was, and although he was inching closer, he hadn't put the puzzle completely together yet.

In the morning Mark sat down with Ben to have a cup of coffee and bowl of cereal.

"You look like shit," Ben said with a grin.

"Thanks for the keen observation. I didn't sleep much last

night. Trying to figure out who murdered Manny and Old Mel."

"I've told you all along I think it's Howard Roscoe. Timing of when he showed up."

"That's part of the key. I've been going over the details in my mind all night. There's something Old Mel said that my pre-Alzheimer's brain keeps trying to remember."

"It's all tied to the fifth man arriving at the court," Ben said, punching Mark's shoulder playfully.

Mark jumped out of the chair spilling his coffee on the table. "That's it! That's the missing piece I've been trying to remember."

Ben looked at him quizzically.

Mark paced the room. "Old Mel told me that he had been instructed to wait for the fifth man to appear before turning off the lights."

"So?" Ben raised his eyebrows.

"The murderer knew a fifth man would appear. Which of the suspects knew that?"

"Maybe the guy who arrived, Howard Roscoe."

"No. He would only come if he thought he planned to substitute. It has to be whoever called Howard to fill in."

Ben regarded Mark blankly.

Mark punched his right fist into his left hand. "Right before the lights went out, an argument occurred. Howard Roscoe called out someone's name."

Ben's eyes widened. "Lee."

"Yes. Roscoe accused Lee Daggett of not calling him back to cancel. Only Daggett knew that a fifth man would appear."

"You're right."

"Daggett invites Roscoe to fill in, doesn't tell him that there are already four players, has him come at seven-thirty when everyone else arrived at seven, sets up Old Mel to turn out the lights, then kills Manny."

"Phone Detective Peters immediately. He needs to know this."

"Not yet," Mark said, putting up a hand to hold off Ben. "There's one piece that still doesn't fit. When he lined him up, why would Daggett tell Old Mel that his name was Manny?"

"Probably planting a red herring."

"No. That doesn't make sense. If Daggett planned all this, he'd have to make it look like someone else committed the murder. Like the police think Ken Idler did it or like you've been leaning toward Howard Roscoe. If Daggett told Old Mel the name of one of the other suspects, I'd believe it. It doesn't fit that he'd plant the victim's name with Old Mel."

Ben took a sip of coffee. "Anyway, Mark, stay away from Daggett. The guy's dangerous. Now, before I go to work, since I can't afford to be a member of the leisure class like you, we have another subject to discuss. We have our final showdown in front of the city council tonight."

The group needed to maintain a tight schedule to be able to complete their regular three sets before the council meeting. Fortunately, Shelby arrived only five minutes late.

After being partners a set each with Woody and Shelby, Mark and Ben teamed in the third and final set. With Shelby serving to Mark for the set at five games to four, forty-thirty, Mark could see sweat glistening on Shelby's forehead in the reflected light. In this game Shelby had already served two faults, an unforgivable sin in this sport where the server had only one and not two chances to get the ball in play. Shelby had a tendency to serve too hard. Sometimes the ball would careen off the corner, but more likely he faulted. Then, when he fell behind, he'd send a puff ball over the net, which would be creamed by his opponent. Kind of like his handling of the Idler investigation. Inappropriate and inconsistent.

Shelby wound up and launched his serve, which struck the

top of the net and dribbled over. Mark raced forward but couldn't reach the ball before it bounced twice.

"What a way to end the match," Shelby said with a snicker as they met at the net to shake hands.

Mark glared at Shelby. "You're lucky that the let rule changed a few years ago, otherwise you'd have had to serve again. You'd probably have faulted the next time."

"It's not my fault," Woody said with a smile.

Mark hit the net with his paddle.

Woody jumped.

"What's the matter?" Ben asked.

"I guess I'm still nervous after Manny's murder and the attack on Paul Crandall."

Mark bent over to pick up his equipment bag. A gun shot rang out. Mark heard a twanging sound as something struck the net post. Heart pounding, he dropped to the court surface, scraping his chin.

"It came from the open space." Ben pointed. "Let's head into the rec center."

Mark jumped up and joined his three companions in a dash toward the building.

Once inside, they stood, breathing rapidly.

"This is my fault," Mark said. "I've pissed off the murderer, and he's been threatening me. I'm sorry to involve the three of you in this again."

"Let's call the police," Woody said.

Mark placed his hand on Woody's arm. "Peters will only give me a ration of crap and tell me to get out of town for a while."

"That's not a bad idea," Ben said.

"I have to get to the meeting to fight for keeping the platform tennis courts. Just find a substitute player for me until things settle down."

"But Manny always substituted for you," Ben said. "And now

he's dead. Our other alternate was Paul Crandall, but he wouldn't risk it again."

Chapter 33

Mark parked in the large lot behind the library. Remembering the castigation from the last city council meeting, he left his cell phone in the glove compartment of his car. He then walked across the footbridge that spanned Boulder Creek and entered the municipal building. His mind spun with images of Manny's murder, his garage burning and Old Mel's dead body. He kept circling the answer like a disoriented fly, but he still hadn't pieced it all together. He had to stay focused. Tonight he had a different mission. He and the other platform tennis players had to convince the city council to keep the courts at the North Boulder Rec Center.

The council followed the same procedure as the previous meetings. People wanting to make comments could sign a list for the particular agenda item of interest. Mark added his name behind five other signatures that would be called in sequence.

He didn't spot any of his group, so he found a seat near the back of the auditorium in order to watch the audience. Ben had said he'd meet him here. Mark recognized a number of the neighborhood opponents from the earlier meetings. Probably not bad people, just obstructionists, as he saw it.

Five minutes later, Ben dashed into the room, looking wildly around.

Mark signaled to him.

Ben threw himself down in the seat next to Mark. "Ready for the fireworks?"

"I have my statement prepared," Mark said. "It's time to force a decision."

Ben scowled. "I hear it's too close to call. Two appear to be already in favor and two already opposed, which leaves three undecided. They sit up there not really caring one way or the other concerning this issue, while we're sweating bullets over the outcome."

The meeting began and the first topic concerned changes to the shopping center. One of the council members, a man in his fifties with bushy eyebrows, grabbed the microphone and glared at the mayor. "How dare you pass the preliminary resolution at the last meeting. I specifically requested that it be held until I returned from vacation."

"Calm down," the mayor and moderator, a woman in a dark-green sweater said. "No one excluded you. We took a preliminary vote to test the waters to gain a sense of opinion on the issue. We deferred the final vote until this evening."

"I put months of research into the subject of land use for the shopping center and know more than anyone else on the council. Proceeding without me was completely unacceptable."

Two of the council members rolled their eyes. The mayor said, "The business of the council must go on. Now you can make whatever statement you want."

The protestor launched into a long and emotional tirade advocating the need to provide low-cost housing along with the expansion of the shopping center.

Ben poked Mark in the ribs. "This guy will want to tie low-cost housing to the approval of the platform tennis courts. Just watch."

"It's obvious the council members have their own pet projects, much like we do," Mark said.

At five minutes after eight the platform tennis question came up for review. Once again the park planner reiterated why he recommended that the courts stay at the North Boulder Rec Center. A representative from the parks board explained their decision to support the recommendation. Then a member of the planning board testified that, in spite of the parks board, they had decided against the recommendation because of concern over the land use at the increasingly crowded site in North Boulder.

"The rec center expanded, so we're supposed to be pushed out?" Ben said, twisting in his chair.

"We're the lucky recipient of the oversight in planning," Mark added. "No one has admitted that a screwup occurred in not including the platform tennis courts in the original rec-center expansion plans."

Next, comments began from the public. Mark listened as a man in a turtleneck sweater gave an impassioned plea to rid his neighborhood of the noise, light and undesirable "paddle-toting miscreants."

Mark's lips curled in disgust. "There's a statement that would be perfect on someone's tombstone. Where do these people come from?"

When the moderator called his name, Mark leaped out of his seat and strode to the microphone to make his statement. He surveyed the city council members. One man twiddled a pencil; a woman looked off to the side with a bored expression; several, including the mayor, made eye contact; and the low-cost-housing man gave Mark a frigid stare. Great. Count one against him, and he hadn't even said anything yet.

Mark cleared his throat. "First, I'd like to ask all the people who play platform tennis to stand up." He turned to the room as approximately fifty people scattered throughout the auditorium rose.

"As you can see, a wide variety of people of different ages, sizes and *shapes* enjoy platform tennis." Several chuckles emerged from the audience. Two council members who had previously stared at him impassively now smiled.

"This sport can be played from childhood through old age. The city has had the foresight to install two courts at the North Boulder Rec Center, providing recreation and exercise to a community of over two hundred players here in Boulder, players who vote. I personally have met a hundred and twenty-seven of these people over the last several years." He didn't mention one of these being dead and another in jail.

He then paused to make sure his point regarding the number of voters had sunk in. "The neighbors have raised legitimate concerns so let me address them. There can be noise. Therefore, the relocated courts will be installed closer to ground level to reduce the amount of noise. Lighted tennis courts currently exist at the rec center so light at night will not be eliminated by not having platform tennis courts. But with the proposed courts being lowered and with the planned low-scatter lights, there will be significantly less diffused light than today. The community of platform tennis players has agreed, in good faith, to limit play so as to complete by nine P.M. to further alleviate the apprehensions raised by the neighbors."

Mark saw one more council member looking up with interest. "Open space being taken away is a valid concern. What used to be a small park will be replaced by a drainage holding area as required by city code, not because of the platform tennis courts, but because of the expanded rec center."

Mark saw a head nod from a councilwoman. "I have walked through the neighborhood and found seven houses and ten apartments that will have a view of the platform tennis courts. If someone watches television in any of these dwellings, they will never notice a light nor hear a sound. Also, a playground exists right on the other side of the apartments. When in use, this park playground produces more noise than the platform tennis courts."

Mark paused and eyed Mr. Low Cost Housing, who gave him a scorching look back. "During the summer, daylight continues past nine P.M., so winter use of the lighted courts until that time should provide no more distraction than natural summer sunlight. The council must decide between conflicting rights for the greater good of the community. Why take away an existing, popular resource when all the stated concerns have been addressed? The real objection from the neighbors isn't the platform tennis courts. It's the expansion of the rec center, and the city has already decided to enlarge the recreation building. The platform tennis players are merely the unfortunate recipients of the reaction to the expansion. I urge you to rule for the best interest in our community and keep the platform tennis courts. Thank you."

Mark scanned the faces of the council members one last time. One woman nodded to him. Two others smiled. The low-cost-housing advocate fixed him with an icy stare.

As he returned to his seat, he heard a smattering of applause from supporters and an undertone of growls from rec-center neighbors. He also anticipated, and saw, a few glowers.

After several more speakers, the mayor threw the issue open for discussion among council members.

The low-cost-housing proponent grabbed the microphone. "I can't support this. It's obvious that an elite group is pushing their own agenda at the expense of residents who live in low-cost apartments bordering the rec center. The families in the apartments deserve peace and quiet as much as someone who can afford a palatial estate."

"What'd I tell you," Ben whispered in Mark's ear. "This guy turns everything into a low-cost-housing issue. Count one against us so far."

A councilwoman next made a statement. Smoothing the hair

from her forehead, she said she had played platform tennis and, although understanding the neighbors' concerns, she agreed that the necessary mitigation steps had been taken.

"One to one." Ben put an index finger up from each hand.

Four other council members took clear positions. The final man, the only one wearing a tie, made a very ambiguous summary of the issues.

"I can't figure out if he's for us or against us," Ben said. "It's three to three with one swing vote."

The mayor called for a vote. As Ben had predicted three hands went up in support of the motion to keep the courts.

Mark watched the one undecided council member. "Come on, put your hand up," he urged.

The man straightened his tie, looked around at the other council members and finally raised his hand.

"The motion carries four votes to three to retain the platform tennis courts at the North Boulder Recreation Center," the mayor announced. "The next topic on the agenda is . . ."

Mark and Ben bolted from their seats and charged out of the auditorium and down the stairs.

Outside the building, they gave each other a high five as they stood in the cold night air.

"We won!" Ben screamed.

Mark gave a subdued smile. "Yes, it's over. After all the obstacles and hearings, we'll still have courts to play on."

"What a battle," Ben said with a smile. "Do you want to stay at my house again tonight?"

"No. I think it's safe to go back to my place. Thanks for putting me up." Mark looked out into the ominous darkness. "Now, we just need Manny's murderer to be arrested."

"Please be careful, Mark."

Ben had parked in the small parking lot next to the municipal building, so they parted. As Mark strolled over the bridge toward the other parking lot, he hummed the Beatles' "I Want to Hold Your Hand," remembering it from the radio earlier in the day. He threaded his way along the sidewalk and suddenly realized the light that had illuminated this corner of the parking lot when he arrived was out. *Uh-oh.* He tensed at the sound of rustling in the bushes. Out of the corner of his eye, he saw some movement in the shadows. Suddenly, a figure appeared. Something flew toward his head.

CHAPTER 34

When Mark awoke, his head spun like a wobbly top, and his cheek burned like it had been branded. He felt some jostling movement, but couldn't figure out where he was. He lay on his stomach in the dark. He couldn't move. Someone had bound his hands behind him.

He wriggled his fingers and felt a substance smooth on one side and sticky on the other—duct tape constrained him. He saw a brief flash of light and discovered he lay in the backseat of a car, on a leather seat, with his face in a pool of drool. His ankles were also bound. The car jolted. It felt like a speed bump. *Must still be in Boulder,* he thought.

He tried to raise himself, but didn't have the strength to sit up. He saw the back of the driver's head, but there didn't seem to be any head peeking above the headrest on the passenger's side.

He decided not to let his assailant know he had awakened. With his limited field of vision, he couldn't spot any identifying insignias in the dark. Now the car made sweeping turns and seemed to be going up an incline. He spotted periodic flashes of car headlights, then darkness again.

The car thumped over a bump, and the back of Mark's head banged into something on the seat. He turned his face to try to see the object, but it remained too dark to tell. Then lights appeared from an oncoming car. Mark squinted to make out the writing on the box. Samoas. Girl Scout cookies. Melinda

Daggett had said that Lee loved Girl Scout cookies. Lee Daggett!

Mark turned his face away from the box. After a while, the car made a sharp turn and the top of Mark's head banged into the door. Then the seat began vibrating and Mark found himself bouncing up and down. He could hear the sound of gravel crunching underneath the car's tires. He no longer saw any flashes from headlights. The car passed over a smooth section of road, but moments later Mark heard the sound of gravel once again, and the car quivered from what seemed to be a washboard pattern on the road.

Mark's face pushed into the seat as the car headed uphill, and then he slumped back as the car crested a hill and headed down. The car lurched and turned numerous times before skidding to a stop. A car door opened and slammed. The door that his head had been periodically bumping into opened. Mark stayed limp.

Someone grabbed him under the armpits and dragged him out of the car. Mark's feet bumped along the seat and then crashed onto gravel before his assailant dragged him along the pebbles and away from the car. Unceremoniously, his attacker hurled Mark to the ground.

"As soon as you wake up, you can join Manny and the old vagrant," a gruff voice announced.

Mark continued to keep his eyes closed.

He heard crunching steps on the gravel and a car door opened. The door closed and footsteps approached. Then a liquid hit his face. He spluttered.

Cold coffee, cream and sugar entered the corner of his mouth.

"Time to wake up, sleeping beauty."

Mark shook the coffee off his face and struggled to a sitting position.

"So why'd you bring me all the way out here?" he asked.

"Simple. You've been a pain in the butt and getting in the way."

In spite of the cold, Mark began to sweat. He tried to think of any bargaining chip he had to play. He only had one ploy. "It wouldn't do any good to kill me. I've left a sworn statement on all I've learned in a safe with instructions to my lawyer to open it if something happens to me. It even has your name, Daggett."

A laugh emerged from the face hidden in the dark. "Nice try. You didn't know enough before coming up here to cause any problems. Now it's too late for you to talk to anyone."

Mark thought back to what he had found out. It was true. He had a smattering of facts, but nothing conclusive. He had mentioned his suspicion to Ben, but he had no concrete proof to support his conclusion.

Lee Daggett reached down and cut the duct tape from Mark's ankles but not his wrists.

"There," Lee announced. "Now you can come for a stroll with me. Time for swimming lessons."

Lee raised Mark up under the armpits and set him on his feet.

"March!"

Mark felt a push in the back and he stumbled down a gravel driveway. Off to the side he could make out the faint outline of a house—a three-story, wooden structure with two decks. He stumbled past a woodpile.

"This place belong to friends of yours?" Mark asked.

"Let's just say it belongs to someone who is out of town. Don't expect to find anyone around to help you. Keep moving."

When they reached the end of the driveway, Daggett steered Mark toward a path that wound through some trees. A few minutes later, Mark found himself facing a steep beach, giving way to a large body of ice-covered water. Another shove directed him to the right, along the pebbly beach.

Mark tried to think where he could be. He estimated they had traveled for no less than thirty minutes, but not longer than an hour. Within that travel time from Boulder, there existed two large reservoirs: Gross and Barker. The route to Gross Reservoir would have entailed more steep grades and hairpin turns than he'd experienced. This must be Barker Reservoir.

He stumbled along, tripping once and sprawling on the gravelly sand. He felt small sharp rocks dig into his chin.

Daggett grabbed him and lifted him up like a child picking up a doll.

"Keep going."

Another push.

They rounded a point, and Mark could faintly see the ice. He staggered on as they curved around an inlet, and he stepped through a dry stream bed. He stumbled again on the steeply slopping shoreline and desperately fought to retain his balance. In the distance he saw the headlight of a car and a faint reflection across the ice surface of the wide body of water. *That must be the Boulder Canyon road,* Mark thought. They were on the far side of the reservoir.

Daggett broke the silence. "How'd you like the present I left on your doorstep?"

Mark didn't answer.

"I found that deer caught in netting I'd put in my backyard. I had to tranquilize it to bring it to your place. Thought it would help convince you to back off. You might have lived if you'd paid attention. You're too stubborn. Even a little fire didn't seem to convince you."

Mark pictured Lee lugging the deer to his front door and slitting its throat. Then he recalled the image of his burning garage. This guy had definitely gone over the edge. He acted cocky and might slip up. Mark had to think of a way to get him cocky enough to slip up.

239

Mark tugged at his wrists. They remained firmly constrained. He needed something to tear the duct tape. Once he could force a break in the tape, he could snap it apart. Just like he did when ripping duct tape to put on his tennis shoes before each platform tennis game.

"Bet you also enjoyed the note I left you," Daggett bragged. "I got the idea from Howard Roscoe."

Mark thought he should try some delaying tactics, keep a conversation going. "Why'd you steal the folder from Barbara's house?"

"I wanted to retrieve some papers."

"I bet the contents of the folder surprised you."

Daggett stopped. "What the hell do you mean?"

"Didn't you read the papers?"

"No. I burned them."

"Well, in that case I won't shake your illusion that you destroyed what you wanted to," Mark said.

Daggett whacked Mark's shoulder. "Are you trying to game me? Move your butt." He gave Mark another shove.

They reached a rock outcrop, and Daggett directed Mark up the steep beach. The sand ended against a pile of rocks. Mark stopped, unable to negotiate the uneven surface with his hands bound behind his back.

"Climb!" Daggett commanded.

Mark placed his left foot on a rock and received a rough boost from behind. He stumbled up onto the rock surface and struggled to retain his balance. After several precarious steps and further pushes, he reached the flat top of the rock.

"Sit down," Daggett said, thrusting him downward.

Mark bounced and came to rest with his hands scraping against the rock.

"I'll give you a moment to review your worthless life, and I'll tell you a secret." Daggett laughed. "So you'll know what to expect, you're going for your last swim. You'll sail off the rock, fall through the ice and drown in the deep water. And the beauty of it is that your body will be under the ice so no one will find it until next spring at the earliest. Now I'll fix your legs."

Daggett wrapped duct tape around Mark's ankles. As he lay there, Mark felt bile rising in his throat. *Think.* He felt a rock jabbing the small of his back. He moved his hands and started scraping the duct tape against the jagged rock. If he could only tear the tape in one place, he would be able to free his hands. As Daggett wrapped yet more tape around his ankles, Mark continued to rip the duct tape binding his wrists and could feel it giving way. He had almost worked it through when two arms grabbed him and pulled him up. Daggett dragged him down to another part of the rock surface.

In the distance another headlight briefly illuminated the ice, and Mark peered straight down. Some instinct made him look up just as a large stick of wood, partially illuminated by the car's headlight, shot toward his head. He ducked enough so that the blow glanced off the side of his head. He felt a push. Dazed by the blow, but still conscious, he sailed through space.

CHAPTER 35

Mark struck the thin ice and broke through into the freezing water. The shock of the cold revived him from the blow. Now he had mere seconds to free his hands. He tried to wrench his wrists apart.

Nothing happened. His heart beat faster.

He needed to free his wrists in order to survive.

With all his strength he thrust his hands apart. He felt the duct tape give way, but not tear completely.

He needed air.

One more violent tug and his hands came apart.

He raised his arms and clawed at the water. Up he went until his head hit the ice. He felt his chest tighten.

He wondered if he could break through.

His lungs burned.

He pushed the ice.

Nothing happened.

He rammed his fist into the ice. The ice cracked. He punched again. The ice gave way.

His head popped through the opening.

He gasped for air.

The cold mountain air filled his lungs. Mark knew he had less than two minutes to escape from the water before hypothermia set in.

He heard a laugh in the distance. Lee Daggett had started back, and it appeared he didn't know that Mark had freed his hands. Now Mark had to find the shore. Looking in all directions, he couldn't make out any objects. Then a faint flicker of a distant headlight appeared. Mark stroked in the opposite direction, breaking the ice as he went. The ice was too thin to hold him so he had to act like an ice breaker to shred his way to shore.

His head throbbed, and the cold slowed his muscles. His arm hit rock. Too steep to climb. He pulled himself along the outcrop, breaking the ice as he went. His fingers had gone numb.

Finally, one of his shoes scraped the bottom. He shuffled onto a pebbly, sloped bottom and pulled himself onto a stretch of rugged beach.

He grabbed a jagged rock and tore at the duct tape on his ankles. His numb hand dropped the rock twice before he completed the task.

He lay gasping for breath, feeling his heart pounding erratically. Putting his hand to his head, his fingers came away with a sticky substance. Blood! He began convulsing in shivers. His body needed warmth.

He raised himself and stumbled along the beach until he came to the rock outcrop he'd been pushed off. He crawled over the rocks and down to the beach on the other side.

He heard a car driving away.

Lee Daggett had left.

Mark looked for light along the coastline. Nothing. He had to keep moving.

He had lost all feeling in his fingers. Struggling along the beach and across the inlet, he rounded the point. Still no lights. He gauged where he thought the house would be—the house he'd seen when Daggett had parked his car.

If he went into the woods at the wrong place, he could wander forever.

Picking a likely spot, he staggered into the forest. For a moment he thought he'd entered in the wrong place. Then he saw a faint reflection off a window.

He passed a small shed and found a door to the house. Locked. He picked up a rock. He held it in his two numb hands and unceremoniously broke a glass pane on the door. He slapped his hands together to try to regain some feeling.

Then he reached inside and found the door handle.

His numb hand fumbled trying to grasp it.

Finally, he got a grip, turned the knob, and the door released.

He pulled back his hand, careful not to cut himself on the broken glass.

Stumbling through the entryway, he found the master bedroom and bathroom.

He clumsily removed his clothes, took a hot shower and wrapped himself in a blanket to keep warm. Other than his head now hurting, he had no other injuries.

Satisfied that he had escaped hypothermia, he explored the house. He found a desk and turned on a light. Rummaging through some papers, he found an address and name of the occupants. He jotted down the information, picked up the phone and dialed a number.

"Ben, I need your help," he said.

"You woke me up. What gives?"

"I've been kidnapped and almost murdered."

"Oh, my God! What happened?"

"Lee Daggett is the murderer . . . never mind, long story. I'm stranded in the woods near Barker Reservoir. Could you come and pick me up? I'll explain everything when you get here."

"If picking you up is what it takes to keep our foursome going, sure. Sorry, Mark, that wasn't funny. Just tell me where you are and I'll be there as soon as I can."

★ ★ ★ ★ ★

While waiting for Ben, Mark found a piece of cardboard and some duct tape. He covered the broken pane of glass. Then he wrote a note and removed fifty dollars of soaked cash from his wallet.

Forty-five minutes later, Mark heard a car pull to a stop in the driveway. He peered out the window to verify Ben's silver Acura.

Mark picked up his soggy clothes and still wrapped in the blanket shuffled outside to meet Ben.

"You look like hell," Ben said.

"I had a little unexpected nighttime swim," Mark answered.

"But your head. There's blood at your hairline."

Mark put his hand to his head and felt the goose egg. "Lee Daggett added a little extra incentive for me to stay in the lake. He tried to kill me like he did with Manny and the street person down on the mall."

"You better sit down with the police when we return to Boulder."

Mark thought for a moment. "I need to do that, eventually, but not yet. Right now it would be my word against Daggett's. He'd deny everything and have some alibi for tonight. Daggett thinks I'm dead. With the right element of surprise, I should be able to trap him."

Ben slapped his forehead. "Come on, Mark. For a smart guy, you're acting pretty stupid. It's time to cut out the amateur-detective crap. You almost swam with the fishes. You're over your head in dealing with these people."

"Thanks for the concern, Ben. I may have stumbled along the way and being pushed off a rock into a frozen lake terrified me, but I'm close to finding a way to wrap this up for good. There remain a few elements of Manny's murder that don't make sense. I have to figure out the rest of it."

"Like what?"

"I'm guessing Daggett murdered Manny to escape a large gambling debt, but it seems he could have solved that problem without resorting to murder. As I told you before, there's the statement made by the street person, Old Mel, that still bothers me. He said the man who asked him to turn off the lights at the rec center identified himself as Manny. Old Mel adamantly stated Manny's name, and it makes no sense. I need to see Daggett one more time to resolve a few final questions. He pushed me in the reservoir before I could obtain all the information."

"You meet Daggett one-on-one, and there won't be any more of you left."

"I need to trap him. I have to figure out a way to do it without giving him a chance to try to kill me again."

"You're sounding as realistic as Shelby when he blundered in to confront Ken Idler. And you should go to a hospital to have your head wound looked at."

"If I could survive the icy water, I can handle a knock on the head."

"I still think you should have your head examined, in more ways than one."

"Let's head home. By the way, how did you find this place so fast?"

"My old Boy Scout skills. I have a forest-service map of the town of Nederland and Barker Reservoir. I navigated the roads using the map. I didn't even need a GPS."

Mark leaned his head back against the headrest. In spite of his fatigue and pain, an idea started to form. He would need someone to assist him.

"Ben, I may need your help with another matter."

They passed through a traffic circle in Nederland. Ben raised his eyebrows. "Remember, I'm off the case. I'm willing to rescue your sorry ass when you end up stranded in the mountains, but I'm not involving myself directly with these characters. Besides, I'm flying to New York tomorrow afternoon." Ben looked at his watch. "Actually, this afternoon."

"I understand. I'll see if Woody or Shelby will be around."

"I wouldn't try Woody right now. It's been exactly two years since his son died in that car crash. He and Amelia are in a bad place with the memories of the event. Shelby's your best bet."

Mark rubbed his chin. Yes, Shelby should be able to help with what he had in mind. If Mark could count on him to show up on time.

When they arrived in front of Mark's house, Ben did a double take. "That's some garage. You're lucky the fire didn't spread to the whole house. Mark, you have to go to the police. Daggett is going to keep after you."

"On the drive home I thought through how to end all of this."

"What do you have in mind?"

"It's a way to trap Daggett. I need to put the plans in place tomorrow. I'll fill you in when you get back from your trip."

"I only hope it doesn't end you."

"Thanks for the concern and for the ride. I'll be careful."

Mark let himself out of the car and staggered to the front door. He pulled the house key out of the soggy pants he carried over one arm.

Once inside he threw his wet clothes in the clothes hamper and headed into the bathroom for another shower. As he soaked in the hot water, he thought back to the flight off the rock into the icy water. Even in the soothing warmth of the shower, he involuntarily shivered. He would be safe for the night. Daggett wouldn't suspect he had escaped, so after a good night's sleep, he could put his plan in action tomorrow morning. For the first time in hours, he let his muscles relax.

After he toweled off and changed into pajamas, he noticed the light flashing on his answering machine. He played a message that asked him to stop by to see Dr. Gallagher at eleven in the morning. Mark's muscles tensed again.

Mark slept until nine and awoke with a throbbing headache. Two aspirins hardly helped, but after a cup of coffee and a bagel, he called a taxi to take him back to his car, still in the lot by the library. Then he began his errands. He first stopped at Radio Shack. He surveyed the electronic recorders and tried several before selecting a compact model that recorded clearly and had an external microphone attachment. Now he had one other piece of equipment to obtain.

From his cell phone he called Shelby at his office at the university. Mark explained what he wanted Shelby to do.

Shelby reluctantly agreed.

"You'll need to arrive at exactly five minutes after nine tonight," Mark reiterated.

"Yeah, I understand."

"Thanks, Shelby. I really need your assistance on this."

Mark's stomach tensed at the thought of whether Shelby could really arrive on time, but he really had no other choice.

Now for the difficult part. He checked his platform tennis list for Lee Daggett's phone number. The first time he called, he immediately heard a recorded message.

Mark waited ten minutes and tried again.

"Yeah?" came the gruff answer—the same voice as last night at the reservoir.

Mark clenched the phone tighter. Using a gravelly voice, as unlike his own as he could make it, he said, "Daggett, you made a big mistake. You were observed committing a murder at Barker Reservoir last night. We have a deal to work out. Come alone to the playground at Scott Carpenter Park. Tonight at nine sharp."

CHAPTER 36

Mark closed the cell phone. He let out a breath as a wave of tension flowed out of his body.

That should catch Lee Daggett's attention. Daggett wouldn't know exactly what to expect, but he liked doing deals. He should be curious and concerned enough to show up.

At ten forty-five, as Mark drove toward Dr. Gallagher's office, his mind filled with a conflicting set of images. What if he didn't receive a clean bill of health? What if the cancer had completely disappeared? He had butterflies in his stomach as he sat at a stoplight and watched an elderly couple cross the street, the man leaning on a cane and his female companion holding his arm.

Would he ever live to be that old?

As he pulled into the medical-center parking lot, he swallowed dryly. What would he tell Sophie if the cancer had returned?

Walking into the building, he jangled the change in his left pocket. He made his co-payment and signed the form and credit-card slip as he shifted and re-shifted his feet. Finally, he shuffled up the narrow stairs, handed over the yellow and pink forms at the nurse's station, and plopped into a chair.

He looked around the room at the handful of people waiting to have their various ailments treated. Would he be back here on a regular basis again, or could he escape for six months? Picking up a three-year-old *National Geographic,* he leafed through the pages, pausing briefly to skim an article describing Costa Rica. He had never visited the rain forests of Central or South America. Would he have a chance to do that?

"Mr. Yeager?" the nurse called.

Mark dropped the magazine on the end table and jumped up. Sweat, not caused by the overheated room, trickled down his ribs from his armpits.

The nurse in her light-green smock and her hair pulled back in a tight bun asked him to step on the scale. "One hundred eighty-one pounds," she said looking over her glasses at the scale. "Within two pounds of your last visit."

Mark decided to take that as a good sign. Stable body weight. No cancer eating away? Or did he merely hold a false hope? He had been exercising, primarily with his three platform tennis games a week.

The nurse directed him to a small room, and he sat on the one chair next to the examination table. If he never saw another one of these rooms, it would be fine with him.

After taking his blood pressure, the nurse left and closed the door.

Mark surveyed the chart on the wall. It showed a male form from the front and back, skin stripped away to reveal the muscles of the body. Mark fidgeted in the seat and drummed his fingers on his knees.

Outside, something fell on the floor. An indecipherable high-pitched voice spoke and a deeper voice responded, but Mark couldn't hear what they said. The door knob moved, and Dr. Gallagher stepped in, a laptop computer in hand.

"So, Mark, how do you feel?"

"I hope a lot better after I hear the lab results."

Dr. Gallagher regarded Mark quizzically and then broke out into a smile. "I see. You're one of the few business people or, in your case, retired business executives I know who has never been treated for tension-related disorders. You're now as nervous as I've ever seen you."

Mark tried to smile, but only twitched his lips. "I can't stand it any longer. Tell me how the lab results turned out."

"Give me a moment." The doctor set his laptop on the counter and tapped away.

Mark felt sweat dripping down his ribs again.

Dr. Gallagher tapped a few more keys and stared at the screen. "The bottom line is that the blood test shows no indications of any reoccurrence of the cancer. I'm giving you a clean bill of health, at least for the time being. When you pass the reception desk, set an appointment to come back in six months. I won't need to see you until then."

I made a copayment of thirty-five dollars for this ten-second speech, Mark thought. Then he felt a genuine smile spread across his face and his muscles relaxed.

Later, Mark prepared for his encounter with Lee Daggett. He put the recorder in the pocket of his pants, where he could easily turn it on, and ran the microphone cord up to his collar. He clipped it on. Then he put on his jacket to hide the cord and pulled a ski cap onto his head.

Driving to Scott Carpenter Park, Mark reviewed how timing would be critical. He needed to confront Daggett, confuse him and trick him into admitting what he'd done. Mark would have the recorder running. Then he needed Shelby to arrive to distract Daggett.

Mark parked his car at the far end of the lot, checked his watch to verify the time of eight-fifty and walked to the playground to wait. He reached into his pocket and turned on the recorder.

At exactly nine a car pulled up, and someone climbed out.

Mark's heart pounded as the dark shape moved toward him. His senses set off alarm bells. The figure appeared shorter and skinnier than Lee Daggett.

Mark considered shrinking into the shadows, but the figure now confronted him.

Cheryl Idler pulled out a gun and pointed it at him.

"Where's Lee?" Mark said.

"He's sleeping. I gave him a drink with an extra ingredient. I didn't want him blowing it again, so I came to make sure you wouldn't cause us any more trouble."

"So, you know all about Lee's attempt to kill me last night."

"Yeah. The dumb ox pushed you in the lake, but obviously he didn't do the job right."

"How'd you know it would be me here?"

"Simple. When you called Lee, his caller I.D. showed your name."

Damn, Mark cursed under his breath. How could he have forgotten that? The element of surprise wouldn't have worked if Daggett had shown up. Now Mark had been thrown off balance. He needed to obtain as much information as possible as quickly as possible.

"I suppose you know that Lee killed Manny and Old Mel."

"Lee and I planned the first murder. The second one needed to be done to cover up his first mistake."

"First mistake?"

"I don't know why I got involved with such an incompetent jerk. He was supposed to kill Ken, but in the dark he hit the wrong person and killed Manny."

Cheryl leaned her head back as the light from a passing car shone briefly in her face.

Mark noticed a mole on the left side of her neck.

It all suddenly made sense to him. "You planned to cash in on Ken's estate after his death and had set it up to put the blame on Manny. Then you and Lee hired Clyde to kill me because I started getting too close."

"That's right. You're smarter than Lee. He screwed it all up, and then we had to scramble to make it look like Ken committed the murder. The vagrant confused the issue. So Lee took care of him. But then you interfered. I gave Clyde a description that Lee had written down. I told Clyde which platform tennis player to attack, but he went after the wrong person. Another incompetent. Howard Roscoe had raved about his skills, but Clyde couldn't handle it and Lee couldn't, either. Now I'm here to take care of you myself."

"Why didn't you let Lee come to kill me? He may be a 'dumb ox,' but he had the element of surprise on his side. I didn't think about caller I.D."

"Two reasons. One, I didn't trust him to do it right. And, two, I've had enough of him." She ran her hand through her long, blond hair. "I have his gun here with his fingerprints on it, and I'm wearing gloves. I'll testify that Lee received your phone call and came here to kill you. I want him out of the way now so I can live on Ken's money by myself while Ken's in prison for Manny's murder and Lee is in prison for your murder. Maybe they can even be cellmates. Now, we're going to walk over toward Boulder Creek."

Mark pushed the stem of his watch to see a time of nine fifteen. What had happened to Shelby? He needed the distraction of Shelby's arrival before he and Cheryl left the playground.

"One last question," Mark said, trying to stall. "What if Ken isn't convicted of Manny's murder?"

Cheryl pursed her lips. "I'd probably have to kill him. I can't stand him anymore."

Mark shook his head. He couldn't understand this callous attitude toward murder. He had dealt with some pretty tough people in the business world, but nothing like Lee Daggett and

Cheryl Idler.

"Okay. Let's move toward the creek," Cheryl said, waving the gun at Mark.

He looked at the long attachment on the end of the gun. Hadn't he seen one of those at the gun show?

"That's quite a contraption."

"Howard Roscoe has been very helpful for supplying his friends with weapons." Cheryl tapped the muzzle of the gun. "This baby has a state-of-the-art silencer. No one will hear what I'm going to do to you."

Mark had a decision to make. Still no Shelby. He reached into his jacket pocket and put his hand around a pepper-spray can. He took a deep breath, hesitated a moment, and then spotted a car racing into the parking lot with its high beams flashing and its horn honking.

"What the—" Cheryl turned her head.

Mark pulled the pepper spray out of his pocket. He said, "Cheryl" in a loud voice, and, when she turned back toward him, he sprayed it at her face.

She screamed, dropped the gun and fell to her knees, clutching her eyes.

Mark picked up the gun as Shelby dashed toward them, waving his hands.

"Am I glad to see you," Mark said to Shelby.

"How'd you like that distraction?" Shelby said, puffing out his chest.

"Very good. But it could have been a little sooner."

"You're never going to believe this, but I had to stop to put gas in my car."

"I believe it. Keep an eye on Cheryl while I call Detective Peters."

Mark pulled out his cell phone and punched in the numbers.

Peters arrived within ten minutes. Cheryl sat on the ground, still rubbing her eyes.

"Manny's death was a mistake," Mark told Peters. "Cheryl Idler and Lee Daggett planned to kill Cheryl's husband, Ken, and Lee Daggett killed Manny Grimes and Old Mel. Both of them also tried to kill me." Mark reached into his pants pocket and pulled out the recorder. "Here's a recording with Cheryl describing the whole plan. You'll find Daggett drugged and asleep at his house."

"What's he doing here?" Peters asked, pointing at Shelby.

"He's my assistant," Mark said.

While Peters read Cheryl her rights, Shelby pulled Mark aside. "There's something wrong with my car."

"Oh?"

"It got thirty-five miles to the gallon at first, then twenty-five, but on this last tank only fourteen miles to the gallon," Shelby said with a quivering lip.

Mark slapped him on the back. "Shelby, you can cheer up. You only have one problem. Leaving your car unlocked so someone can release the gas cap door."

Shelby narrowed his eyes. "What do you mean?"

"You've been the victim of a little prank. I won't mention any names, but someone added gas to your tank at first so you'd seem to get extra good mileage. Then he left it alone for one tank full. Recently, he siphoned gas out of your tank."

"So, it really gets close to twenty-five miles to the gallon?"

"I'm sure it does."

Shelby's smile returned. He strutted around and punched his right fist into his left hand. "Boy, we sure solved this case, didn't we, Mark?"

"Yes, Shelby. *We* did."

CHAPTER 37

Mark entered his house, ready to collapse from exhaustion. He stumbled up to the bedroom and dropped onto the bed.

The phone rang.

He almost let it cut over to voice mail, but after three rings he picked it up.

"Mr. Yeager," Detective Peters's tense voice said, "you may be in danger."

Mark's mind became immediately alert, and he sat up straight. "From what or whom?"

"After I left you at Scott Carpenter Park, I went to arrest Lee Daggett. I expected to find him drugged at his home, but he'd disappeared."

Mark's heart beat faster.

"He may be on his way to your house. I've dispatched two cars, but they won't get to your place for ten minutes. Don't let anyone in until the officers arrive."

As Mark hung up the phone, he heard a crashing sound from downstairs. Someone had broken a window. Daggett!

Mark needed to buy time. He quickly unscrewed the light bulbs from the two bedside lamps and climbed up on the low, horizontal dresser to remove the bulb from the one overhead light. He dropped the bulbs into a drawer and closed the bedroom door. Too bad it had no lock.

He heard footsteps on the stairs. He turned around. Where could he hide? The closet?

He groped his way along the wall to the closet and stepped inside. He pressed himself back against his shirts.

The bedroom doorknob turned and a faint shaft of light from the hallway shown into the bedroom, barely visible from the closet. Footsteps entered the room and then stopped.

Mark controlled his breathing to stay as quiet as possible.

"I know you're in here, Yeager. I'll find you and finish what I should have completed at the reservoir."

The light switch clicked and nothing happened. "Shit," Daggett said.

Several more footsteps and then a pause. "I'll bet you're hiding in the closet. I think it's time for a dead body in the closet." Daggett laughed.

Mark shuffled his feet backward. His right foot bumped into something. His equipment bag. Mark reached down and pulled out his platform tennis paddle from the bag.

More heavy footsteps approached.

Mark could make out the faint outline of a head leaning into the closet. With all his strength, he raised the paddle and bashed it down on Daggett's head.

The closet reverberated with a dull thud, followed by a thump as Daggett collapsed on the floor.

Mark felt the blood pulsing in his veins. He realized he'd been holding his breath and took a lungful of air.

Daggett didn't move.

Mark stepped over the body and raced downstairs. He grabbed his roll of duct tape and ran back up the stairs, taking them three at a time. He screwed a bulb into the closest bedside lamp and turned it on.

Daggett lay motionless with blood trickling down his forehead. He breathed unevenly.

Mark turned him over and thrust the limp arms behind Lee's back. He wound duct tape around both of Lee's wrists. Then he wrapped Daggett's ankles as well.

Moments later Mark's doorbell rang.

He dashed downstairs and opened the door. Two police officers stood on his front porch.

"He's upstairs." Mark pointed.

The first officer pulled out his gun.

"That won't be necessary. The intruder's unconscious and tied up."

Up in the bedroom, one of the police officers added handcuffs to the duct tape and cut the tape from Lee's ankles.

Daggett moaned as he started to regain consciousness. The officers helped him to his feet.

Still groggy, Daggett tried to lunge at Mark, but one of the officers restrained him.

"Asshole," Daggett muttered.

"A pleasure doing business with you, too, Daggett," Mark said.

CHAPTER 38

First, Mark punched in Norm's phone number.

Dawn answered.

"Hi, this is Mark. Thanks for providing Sophie a home away from home."

"We've certainly enjoyed her visit. When will you be coming to see us?"

"No specific plans, but I think it's time for you to have your place to yourselves without a visitor. May I speak with my bride?"

When Sophie picked up the phone, Mark said, "I'm done with all the investigating. I'm sorry for everything I put you through."

"That sounds like the beginning of a good apology. Keep going."

Mark let out a breath. "I love you and won't do this again."

"And you're ready to return to normal?" Sophie asked.

"Yes. I sure miss you. Will you come home tomorrow?"

"I think that can be arranged. We've been apart too long. Expect me back late afternoon."

Mark felt a smile cross his face. "That's one of the two best pieces of news I've heard in weeks. The other good news is that Dr. Gallagher gave me a clean bill of health."

Mark awoke at nine-thirty the next morning. He couldn't recall any troubling dreams for the first time in weeks. A ribbon of sunlight danced on the rug as waves of radiant heat from the baseboard gently nudged the curtains. He stretched and pulled himself out of bed. He hadn't slept this late since college.

He fixed a cup of instant coffee and two pieces of raisin-bread toast. Before he could decide what to do next, the phone rang.

"Mr. Yeager, this is Detective Peters. I need you to come here and make a complete statement."

Mark looked at the sun-covered hillside and thought how it would be nice to take a hike. On the other hand, he had a platform tennis game at lunchtime so would have a chance to exercise then. And the courts would be staying at the North Boulder Rec Center.

"Sure. I can be there in half an hour. By the way, what happened to my 'friends' from last night?"

"Lee Daggett remains in custody for mutilating a deer. Under the animal cruelty law he could receive up to eighteen months in prison and a minimum fine of one thousand dollars."

"That's all?" Mark said, and heard his voice rising.

Peters chuckled. "Just testing your sense of humor. Daggett also faces two counts of murder and one of attempted murder. After we obtained a search warrant for his house, we found a dented platform tennis paddle and a pile of cracked coconuts in his backyard. Guess he practiced. We've also arrested Cheryl Idler for attempted murder and conspiracy to commit murder."

"And Ken Idler?"

"No charges for murder, but he's still being held. We have enough evidence to try him for drug smuggling."

Mark smiled to himself. "Did you check the background of the rifles in the storage shed?"

"Yes."

"I bet they turned out to be modified from semi-automatic to automatic."

After a momentary pause Peters said, "That's correct."

"You should be able to track that modification to Howard Roscoe."

"I can't discuss an ongoing investigation."

"Peters, you play it so much by the book, but I know you'll lock up Roscoe. Answer this one question for me: Who did Manny plan to sell the rifles to?"

"I don't have to tell you that."

"I know. But Manny's already dead so the information won't affect your investigation. Please soothe my curiosity, and I'll stay out of your life from now on."

Peters chuckled again. "You've heard my lectures, and none of them did any good. It will be worth it to get you out of my hair. I'll tell you this much. A group of survivalists in Montana planned to buy the weapons."

"Now, you only have to remove Jacob Fish from the streets of Boulder."

"A warrant has been issued on federal charges of software piracy. The FBI will put him away for at least ten years."

"Well, Peters, you made a clean sweep."

Mark owed a friend a phone call. He punched in the number for Al Lawson at the *Denver Post.*

"I promised you a full report, Al, and here it is."

"I'm eagerly waving my fingers over the keyboard."

Mark recounted all he had learned concerning Idler, Roscoe, Fish and Daggett.

"I don't know how much of that I can use, but you've given me several juicy stories," Al said.

"Have at it and enjoy yourself."

When Mark returned the phone receiver to its cradle, he thought that Ben's comment when they found the rifles in the shed might have been right. Maybe Manny wanted to start a war.

Mark sighed.

Manny sure had failed him. And yet he had Manny to thank for insisting that he go in for a prostate checkup. He remained alive because of Manny, and Manny had died, caught in a strange web of illicit dealings, identity confusion and bad luck.

Mark finished his cup of coffee and took one more fleeting look out the window at the hillside. He saw a deer grazing amid patches of snow left over from the last storm. He smiled, thinking of Sophie and her battle with her garden marauders. Then he sauntered upstairs and removed his tennis shoes from the closet.

Extracting his roll of duct tape from the pantry, he sat in his favorite easy chair in the living room and carefully applied strips of tape to the bottom of his tennis shoes.

Sophie would be home this afternoon. After speaking to Peters and playing today's platform tennis game, he'd tidy up the place and be ready for her return. Then he'd be seeing his daughter and her fiancé. Maybe after Audrey and Adam's visit, he and Sophie should complete plans to take that trip to Hawaii. Somewhere to really relax before he started consulting. Just the two of them.

He stretched.

After surviving the last few days, only one wish remained.

He thought again of Sophie. He felt a long overdue stirring he had not experienced since his prostate-cancer surgery. Maybe tonight.

ABOUT THE AUTHOR

Mike Befeler is author of six novels in the Paul Jacobson Geezer-lit Mystery Series: *Retirement Homes Are Murder, Living with Your Kids Is Murder* (a finalist for The Lefty Award for best humorous mystery of 2009), *Senior Moments Are Murder, Cruising in Your Eighties Is Murder* (a finalist for The Lefty Award for best humorous mystery of 2012), *Care Homes Are Murder* and *Nursing Homes Are Murder*. He has four other published mystery novels: *The V V Agency, The Back Wing, Mystery of the Dinner Playhouse* and *Murder on the Switzerland Trail,* and a non-fiction biography, *For Liberty: A World War II Soldier's Inspiring Life Story of Courage, Sacrifice, Survival and Resilience.* Mike is past-president of the Rocky Mountain Chapter of Mystery Writers of America. He grew up in Honolulu, Hawaii, and now lives in Southern California, with his wife, Wendy. If you are interested in having the author speak to your book club, contact Mike Befeler at mikebef@aol.com. His web site is http://www.mikebefeler.com.